Sophie Parkin has contributed to two successful collections of writing, *Mothers by Daughters* and *Sons and Mothers*, as well as to many newspapers and magazines. She has broadcast on television and radio. She has two children, Paris and Carson, and lives in London. This is her first novel.

Tanja Howarth
Literary Agency

19 New Row
London WC2N 4LA

Tel: 020 7240 5553
Fax: 020 7379 0969

Email:
tanja.howarth@btinternet.com

all grown up

SOPHIE PARKIN

review

First published in 1997
by REVIEW

An imprint of Headline Book Publishing

First published in paperback in 1998

10 9 8 7 6 5 4 3 2 1

ISBN 0 7472 5740 X

Printed and bound in Great Britain by
Clays Ltd, St Ives plc

Headline Book Publishing
A division of Hodder Headline PLC
338 Euston Road
London NW1 3BH

To my wonderful Mum and Papa
without whom I wouldn't have
been born, let alone got to be
'All Grown Up'

All my love and thanks go to Geraldine Cooke, the perfect editor, Lisa Eveleigh, for holding the faith; Shaun de Warren, for giving me faith; and to all my friends and family for their support and belief, but especially Paris and Carson, for living with me through it all.

CHAPTER ONE

The bed is low to the ground, heavy with blankets and it is dark. So dark, in this blackness I can't make out anything else in the room. There seems to be nothing, there is nothing but the bed and the blackness. I wake up thirsty, not just dry-throated but parched. I must have some water, I've got to have some water.

'Mummy, Mummy,' I call out into the darkness.

As I call, a tall, angular, modern standard lamp in the corner of the room appears, swivels and turns on. Mummy is under the lamp, standing in the spotlight. She comes smiling to my side in her pale hessian A-line minidress.

'What is it, chicken?' she asks soothingly. I tell her and she brings me the cold water and waits balancing down by my bed, smiling for me to finish. I'm soon snuggled back down inside my covers, warm, with my newly kissed forehead. She leaves me and the light turns off.

'Night, night chicken,' she says, and I'm asleep.

I wake again and ask, more water.

The light comes on and a figure steps out of the shadow, not my mother. It is a man with an axe and a hat covering his face. This man takes my mother's arm and with the axe chops it off. Blood is spurting from her body, but she doesn't cry or scream and I have to have the water, she brings it to me again. I am no longer warm and comfy in my snug bed, I am scared cold.

The light goes out again and the bed feels wet and uncomfortable from urine. I don't even know if it is mine. My thighs feel sore, pink and chapped, goose-pimpling under the covers.

Each time the light comes on, another of her limbs is severed.

1

If I call out again there will be nothing left of her, she'll have become a disassembled mannequin's torso. If I can't call, I will be left alone with the mad axeman and my mother, lying disembodied in a pool of blood.

I am so scared that I cannot cry. I know I must be very, very quiet. If I don't make a sound, nobody can find me, I can be hidden in this blackness. I can disappear and only the blood will seep through the cold black night towards my bed.

I run into her room to wake her up but she is hard to rouse through her drunken comatose sleep. How can she sleep so? She stirs with my crying.

'Mummy, Mummy! I've had that dream again. That bad dream. Mummy, Mummy, wake up. Mummy!'

I am by the side of her bed, my tears upon her sheets. I don't care about the man next to her who snores naked by her side, and she is as oblivious to his presence as he is to mine. She tries to console me, with an arm upon my head that flops away as sleep pulls her back. I know it is only a dream, but it seems so real. Wake up, wake up! I try to will her there for a minute, but she is gone again.

I am alone in the dark, stumbling back to my room, snagging my nightie on a nail, stubbing my toe on the stair. I crawl back into my still warm bed, grateful for its dryness, only ever wet in my dream. I pull my cat off the end of it and inside the covers with me to let him suck my hair.

'If only I'd stop having this dream, this horrid bad dream, Ralphy,' I say to my sleeping, sucking, purring cat, before I follow him down into the abyss of sleep.

CHAPTER TWO

'Mummy, why are you crying?' Joan asks from thigh height, looking up at Coco in the warm yellow kitchen.

Chop, chop, chop, goes the knife on the board, slicing and dicing its way through to the end of the onion.

I can't stop now, thinks Coco, not even to answer her daughter's question. Nearly at the end. Finished. She runs over to the sink, hands straight under the gush of water, her eyes close by, blinking in the negative ions to dry her tear ducts to order.

'That's better. I'm sorry, Joan, what is it? I had to get that wretched onion finished, otherwise I would never have gone back to it.'

'Why were you crying Mummy, I said,' said Joan. 'Was it the onions or what Granny said on the phone?'

'It was the onions, sweetheart. I chopped it the wrong way round by mistake. I didn't chop the root off first.' And she was certain of that. Long gone were the days when her mother could make her cry from anguish, sympathy, anger or the carelessness of some remark or unthinking innuendo. 'Granny doesn't make me cry, Granny makes me laugh.'

'Oh. She makes me cry sometimes, she makes me wash my face and I don't like it.' Joan followed her remark with a pensive silence as she considered the horrors of flannels invading her face, with a pencil-sketched frown; nothing held or marked her young elastic skin. Coco could see it was not a time to interrupt her daughter's train of thought: she wouldn't have heard anyway. Joan's mind had retreated to its private sphere.

'Why do you have to chop the root off first?'

'One of the mysteries of life, like, why does running water

stop you crying when you put your hands under it.'

Joan looked questioningly up at Coco. She was almost four and at the age of asking everything and pondering busily over the complications of life's unfolding. In between, she had to fit in showing everything she could do. Joan looked like a Mabel Lucie Attwell drawing of a fairy. Still squodgy with baby fat and marked by the dimples that sat in her face, her brown-blonde ringlet hair always swung into her eyes from her low brow. Joan was a child to fall in love with, nobody could help it: her smile was always instant even as tears were still rolling off her face, and she carried her barrel tummy with such pride, it was hard not to want endlessly to hug her.

'Or tell me this, Joan. Why does every woman that marries a king become a queen, and every man that marries a queen, become a prince? One of the mysteries of life. I suppose there's answers somewhere. Maybe you'll find them one day.'

'I don't know, because Cinderella became a princess when she married the prince, and did you know I have the book upstairs? Shall I show it to you and then you could read it to me.'

Life was simple when you held the right puzzle pieces and discarded the rest.

'Alright. Go and get the book. But remember, Joan, quiet when you go up the stairs. Mummy has to get on with the cooking now.'

'First, I think I will have to give you a kiss.' Coco leans down to her daughter's will, cemented in the mischievous, twinkling blue eyes. Joan's arms automatically wrap around her mother's neck, her lips to the waiting cheek where she deposits a noise of wet farts and saliva.

'Ha, ha, ha, ha,' Joan cries with glee. 'Splatter kiss!'

'*Uch*, you little monkey! Come here and be tickled!'

But Joan is off down the corridors, a tinkle of laughter running away. An ambassador of joy, stamping a thrill in Coco's heart that makes her smile for the rest of the morning.

★ ★ ★

On the large industrial stove stood four pots boiling and simmering, steam gasping occasionally from their lids.

The oven was full of old-fashioned treacle tarts with golden pastry laced over them like nets upon the sand of syrup-sodden breadcrumbs.

The lemon and vanilla-pod ice cream still had to be made.

Coco sat down at the large wooden kitchen table, scrubbed pale after each day of preparation and children's meals, and looked at the hardly legible menu, written, crossed-out and rewritten. Her legs felt tired and it was only the morning, her stomach too heavy and full, a little foot lodged uncomfortably close to her bladder, and she hated the dress she was wearing because none of the others in her wardrobe fitted her any more.

Another day, another meal to be made. Soon it would be the afternoon, evening would draw in the night-time blanket over them all, and as they slept this new baby inside Coco would keep growing. Coco was thirty-four years old and she was carrying her fourth child, if you didn't count the abortion she had had on her nineteenth birthday. She could've imagined having nicer birthday presents from her mother that year, but you don't always get the presents you want, sometimes you just get the ones you need. And she needed the abortion. Did her mother remember taking her to the clinic, sitting and waiting the three hours to collect her groggy, bleeding form to take home in a taxi and put to bed? She didn't imagine she did. They never spoke about that time.

The sun filtered through the litter of passion flowers that grew across the kitchen window, and glinted off the glass cupboards full of herbs and spices. Cupboards full of jars marinating artichokes in garlic and lemon, pale as the moon; olives packed with chillies and thyme, their black skins pressed hard against the glass, shiny as new, wet wellingtons. Other cupboards held home-made jams from the plum and apricot trees, blackberry bushes, and strawberry nets in the garden. Everything that grew there got consumed immediately, or got its shelf-life. Pears in *poire William*, peaches in brandy, cherries in kirsch, the thick syrups suspending their fruit, bottled for the winter and served hot, dripped over cold ice creams or warm pancakes. All except the pears. The pears would have a rich, dark chocolate sauce melted across their curves, as round and as soft as Coco's belly, or the downs that surrounded the big Georgian hotel which Coco and Ben owned, and where they and Mary, Bill and Joan, their children, lived.

'Oh, I can't think about that now!' Coco heard herself say out loud in exasperation about what she should put on the menu, and made herself laugh remembering that it was Scarlett O'Hara's line in *Gone with the Wind* when faced with starvation or dressing up for Clark Gable, and here she was with this glut of food. 'I'll know what to replace it with after I do this bit of washing-up.'

It really wasn't the weather for ice-cold gazpacho, no matter how much the sun shone in this Indian summer of late October. The nights were cold and everybody clambered around the big stone living-room fire as soon as the light faded. Another summer come and gone so quickly in the countryside, where one season seemed to take over so clearly from the next. Not like the city, the London where she had grown up, thought Coco, where you have to drive to a park to see if autumn's arrived, and where the stars are never visible through the orange glow of street lighting. What use knowing about the Big Dipper then? No understanding of the expanse of the universe, a child's blinkered vision shrunk in its perspective, like New York viewed from an aeroplane.

No matter the excess of overripening peppers and the last of the batch of cucumbers, something could be done with them. The vegetables turned in her mind, every variation of what they could be conjured into. Cucumber soup, peppers stuffed with basil and plum tomatoes injected with slices of garlic, served warm with chunks of hard-skinned soft white bread, to soak up the juices. Pepper and coriander mousse. Cucumber sautéed in butter and black pepper. *Pipérade*, soft cooked peppers and onions bound with egg in a multicoloured scramble . . . Bill always said, 'Yuck, we're not having egg car crash again, are we? More blood – pass the ketchup.'

Before Coco emptied the sink, she put the kettle on, marking the end of that part of the morning's work. A daily routine, like her list-making that she had to follow to keep herself paced. The sink was full to overflowing, she'd been chucking things into it since breakfast. Once emptied, she swilled it out and turned the hot tap on full and then the cold. The torrent of water made fresh white foam appear instantly, and Coco was sorry not to have her small companion Joan with her to shriek with glee at its magical appearance. She felt the warmth of the water and added more cold. She didn't want to have to wear the pink rubber gloves that hung above the sink. She couldn't stand the smell of them, never could, it clung under your nails and sunk into your pores like a heavy perfume you only test-try and can't scrub off. Besides, it always reminded Coco of dirty macs and Lord Hattersby. Lord Hattersby and Brockingford. Lord Hattersby and her mother. Lord Hattersby and his rubber room. The sick smell of rubber.

CHAPTER THREE

Brockingford is a huge, sprawling, eighteenth-century mansion owned by Lord Cecil Hattersby. Every calls him Mad as a Hatter, and it's not hard to see why. He looks like a strangely tall Victorian gentleman, distinguished and clever, sad but not kind; always dressed with a little rubber. He stoops timidly in his full-length black, shiny raincoat and wellington boots with gloves to match and a crop that most would take for leather.

Along with all the rubber, he has formed such an addiction to my mother that it is embarrassing. They conduct a love-hate relationship. He adores, loves and adorns her, she openly despises, humiliates and loathes him. Taking, with contempt – that's their relationship. He steals glances from her; takes long, obsessive, drowning unwelcome looks, and her cruel words to comfort him when she's gone. She takes his gifts.

No matter how bad it gets between them, how horrible Mummy is to him, or how annoyingly irritating his presence and presents, some bit of glue keeps them together.

The house, the mansion is one of the sticky bits and in the summer we go down every other weekend. It's like our own private country house, without the responsibility (except for Cecil) or the bills. Cecil pays for everything. We take whoever we like down there, cousins, friends, Granny, and play all weekend. We try to play tennis, hacking at the perfect smooth green lawns with rackets with 'Made in 1927' on the handles, volleying our balls across the net behind the Victorian glass conservatory. Inside, we hide our bath chairs for the races around the cherub-spouting fountain and the tree-high potted palms that make you think you're trapped in a terrible jungle. In the pond, golden and yellow fish swim around and below the tangle of water-lily plants. In the afternoons there are fancy-dress competitions, with clothes from the trunks in the attic, full of Cecil's aunt's and granny's clothes. We collect peacock and pheasant feathers from the woods and from around the old Chinese summer house to make our costumes even more elaborate, sticking them on with Sellotape.

The dresses are old, after all Cecil's ancient, almost as old as Granny, so some of these clothes are falling to bits. I find it hard, though I am almost eight, to think of being that old and having all the run taken out of you, to be only ever able to walk places. You have to walk to be like them; grown-ups can't run. Cecil's mother's and aunt's eyes follow us as we slide down the banisters in dresses they once wore to parties. There are tears in the beautiful lace jackets, moth holes in velvet gowns, and silk petticoats rip and shred after we've finished careering around the corridors or investigating forbidden places in the eaves. We dare each other down into the cellars where prisoners were once kept and the chains still hang on the walls next to the racks of cobwebbed wine bottles. We pretend to go down to find the rocking horse Cecil rode on as a child and his strange, ancient toys, but really we're looking for skeletons. Skeletons and secrets. Adventure.

As you turn off the main road into the half-mile driveway to Brockingford, the trees bend across, reaching to hug each others' branches. In daylight it's an ice-green glade, everything dappled in the sunlight and a thick special magic as though you're entering a fairy glen of cold green-yellow light. At night, the mystery glows as the wheels of the car crunch to a halt on the gravel and the pale spectre of the house rises against a dark sky. The massive oak doors open on to the marbled hallway where the wooden staircase turns in. Family portraits through the generations follow the banisters up the hand-printed William

Morris walls; the best banisters in the world for sliding down. It's hard not to think of horror films, walking through the front door: I always look for the Mary Poppins umbrella with its parrot-head handle to touch for good luck, before I feel better. One of the paintings looks like Mary Poppins, well, the same clothes anyway.

I wish my cousin Barbara would stop bringing the Ouija board down here, it gets too scary, like a real horror film. Sometimes I think Cecil looks like Dracula with his big, black cloak on, oily hair and starry eyes. I've seen bats fly through the house sometimes . . . Mum laughs and says, 'Darling thing, it's nothing to worry over, it's a coincidence.' I don't think I believe her.

Barbara's American friend Cindy first brought the Ouija board down one weekend and none of us could bear the anticipation to begin. We sat ourselves in the White Room, cross-legged in a circle with a glass of water all ready to start. Smothering nervous giggles, my cousin and her friend sneered at us babies, just because they were older than the rest of us. Really grown-up – *not*!

The children never sleep in the White Room because that is the really haunted room in the house, everybody knows it – nobody sleeps there. That room is so spooky you can feel it in the day with the shutters wide open and the sun streaming across the heavily draped four-poster bed. There always seem to be more dead flies and insects there on the window seats than anywhere else, handy when we're playing tricks, but I wouldn't go in there by myself. Not even for dares. Not even for a whole packet of wine gums or Chocolate Éclairs. Wine gums, Chocolate Éclairs and Refreshers, then maybe I'd think about it.

'Now, we all think of somebody that we once knew, but they've got to be dead. Then you gotta all drink from the glass of water in the middle and then put your fingertip along the edge, like this. Now close your eyes tight and concentrate,' says Cindy.

'And stop giggling, it won't work if you giggle or if you look, so no peeking.'

I'm trying to think, trying to concentrate but at my age I really don't know anyone who's died, all my relatives seemed to have died before I was born. I did meet Cecil's mad brother once. He's dead now. He was so scary I can hardly think of him. I push myself to do it.

One weekend Cecil takes Mummy and me to meet his brother and sister-in-law in another large country house. We go into the library for tea and sit at a long table covered with cakes, sandwiches and the sort of silver and crockery that you see in museums. In the corner is a neat, pale woman in tweeds, twinset and pearls, very posh, nice, distant.

'So nice to meet you, do come in, won't you sit down?' she says. Her voice is like the queen's, and so is her hair. She stands gently leaning, with a quite normal fixed smile as though nothing is strange, upon a wheelchair containing a dollop of human flesh that screams, rants, babbles and drools.

That's Cecil's brother.

I am scared of the noises, I am frightened by the swivelling eyeballs, I can't understand why everybody pretends to be normal amid this madness, but the tenseness isn't normal. I don't want to be in this room. I slide beneath the table to put my face in my mother's lap, to cling to her legs and join the sounds of bewildered tears.

The cook is finally sent for with her five-year-old daughter, who is slightly older than me and who leads me out of the terror down to play in the kitchen, in the staff quarters.

I ask, 'Why don't you have to have tea with them and we do?' Cook doesn't answer except to say, 'How about a nice glass of squash with your jam tart, eh? Show her your dolls, Jenny, that should cheer her up. I've got the rest of the baking to get on with.' She gives me a warm, soft smile dusted in flour that makes me feel better.

'I got a Barbie doll for my birthday. Do you want to come and see her?'

I know who is the more privileged, the happier.

'Now we all taste the glass of water in the middle of the board. It says in the instructions that the water should've turned to sour milk.'

Cindy instructs.

'How could it have? We've all been sitting here,' I ask, mystified, and Barbara gives me one of those 'Shut up don't be stupid' looks.

And so I do, because they are older and I want to be liked.

'Simple. Because of the spirits passing over the glass, the water changes the consistency of the metaphysical matter.'

'Oh.'

'It doesn't look much like sour milk,' I say timidly, the first to sip from the glass. 'Ugh, it tastes like sour milk.' I spit it straight out on to the Victorian Persian carpet we're sitting on, and a pale stain seeps into its dark red woven depths. I swill my tongue around, rubbing it against the roof of my mouth to rid it of the sour-sick coating.

'Me next!' Barbara says urgently.

'Pass it here, Coco,' says Wanda.

'Bagsie me last,' says Hillary, her sister. 'We don't all have to taste it, do we?'

'We do if you want to go into the next stage and make something really exciting happen,' says Cindy, endlessly enthusiastic with her dangerous new toy. 'If we're serious about contacting the dead.'

Hillary doesn't want to be serious, and goes downstairs to find grown-up comfort in her mummy and daddy. I am sorely tempted but too boastful and proud: she's my friend but I'm too tomboyish to back down. I'm not the sissy of the outfit. No fear! I wear jeans, climb trees and I'd cut off my own pigtails if I could (I did it with my fringe last summer).

We begin again.

This time I am concentrating hard on the madness within Cecil's brother's eyes and just as they seem to be staring back at me, there's a high-pitched scream and a sack of coal falls down the chimney.

No amount of bravado can keep me in that room for a second longer. I'm out and up through the doors, along the corridor and up the stairs in search of Mummy. I run through her bedroom and almost leap into the bath with her. I'm babbling now. My wits are scared out of me. My cardigan arms grow soggy in my rush to find the comfort of her flesh.

'Mummy, Mummy, it was horrible . . .' My head on her shoulder, my hair trailing into the water.

Upstairs, one dark corridor leads to another with endless rooms leading off them. Bedrooms full of immaculate antique furniture and marble fireplaces, bathrooms with ancient grand tubs with lion's claws as feet and hand-painted wallpaper filled with flowering birds. At the top of the house, away from everything, right upstairs, are the nurseries, obsolete and packed with the house's detritus. The nurseries have a sadness bigger than any of the rooms. The carpets have been taken away, one of the windows is broken and even the paint is peeling to get out. We only go there for guy-making material at bonfire time, stuffing Cecil's old trousers with wartime newspapers. Metal cribs and tin baths, broken chairs and unloved dolls with scary, starry china-blue eyes tell you to go downstairs. Barbara's read me a story from her *Pan Book of Horror* about dolls that come alive and plot poisonous, murdering revenge, so I know that it happens.

Then there is the Blue Room, with a double four-poster bed, rosewood carved dressing table and Chinese silk wallpaper where Mummy sleeps. The Red Room is full of heavy red silks, velvets and exotically patterned carpets. The Grey Room is almost simple with the single bed's muslin drape and the portrait of Lady Jane Grey's innocent young face painted on the fireguard, in its place. The children sleep in the Flower Room with the biggest bed, so we can all cram in together, we like it together, warmer and safer. Mummy says at bedtime that we look like fairies huddled in the flower patch and we giggle; there is a magic there.

There is also Cecil's room. You could almost forget Cecil's room, halfway down the hall and up the small staircase to the right, but I can't any more.

Children are not supposed to go in there, I'd forgotten that, 'conveniently' Mummy would say. We've been told over and over again not to go in, it's Cecil's and it's private and usually locked so of course I've been. Sneaked and peeped with my friend Thomas. I thought that we weren't allowed to go in because it must be very precious, full of old rare things like the rest of the house. Things worth a lot of money, millions! Really? That was before Thomas and I saw it.

It is probably the smallest room in the house, outside the maids' quarters, and it is covered in rubber. From the walls hang tall fishing boots, mackintoshes, sou'westers and whips, there are red and black rubber sheets on the single grey metal bed, a bed like you'd see in any hospital. Like a hospital sterilisation department there are buckets full of medical equipment, rubber hose-pipes and unemptied potties. The place looks like a slum and it stinks, stinks of old pee and rubber. The Rubber Room. Now that I know, now that I've seen, I smell it every time I walk past the door and it makes me feel sick. Every time Cecil's bespattered old face appears shyly twitching into any of his own rooms, like an intruding unwanted guest, I smell rubber.

'Erg!' Thomas and I say to each other. Frowning up our noses and skulking away from the forbidden territory, we both wish we hadn't been there and we don't mention it again, there's something not so funny about it all. We know we can't tell the grown-ups. Downstairs again, we go and play the Wheel of Fortune, What the Butler Saw and the fruit machines that fill up the old gold and white ballroom. Once they held dances there just like in *My Fair Lady*, Cecil said, when he was a boy. There are always things to find, and in the cupboard in the corner there are some dusty red-and gold-braided uniforms and we dress up and have sword fights with the chair legs, our muddy boots battling and scuffing across the empty wooden dance floor.

Inside, we spend our time in the space closest resembling a sitting room. When I say 'we', I mean us, the children. The grown-ups, where are the grown-ups? Not out of bed in the morning; on walks in the grounds; down to the pub; long lunches and dinners around the brown bus of a dining table. Lunches that last until five o'clock, dinners that start at seven with just enough time for a bath and a snooze in between. Sometimes they manage to fit in tea in the gold and white drawing room, but I don't feel comfortable in there. One look might break a Louis-Seize chair, shatter all the delicately arranged porcelain, or the rickety glass-case box, like a waiting room crowded with painted faces, family miniatures.

Our crammed room is full of a grand piano, walls of busy blue and turquoise fighting swirls and a red leather chaise longue with matching overstuffed chairs. The crowning object in this room is the massive glass dome protecting a quarter of a tree that has disappeared under its covering of rare, tiny, brightly coloured stuffed birds – all dead. All the colours of the rainbow are crammed on to every mossy surface and corner. Horrifying and fascinating in its detail, worms hang from their mouths, insects lie trapped beneath their clawed feet; frantic pinned movement. Everything is as still as a photograph, as dead as a doornail with no chance of escape.

On Saturday nights, after the grown-ups have left for the pub, we creep down to watch horror films on the portable black and white television in the corner with a coat-hanger as an aerial. One night of horror, Barbara and I are trapped watching the late-night film *Psycho*, too terrified to go up the stairs back to our room, too scared to watch the film we've been banned to stay up and see. We wrap ourselves in a tartan car rug and pretend to sleep, snuggled close waiting for whatever arrives first, dawn or grown-ups.

That was in the days when Cecil and guests were still welcome in the local hostelries of the area, before the whisky had taken its firm and steady grip and he was able to keep up the house, the staff, the grounds, the stables, my mother. By the end, everything was falling apart: Cecil, the conservatory, the antiques, even the cats had holes in their tails and missing eyes. But that was at the end, when the dog got shot, when the horses bolted from the stables to turn wild in the forests, and the gypsies moved in.

At first I couldn't persuade Mummy to marry Cecil, not for anything, not for all the nagging in England. The exchange of a stable full of ponies, a boarding school full of adventures and a new bike that he'd promise me every time I saw him, just wasn't enough for her, I thought it a good enough exchange. Mum accepted everything he gave her with a sneer, as though his touch or thought had soiled the goods, rubber-stamped them SPOILT. With Mummy's lead, I started not to like him much either. When he offered Mummy the Rolls-Royce that he'd scoured all of England for to make sure it was made on the date of her birth, she gave it a contemptuous glance and said, 'What would I want with a black Rolls-Royce, bring it back when it's pink!' and she shut the door in his face.

She was always doing that, or making him wait on the doorstep like a delivery boy with his presents, but the truth was she'd treat a delivery boy better. Cecil would wait sheltered under the porch when it rained and I would watch him silently through the window. I know why she made him wait outside, because once he came into the hallway and tried to kiss Mummy. She couldn't have wanted him to, I'm sure she didn't: maybe she was too frightened to get away or something, something like that. I saw from the top of the stairs and I felt sick seeing him that close to Mummy. I wanted to get a knife and chase him away, but the knives were in the kitchen so I ran into them, wedging myself in the space between their legs, close enough to bang at his balls with my fists and stamp on his feet. That soon got rid of him!

Mummy had always told me that men don't like being hit in the balls.

I thought she'd be grateful to me for saving her. I don't know why she sent me up to my room shouting cross words, to see Cecil out by herself. Her voice was different, she must have been merry (she always calls it that when she's been drinking), and my angry, tear-stained red face just served to make her even more cross. I hate it when she's like this, her voice and eyes change and suddenly all the rules go with them.

Drunk and driving home in the Rolls one night Mummy stopped at the bus stop where we caught the bus to school. At seven in the morning she was arrested, drunk in charge of a pink Rolls-Royce and illegally parked at the number fourteen bus stop. It was so silly, she was just around the corner from home. Banned, Cecil gave her the chauffeur and for a whole year I was never once late for school. But with the chauffeur, Cecil came more and more to the house until the break-in and all of Mummy's knickers and bras and her high-heeled shoes were stolen, and then he was arrested. Mummy was cross at having to go out and buy new underwear with the money she demanded from him. I couldn't understand what he would have done with it all, how it could've been worth the trouble and the police. He pretended he didn't do it, but you can always tell when somebody's lying, their voice goes funny just like when they're drunk.

★ ★ ★

There are lots of nice things about Cecil once you get to know him, and I know it's important to try and see the good things in people. He is kind and generous and happy, when he is able to provide for others' happiness. One day Mummy said, 'What the hell! I give in', and married Cecil last Christmas. He took Mummy, me, Maureen (Mummy's best friend), Tony (Mummy's theatrical manager), Jim and Annie to Ibiza. Everyone thought it a strange way to spend a honeymoon, but Mummy insisted and she always gets her way with Cecil: the registry office, the party, the honeymoon, everything.

We all had separate huts on the beach and there was a band that played around the swimming pool every night and the children were all allowed to go to the disco. That was where Mummy first let me taste crème de menthe – delicious, all ice-cool green, like chewing-gum sorbet with a straw, yummy-yum. I mean I'd drunk wine lots of times before, sometimes even without water and I didn't like it that much, but Mummy said it was sophisticated to be like a continental child, so I did it to make her happy, even when I felt sick. Crème de menthe was something different, I really liked it and Mummy couldn't tell late at night how much she'd drunk when she came back from the dance floor, and I'd always get the watery leftovers. It tasted like Consulate cigarettes that Mummy would give me puffs on for being good. Cool and minty, like Polos.

I'd run around the swimming pool, play catch with the other children, until the grown-ups snogged in slow dances and I'd ask Mummy to put me to bed. In the morning, having woken up late, I saw Mummy just coming in, wiping off last night's make-up still smeared down her cheeks, lipstick across her chin. Her stained party dress was thrown in a corner and replaced by today's, a crisp orange mini sundress, new lipstick, fresh eyeliner and a cigarette for breakfast. Playing on the beach, riding the donkeys, staying up late, jumping in the sea; but Cecil didn't seem to enjoy it much. He didn't like Mummy going off with the waiters or the handsome, dark singer in the band. Mummy says he's an old stick-in-the-mud.

I see him sitting by himself, all alone and miserable. 'What is it, Cecil?' I ask, putting my hand on his, and his face appears like a tortoise's from a shell and smiles, pretending to be happy, but it's only a change in the shape of his mouth.

'Oh, I'm alright, but you should be off having fun . . .'

'It's Mummy, isn't it, I know, she makes me feel like that too sometimes. It's hard to remember it's only a bit of her and that all the rest is nice, when we want it nice all the time,' I said to cheer him up, but all he did was pat the top of my hand and retreat back into his shell.

'You just don't want me to have any of my own fun, miserable git. If you don't like it, fuck off out of it.'

'Of course if that's your idea of fun, as you so succinctly put it, my dear, then that's what you must have. I know I'm dreadfully old-fashioned but I don't like to see you degrading yourself with people of a lesser class.'

'Lesser class! *Bollocks*! That's what I say to you. Now piss off. I've had enough of you standing around here. Make yourself useful, get us another bottle of champagne and some more Coke and crisps for the kids whilst you're about it. Alright!'

She kicks him neatly with her sharp black and white stilettos. Make sure he's got the point. Me and my friends from the beach giggle. That was the end of the honeymoon.

I thought that when you got married you all lived in the same house, but Mummy refuses to move and she says she won't have Cecil living here. She says she was drunk when they got married so it doesn't count. Instead we go to Brockingford every weekend now and I have my pony Lollipop in the stables, and Barbara, my cousin, rides Henri, the brown mare. We spend the weekends riding across the fields and through the forests. We take sandwiches and bottles of lemonade in our pockets and don't come home until tea. We make jumps in the fields and secret dens in the woods. We gallop and canter, walk and trot, climb trees and play Robin Hood, Tarzan, Swiss Family Robinson. Tim, the stable boy, asks us to play other games with him, where you have to take your clothes off and lie down in the hay next to him; he says all grown-ups do it.

'We know that! And it's stupid and dirty and sissy and we'll tell your mum. Anyway we're not grown-up, and don't want to be if we have to do that,' we say.

Tim's mum, Mary, is the cook and she's round and warm in her apron and her hugs go right the way around you, like a pillow-sausage roll. Mary smells of flour and barley sugar and there's always one to pop in your mouth from her huge pockets. She lets me lick the cake bowls, roll out pastry on the marble slab (so it doesn't get warm), and grease the tart tins. When we make jam, I draw the labels for the jars and test its setting point on cold saucers, watching for the glossy red skin to form. The foam we skim off the top, Mary makes into strawberry toffee that I take back to London and save to suck slowly, one piece a day. She's always working but never too busy to stop and set out an extra knife and chopping board for me to help. She teaches me to knead dough, make profiteroles from the beginnings of a white sauce, break eggs and save mayonnaise. In the mornings I collect the eggs for her from the chickens out around the back courtyard. I like it in the kitchen, especially in the winter when the oven never goes off.

Mummy says Cecil has put his foot down and next holiday, he's only taking family: me, Mummy and Granny. I expect I'll be able to lose Granny like I did in the hotel in Rome, before Cecil. That'll be fun. I wonder if I can take Barbara – imagine the tricks we could play then; or a friend, my age and not so bossy. I hate being the only child with all the grown-ups, being made to sit at some starched hotel table with too many knives and forks. Being told not to interrupt, to think before I talk, to listen, to grow up. I sit and eat and concentrate on the food while the adults drone on and on. I know I'm wasting valuable time, I could be running around the corridors, playing with the twins in the lift, sneaking down to the fridges in the kitchens, being naughty, having fun.

The Mamas and the Papas are on the portable record player: 'I'm In With The In-Crowd', and we're twisting and dancing under the pine trees in a wood outside Rome. I'm staying with Maria, my au pair girl, with her parents in their Rome apartment. There seem to be wild teenage parties every other day that Maria has organised, in the apartment, on the beach, in the woods and I am the cutesy English girl. I am learning to eat six-course Italian lunches, breakfasts of golden apricot lattice tarts straight from the oven with our glasses of milk and wedges of bread spread thick with Nutella; to pick pine nuts out of their kernels and grill sardines by the sea as the sun sets. I am happy. Yes, I am happy. I don't ever want to go back home. I like sleeping in the afternoon and hearing the sea roll outside my window, staying up late in the warm starry nights and speaking Italian, being the centre of attention and eating home-made sorbets out of the skins of real lemons.

Mummy and Granny come to collect me, and I cry the night before into Maria's lap to let me stay. I'd live with her for ever and ever. Mummy takes us to a large cool hotel with fig trees and table football in the garden. The hotel owner says her son has fallen in love with me. He plies me with presents of disgusting handmade marzipan fruit – doesn't he know I don't like boys or dolls, and sissy life-size dolls. I want to be back in among the pine trees, being swung by the arms by adoring handsome men; sitting in Maria's lap, my hair being brushed and plaited, brushed and plaited; falling asleep to Latin lullabies being sung by her mother cooking in the kitchen.

'Say thank you to Giorgio, Coco, for the beautiful presents. The doll's fabulous, isn't it?' Mummy urges, reminding me with her nudging elbow.

Giorgio stands doe-eyed, unable to speak English, smiling. I pretend I can't speak Italian.

'Mummy! You know I hate marzipan, it's disgusting and makes me sick and I've never liked dolls. I like teddies, not dolls. Do I have to take it?'

One steely-eyed glance from Mummy, and I'm smiling sweetly again.

'*Grazie*, Giorgio, *grazie*.'

I even let him kiss me: our parents coo as though I'd agreed to marriage, soppy, sissy boys.

CHAPTER FOUR

Slish, slash, slish, slash. The knives grind through the machine, glinting with approval: now they have an edge that pricks blood when placed against the skin, mild pressure will sever a leg from a chicken's body, an avocado's flesh-wrapped skin from its stone, and a tomato will glide in two.

Always keep your knives sharp.

Always keep your knives.

'Mum, Mum, is this a'right?' Mary shouts. 'I can see my reflection in all of it.'

And you can: the glimmers of light paint the chestnut table white and dark from the arch windows and the loving care of Mary's polish.

Mary is eight and tall, strong and kind. Her long dark hair throws a glossy wrap around her straight shoulders and as she moves it shimmers, a heavy surround. She can climb trees with Bill and dress dolls for Joan, cook with Coco, make beds and polish with Carol, and with her dad can almost drive the tractor lawnmower and chop the firewood.

'That's beautiful, Mary, thank you. Would you like to lay the table with Carol? Remember the glasses always need an extra polish from the cupboard.'

'Of course, Mum, I haven't forgotten, but I'm not having Bill help us. Fat lot of good he turned out to be last time.'

'Ahh, let him help, Mary, if he wants.'

'No. Not after those two glasses, wasn't it, Carol? The two glasses that got broken last time.'

'Never mind.'

Carol says nothing, just gets on with the job she's employed to do, walking from the village each day up to the big house.

'Mary, Carol, can I help doing the table?'

'No, Bill, and I've already told Mum why not so don't go whingeing to her. You're to play with Joan and stay out of the kitchen.'

'Miss Bossy Bum Poo. Mary, do you want to hear my new poem from school?

> *Here come the horses,*
> *the carriage is about*
> *And here comes Mary with her tits hanging out!*
> *He, he, he, can't catch me.'*

'You gross little pig, when I get my hands on you I'll give you the kiss of a slug . . .'

'Ignore him, Mary, it's the best way,' says the ever-sensible Carol, grown-up and seventeen. 'I should know – years of experience with my four brothers and they're still terrors,' she adds, in her soft local burr.

'Bill is just so annoying and childish. Sometimes I think Joan is older than him,' Mary says in an exaggerated voice for Bill to hear as he passes the door on his way to his den.

Bill's den is at the bottom of the garden and the start of the fields. It is his hideout, a Stig's dump full of Borrowers' treasure. Useful pieces of string; interesting bits of metal and wood collected from the beach; real flints; birds' nests and some bone that was sure to be a *Tyrannosaurus rex*'s found by his dog, Perry, and him in the flower bed this summer. All this treasure lines the floor and walls of his self-made ('Dad only helped, I did most of it') wooden hut.

'Bill is so childish I think Joan is older than him, just something went wrong with his birth and he turned out larger,' she adds for effect, rather pleased with the clever scientific additions.

Bill doesn't hear Mary; he often doesn't hear the rest of the world and the repeated jibe is wasted as he strides out, boots on, sling in pocket and wooden stick-cum-sword in hand. Safe to survey his land, to tell Joan, if she dares to come down and plead to be his willing slave, not to break the glasses or burn the food on the collection of sticks in the middle of the hideout he calls the fire. Maybe Perry is about, to go rabbit-hunting with. He puts his hand in his pocket remembering the toffee saved from yesterday, sticky and hair-covered but still edible, he decides as he wedges it into his neat mouth.

A small incision and you can pull the flesh off the chilli pepper without any of the deadly seeds being used. It's the seeds that set your mouth a-fire till you're calling for the water jets; the flesh flavours and puts in the mild heat, when used in the right quantities. Coco adds two to the Italian smoked pork; the fat sizzles and spits the olive oil over the sliced peppers, chopped cucumber, onions and garlic, mini firecrackers releasing the pungent flavour, until flooded quiet by the quarts of tomato juice and stock. Gazpacho *caldo* to start with, hot and nourishing and 'nice and warm for my tummy', thought Coco, and smiled remembering the catchphrase of an advertising campaign from her childhood.

That was the thing about having children: every day they reminded you about how you were, how you wanted to be, what was fun and what made you cry. It had surprised Coco, having her children and realising that their individual characters were there from the moment you looked into their little wrinkly faces and that, as they grew older, they just grew stronger. Of course experiences change things, make some things drip heavy with pain, while others light things up with pleasure, and for those who don't have those exact experiences, their associations to the same things will be completely different. Like Mary with chocolate: she'd eaten so much one Easter she'd been sick for two days with tummy ache and she'd never touch it again, whereas Bill didn't seem to have a point where he could stop.

Mary was how Coco would've chosen to be as a girl, with a splash of Joan and a stripe of Bill. Maybe she had been like that. It's hard to look back, to separate the past and our behaviour when memories became smudged by feelings and an ageing perception. She was looking absently at Mary, smiling with contentment and pride at her child, so serious with endeavour, engrossed at removing every smudge from every knife, until she felt her mother's gaze upon her and looked up, smiled – an accepting child – and back to her endeavour.

Chop, chop, chop. Coco was automatically dicing croutons to be fried in the golden-green crackling oil, to be heaped into the soup with cold chopped peppers and cucumber later like vegetable islands. She sat down to rest her bloated feet; at seven months her veins and her tummy were beginning to match the landscape.

'Ouch. Hell, I wasn't looking. Carol, can you quickly get me a plaster and cotton wool, I've bloody cut myself. Ahh, the knife was too sharp.'

The blood was already dripping through the fingers of her other hand and on to the tiled terracotta floor, dot, dot, dot. The blood coloured the sink pink and rimmed it red; the tap was smudged with the mess of it and dripping rivulets as she turned it on.

Coco didn't mind the sight of blood but she always felt she should be like the girls at school who had fainted at the sight of it. Maybe the pleasure at seeing it return each month to stain her knickers, as a promiscuous teenager, had overridden the pain of that first flood.

It was the bonding of teenage blood, first periods and how to use a tampon, like slicing your wrists and fingers with pieces of glass and rubbing them in best-friend unity.

'Carol, hurry up, can you take the oil off the fire before we all go up in flames.'

The torrent from the tap pulled the wound open, froze her finger and washed the redness away. Only the pulse of the pain was left as she bound her finger, and a smear of blood around the tap, and she returned to chopping the rest of the food.

CHAPTER FIVE

There are pills everywhere, like a mess of Smarties, and blood spurted all over the floor and walls. I open the door first and find her lying there. I shout out to Mummy to come quick. I know Granny's not dead. I know in the same way that I know the glinting, scattered razor blades on the floor are the ones Mummy uses to shave her legs. Granny has used them to slice her arms and her hands, letting out her messy, red blood. The blood that has been carelessly smudged in waves across the delicately sea-coloured stone floor is now a dirty brown. Bags of pills, their contents emptied, assault the mess.

Granny's gone mad again. Again.

It is horrible, but I don't feel so sad; I'm sorry but cross. Why does she always have to spoil everything, bring attention always to herself? It's not the first time she's done this. I suppose it means the 'Nerve Home', again. Why does Mummy always insist on making things nice for Granny – Granny this, Granny that, as long as Granny's happy then that's all right. But she never is. It's worse than having a baby around sometimes, a grown-up baby.

The doctor arrives, tells everybody off in loud Italian shouts – the hotel manager joins in, half translating – and binds her wrists. The next day she leaves, she couldn't possibly stay, she says. No, she couldn't, because it's illegal in this country. You're not allowed to do it. I wish somebody had told Granny before.

I wonder if I am supposed to feel guilty because of getting lost the night before, but I don't see why I have to stay with her all the time. I'd made friends with some American children and their parents. Granny was supposed to be looking after me, but I think she was more interested in talking to the next table and ordering

31

'just one more small drink from the handsome waiter'. I told her I was going with my friends to listen to ghost stories around the lit-up pool, but she didn't hear. She told the hotel to ring the police, she said, to the interested audience that gathered around the lobby in the commotion, that I'd run away from her on purpose, because she'd told me the truth about my father and made me 'tearful'. She did make me cry over dinner, telling me horrible things about Daddy which I didn't want to know, but he's my Daddy, not hers and nothing to do with her, he's part of me and none of her business. But you're not allowed to say that to grown-ups. Granny gets too excited in big hotels and drinks too much, gets difficult. By the time I lost her, she was already lost in the bar.

We have to leave too, but not until Mummy finishes the filming, her work, why we are there. It's a film with Herman's Hermits. I am allowed to watch them shooting around the pool, where the ladies all parade with big hairdos and bikinis held together with chains, or swimsuits with holes all over them, whilst the pop group plays and we sing along to 'Something Tells Me Something's Going To Happen Tonight'. How did they know?

The packing with Mummy is always hectic. I know that other mothers pack before they go on holiday, sometimes even a couple of days before. Mummy always leaves it until the last moment; sometimes she does it as we're waiting for the cab to arrive to take us to the airport, and sometimes while the cab is waiting. We never somehow manage to get to the airport with time to spare, there's always a rush, and often I have to pray on the way to make sure there's a delay. It usually works, we haven't missed a plane yet. But sometimes I swear to myself, when I'm catching my breath and we're the last to do up seat belts, that it's not going to happen again, well, not when I'm grown-up.

It usually happens when Mummy doesn't come straight home from work, and then I start pulling out our cases and packing for myself. When Mummy heard she'd got the lead in a horror film the day before we were flying to Formentera on holiday, the warning signs were up.

'Mummy, Mummy, *wake up*!' I shout into her comatose ear. I would've been glad if I was having a maths test and wanted to remain ill off school. Then, later, when she woke, I'd innocently say, 'But at seven this morning you said it was all right for me to stay home today'. She could never argue; how could she know what she'd said?

'*Mummy*! We've got a plane to catch! Here's a cup of tea, the cab's about to arrive, so get dressed.'

Granny's downstairs in the hall waiting, 'Just having a last ciggie.' As though there'll never be another opportunity again. Granny takes her smoking seriously, something to be sat down and concentrated upon, a task.

Somehow she gets dressed. At least she doesn't have to spend time putting make-up on, it's still there smudged on her cheeks from the night before, her top false lashes only just holding on. Goodness knows what she's packed and the cases aren't doing up, but we squeeze them and us all into the cab and set off late. I can always tell when Mummy's drunk, her tone of voice changes and this morning it's silly and girlish, laughing too much, too loud and still slurring her words. Granny's getting annoyed with her, I'm just trying to keep the peace, make everything still nice for our holiday, and Mummy has just got the job to pay for it all, as she keeps on reminding us. I stuff any nasty feelings away, no time for them. Sometimes I can't bear it, I pretend to look out of the window but instead climb up the ladder into the space inside my head.

We arrive at the airport. 'Be a good girl and run ahead, stop the plane from going without us, Coco.' I do, I don't mind that, but I hate that embarrassed wait at the top of the steps for Mummy and Granny. We're so happy to have made it on to the plane, Mummy and Granny have to celebrate with champagne, ignoring the comments of fellow passengers: 'Disgraceful', 'Outrageous behaviour', 'Poor child, with a mother like that'.

I poke my head around the seats and stick my tongue out at anyone daring to stare. It's nobody's business but ours.

When Daddy takes me away he brings girlfriends, then we go just the three of us to a hotel somewhere, if Daddy isn't working, filming in Spain, Malta, the West Indies, when he's back from America.

Lots of my friends at school now wish their parents would get divorced too, then they'd get to go away as much as I do.

'You see, it's much better for children because you get double the amount of presents at Christmas, double presents on your birthday and at least two and probably four holidays away a year. Twice in the winter and twice in the summer,' I tell them. 'Besides all the chocolate, toys and comics from boyfriends and girlfriends; you see, they always want you to be on their side.'

'I see, I think,' says Hillary, my inexperienced best friend. 'So what's the difference, you never get to see your Daddy? I never see mine anyway, he's always boring working!'

'No! I do see him, but not at breakfast time.' Sometimes I'm dumbfounded at her stupidity.

'Who do you see at breakfast?'

'Maria, my au pair. Mummy's never up for breakfast because of her head, so I take her a cup of tea, two cups. One for anyone else who's there, of course! It's only polite.'

Poor Hillary, I don't think her parents will ever get divorced, it doesn't sound like they are ever in the house long enough to talk or argue. She only gets one holiday, and that's a week in Torquay with her grandparents.

In the summer Mummy and I sit on the bench in the garden and have Women's Talks, secrets that men don't know about. In the winter evenings we have them in front of the electric Magicoal fire, with the orange dancing flames encased in plastic. Mummy combs and dries my long fair hair, ridding it of rats' tails, plaiting it or tying it in rags, so I can look like Shirley Temple in *Rebecca of Sunnybrook Farm*. My toenails and fingers she paints alternately, pink-red, pink-red. When my cousin Barbara stays, Mummy paints her nails, too, like in a beauty salon, real make-up and everything neat and tidy in its place, that's why Barbara likes coming to stay with us. Auntie Anna complains about what Barbara finds out at our house, that there isn't any discipline, but Barbara says her mum is really pleased to have her out from under her feet.

'Do try not to mention John's name to Henry, Jerry or Sebastian because sometimes they get a bit upset. Like John did yesterday when you told him about Henry being in my bed in the morning, Barbara. I don't know how I'm going to get out of that one.'

'So why do you have to go out with three men, Mummy?'

'It's four, not three, if you add John, silly,' says Barbara.

'Because I like them all for different reasons.'

'Do you love them all?' I ask in amazement. How much love is there?

'Yes, I do. In different ways.'

'Like you loved Daddy in a different way, Mummy?' I say.

'Well Daddy I'll always love because he gave me you, so he'll always be special.'

'I like Sebastian the best,' I say.

'You only like him because of the bags of chocolate he brings you, even at breakfast time. Auntie Ricky, Coco only likes Sebastian because of the chocolate.'

'That's not true. I like the felt pens he gave me as well, and he looks like a teddy bear. So *there*!' I retaliate, to my cousin. My favours are not simply bought with chocolate alone. Hers would be, Cadbury's chocolate and strawberry Mivvies.

'But Mummy, why do you like Jerry Brigg?' This genuinely

perplexes me. This is the one man of all the ones that she sees who carries no favours with either Barbara or me. It's probably because he never brings us any presents and never says 'Thank you' for his cup of tea in the morning. Now that's rude.

'That's because he's married and likes to pretend he's not there at all,' Barbara says.

We have never known him as Jerry, always Jerry-Brigg, because together we talk about him more than we ever see him.

'I like him for lots of reasons. He makes me laugh, we have a good time together, I like going to bed with him . . .'

'But you said to Annie that he only had a small one. Remember, Barbara, Mummy saying Jerry-Brigg's got a small one?'

'Well, sometimes men with small ones try harder than the men with big ones who think they don't have to do anything at all.'

'Oh.'

'Who's for some scrambled eggy on toast, now that we've finished this hair, then?' Mummy says, trying to move things on.

'Me, me, but I don't want any of the white stringy bits in it because they make me feel sick.'

Barbara's always that way about eggs, and fat on meat.

'Mummy, you know Lucinda at school said she didn't believe that men and women had sex even when they weren't making babies? I said of course they did, that you did it all the time, but she said her mummy and daddy didn't do it at all because she'd listened outside their door for funny noises and there weren't any. I told her that's because her mummy and daddy are so old. They're as old as Granny. Then she pinched me really hard and tried to stick a pin in me, so I hit her with a ruler.'

I'm not going to be friends with her any more, even though Mrs French told me I had to.

'Mummy, she's wrong, isn't she?'

'Well, she might be right about her mummy and daddy, we don't know, do we? And you shouldn't sit next to her in class if you're going to argue with her all the time, should you?'

'No. But she said she wouldn't invite me to her birthday party unless I sat next to her all this week.'

'Lucinda had a horrible party last year anyway, nobody was allowed to win any of the prizes except her. The Pass the Parcel only stopped at Lucinda and she got first prize for the fancy-dress competition as well. You said there wasn't any point in going, they'll probably only show that boring balloon film again. Everyone at school knows that Lucinda Jameson's a spoilt baby, that's why she pinches all the time. Anyway, I heard Mrs Brody say so.'

'There you go Coco, Barbara says it's not worth going anyway. We'll all go to the pictures instead, shall we? There's a re-release of *Gone with the Wind*, you'll love that—'

'Not again!' we interrupt in unison.

'Or there's the new Steve McQueen, I think it's called *The Thomas Crown Affair*.' We can buy a big bag of toffees each and have an ice cream in the interval.

'Now who's making the tea, Barbara? And Coco, quick, butter the toast otherwise the scrambled eggs are going to be overcooked.'

'Are you going out again tonight, Mummy?'

'Yes, you know I am. I'm going out with Simon Eliot.'

'Why do you always go out at night if it makes you feel so awful in the morning?'

'Well, I always get a hangover.'

'You shouldn't drink so much to get merry, Mummy.'

'Don't be so cheeky, Coco, and eat your eggs before they get cold.'

For a long time now there's just been my mother, Ricky (thirty-five), and me, Coco, almost eight and named after Chanel. Mummy says with a name like mine I'm already famous; when I'm grown-up I'll hardly have to try at all.

It is comfortable in this house. We are happy and since my

father left, it is all girls. Of course there are men around, like bees round a honey pot with my mother, but they don't intrude. They are allowed to spend the night and wake up in the morning in our house, but not to stay. Even Cecil was never allowed to stay, and is unlikely ever to, now they are almost divorced. Mummy is always here in the morning, except when she's away, of course. There are au pair girls then, Maria, Annie and the horrible German I can't remember, neither of us want to after her hitting, screaming fit and running away with Mummy's red, yellow and blue rabbit-fur coats.

Mummy works hard when she works, plays harder and spends as much time as she can with me. I must allow her her freedom and I must not nag at her for going out at night. She must have her fun and parties as I have mine, it is only fair. There are rules that have to be acknowledged if we are going to live in harmony, as we do, she says. It is a happy family. It is only sometimes, maybe after very long Saturday or Sunday lunches that it's not very nice, when it starts to get scary, when merry spills into horrid. But the weekend only comes around once a week.

'I'm coming to get you, little girl, ha, ha, ha, ha. There's nowhere you can hide. I'm going to get you. Here I come!'

And there is howling and the lights have all been turned off and I'm running up the stairs as quick as I can and I'm scared and I can't run fast enough, and if Barbara is there she escapes laughing and I'm left by myself, not seeing the fun, and I've tripped and I'm frightened of what's going to happen to me . . .

The distorted face comes closer, the eyeballs bulging, the red, smudged mouth with the fangs hanging out either side, like Dracula. Like a witch.

I'm little, I'm scared, I'm crying. I'm alone.

'Stop. Stop. Mummy, *please! Stop*!'

I'm crouched in the corner of the stairs and she won't stop the cackling and I smell her hot stinking breath on my face, all cigarettes and drink, and I give up, covering my head with my arms and just cry, helpless.

The lights go on, the teeth are put back in place and Mummy is sitting next to me, cooing and comforting.

'Shh, shh, chicken, it was only a game. Only Mummy having a bit of fun. Nobody's going to get you. They're only my false teeth,' and she takes them out to show me, not draped over her lips but sitting in the palm of her hand. There, nothing. But it's what happens to her, I can't explain.

'I know it's only a game,' I sniff, 'but I don't like it. It's horrible and scary and I have nightmares.'

'I know, I know. I'm sorry, it's only a joke.'

I never do get used to that joke. This side of her I can't understand, she turns so quickly, when her voice changes. I can always tell when Mummy's drunk, but we're not to call it drunk, that's rude. When Mummy's merry.

It's not just me I worry about, more Mummy becoming like Granny. Barbara said madness grows in families. Bagsie I not have it.

All our favourite restaurants are around the corner from where we live, so Mummy doesn't have to drive far after lunch. We have lunch with a lot of Mummy's friends. Sometimes they bring their children and we play around the restaurant.

After the grown-ups are drunk, we get double pocket money and go to the sweet shop on the corner to buy American comics and lemon sherbets. We sit under the tablecloths for the rest of the afternoon, eating and reading, until evening comes and our bags of sweets are finished. Then we say, one, two, three . . . 'We wanna go *home*!'

On our arrival a starling flock of waiters and managers swoops to welcome my mother with outstretched, upheld arms.

'Eh, it is the beautiful Signora Johnson. How wonderful that you have come to see us and how are the bambinos? Come this way, we have the best table waiting for you.'

Our cheeks get pinched until we learn to cover them with our hands. My mummy is the star. Our parents always take us to Italian restaurants because they know of the warm reception, the love of children and that things are tolerated here that wouldn't be in French or English restaurants, and that includes the grown-ups.

We are always allowed to choose two things from the menu, one course and a pudding. I always have chocolate profiteroles and by the time the pudding trolley comes around the grown-ups order their *sambuca*. It's funny that a drink so dangerous, with its flaming head and sizzling coffee beans, should be allowed to be served at the end of the meal with everyone so drunk. Mummy has knocked her glass of lit *sambuca* over lots of times, setting fire to the tablecloth, but everybody always laughs. Then the other thing they do is forget to blow out the flames before they drink it, then they scream for emergency ice cubes to put on their burnt lips and tongues. It doesn't seem to put them off, they just have another to stop the pain. If they get drunk, we get to choose another pudding and if they get really drunk, we get three.

These lunches are like daytime parties. The only time I don't like them is when Mummy and Daddy have lunch together, just with me. Then it's horrible and I can't explain why. They always start off by saying: 'Isn't this nice, we're all going to have lunch together,' and you know straight away it's not, because everybody's acting strangely. By the time the food has arrived, Mummy and Daddy have given up talking to me and are saying, 'Run along and play' – play where, with who? – while they sit there having a good argue for the rest of lunch about money, or Mummy's boyfriends, or Daddy's girlfriends and money again. It always ends in tears. Tears and spilt wine.

Why does food always go with fighting? When I was a baby,

sitting in my high chair in the kitchen trying not to eat my bowl of fatty stew, I remember Mummy giving Daddy a boiled egg and the row starting and them shouting at each other. All I could think was . . . 'I wish I had that boiled egg instead of this horrid stew.'

That's what I remember of living in the same house as Daddy, stew and rows. He lives in America now, so there are not so many rows; instead he sends presents.

Now that I'm eight I don't eat stew any more, because I do all the shopping. I've got a system: usually I just ring up and they deliver it and put it on the account. Mummy says that since she hardly ever eats in the house and she never knows what me and my friends want to eat, it's much better if I choose and order what the house needs. After all, she says, she has to go out and work to pay for it all. I don't mind, I order chocolate Digestives, Frosties, fish fingers and baked beans and chicken supreme in a can with the rice at the other end – my favourite, I can have it every night of the week if I like. There are also rules, like no sweets or cakes (that's 'cos Mummy's always on a diet and otherwise she'd eat them all and be too fat to go to work, and that is why she has to take her slimming pills), and lots of fruit in a bowl on the dining table, that must be eaten.

'When you're hungry, always eat some fruit first, if it's between meals,' Mummy's always telling me.

When do you ever feel like fruit when you're starving hungry and you're just back from school, where all they gave you for lunch was disgusting greasy toad-in-the-hole and semolina frog-spawn? Anyway, I don't eat sausages because I'm a member of the Piggy Club. It's not a very nice thing to do to pigs, make them into sausages, so we sneak them out of lunch under our jumpers and bury them properly in the playground during recreation. Lots of children at school want to be members of the Piggy Club, but you can't be if you eat pigs and there's a strict initiation course. The boys have to have washing-up liquid poured down their shorts in the cloakroom during milk time, poor Tom Smie and Jim Payne, how they screamed. Hillary and me laughed till our tummies ached.

The thing I really hate is when I forget to order the shopping, and I have to stop by on my way home from school. The shop is only at the top of the road, but it seems ages to get home when you're struggling with a satchel and two carrier bags with the string biting into your hands. I sing songs loudly and count my steps between each lamp-post.

'What's new, pussycat, whoooa . . .'

I promise myself a rest by the next lamp-post-but-two away, and then don't give it to myself. I'm so nearly home that if I can just make it that bit more, I'll be able to put the bags down and never pick them up again. Of course I have to take them down to the kitchen, but that's different, I'm home. Once I left all the meat in the hall with the shopping and Ralphie and Tabby got to the fillet steak first. Mummy wasn't very pleased. The cats were. I have to be able to be trusted, so I take them downstairs, unpack and put it all away.

I wasn't trusted for ages after bringing the milk bottles down when I was four, tripping up and dropping them all. They broke and so did my nose, and I bit my tongue open, there was lots of blood, but Mummy gave me an ice lolly and told me not to fuss and said I wasn't allowed to collect the milk bottles any more.

Now they get left until Jen the cleaner arrives.

I know our household arrangements are not normal. I have friends who have mothers and fathers who don't live like this. I go to tea, stay over, for weekends sometimes and experience 'normal' family life among the middle classes. They have tea at four o'clock in their nurseries full of games, or with their mummies baking cakes and preparing dinner in the kitchen. It's nice. I wouldn't say their way is better, just different. My friends are envious: they don't have the freedom I have to go swimming, to the library, the cinema and museums whenever I like, by myself when I don't have an au pair.

When I go into school teachers say, 'Your mother was terribly good on the television again last night, Coco. Was it Saturday Night Playhouse?'

"No, I don't know, Mrs Sylvia, I was in bed."

But too late, all the class is looking at me. It doesn't matter that John Lennon's son is in Nursery, that's babies; I'm in Juniors and nobody else's parents are divorced in my class, let alone on television talking about it.

I am different.

One day the teacher, Mrs Sylvia, starts a discussion and each child in the class sitting cross-legged on the floor before her has to talk about what work their daddy does. Well, Hillary's daddy's a designer and Mary's daddy has a firm and Lucinda's daddy owns a bank and Joe's daddy is in antiques . . .

'. . . And Coco, your turn. We all know what your mummy does. What does your daddy do?'

'Coco's daddy doesn't do anything because she hasn't got one,' horrid Charles shouts out.

'I have. I have got a daddy.'

'He doesn't live with your mummy!'

I get up off the floor and run away crying, into the street. Stupid, nasty boy. Mrs Sylvia makes him say sorry to me in front of the whole class – serves him right.

'I do have a daddy and he lives in America on a big ranch with horses, and he makes films for the cinema and he's had dinner with the President!' I say proudly. And some of it is true.

We live in the pink house, with a matching Rolls-Royce and pink sports car outside. They match the pink flowers in our garden, fuchsias.

Sometimes I am collected by the chauffeur in the pink Rolls. This is part of being different I like, lying luxuriously in the back playing with the electric windows. Mummy has this thing about being 'ordinary', so even my Clarks brown sandals are painted red and bright green. All I've ever wanted is a pair of brown polished StartRite lace-ups, like everyone else in my class. I understand when Mummy points out that they wouldn't go with my other clothes, my red denim bell-bottoms and purple thick cord ultra-miniskirts. It's just that sometimes I wish . . . Sometimes I get the bus home with Barbara. When Granny is staying with us she collects me from school. Granny smokes Players No. 6 cigarettes, sixty a day. She keeps them in her tight-clipped purple leather handbag along with her packet of Liquorice Allsorts, her bottles of pills and a box of Swan Vesta pink-tipped matches, because fuchsia is her favourite colour too. She wouldn't use any other brand, she says.

I like cooking best, and Granny is always full of promises to make Madeira cake or 'the lightest of pastry', but she never does. Once we made toffee apples but that was when I was on holiday staying with her and my big second cousin, Jane, helped.

Once we are home from school, she locks herself away in the living room for the afternoon, where she is sleeping on the put-U-up sofa. She always seems so old and frail, little. I always have to help her, find things, remind her. It always seems with Granny as though I am stronger, know more of the world. I find her her pills and get her a glass for her whisky, 'just a tot to help them go down'.

Poor Granny, she isn't feeling well. It's always been like this. Sometimes she has to go back, to the 'Nerve Home', when things get really bad. She's supposed to look after me but it always feels, especially when Barbara is here, that we do the looking after with Granny. Maybe it would have been different if Grandpa was still alive but he died before I was born. She's always saying how much she loved him, how she misses him.

I leave her in the darkness of the basement living room, with the curtains pulled, her ashtray and cup of tea next to the bed, all her concentration focused upon smoking the cigarette in her mouth.

I go and play upstairs in the brightness of my room, where the windows go from the bottom of the floor to the top of the ceiling, where the walls are painted yellow and white and the rugs are pink and orange Casa Pupo swirls. I open my full toy cupboard and decide to give all my dolls chickenpox and haircuts, till Mummy comes home from rehearsals and weekend starts. Yippee! We're all going away to Brockingford tomorrow and I'll run through the woods alone, climb trees and make a new den.

CHAPTER SIX

'Don't do anything more, sweetheart. Thank you for everything you've done, it's wonderful.'

'I like doing it, Mummy. Do you want me to do anything in the kitchen? How's your finger, does it need a kiss better?'

'No, that's all right. You could give me a hug, though.' Mary wraps her arms about Coco's neck and squeezes her warm, soft cheek to hers. Coco smells the vanilla-cream scent of her daughter's apricot-soft skin. Feels Mary's hand pat her back in comfort, a gesture she's always done from a tiny toddler. It makes Coco's throat constrict, no sadness, just joy at the well of love being refilled. 'I love you, Mum,' she says, kissing her cheek, then lowers her head to Coco's stomach and, stroking it with her hand, whispers to its contents. 'Alright baby, are you happy in there? You get busy growing and come out big and strong to play. We're all waiting.' And she smiles, listening, waiting for the reply.

'I love you too, sweetheart. But a baby never comes until it's ready, whoever's waiting. Can you remember Joan being born?'

'Of course!' Mary replies indignantly. 'It was upstairs and all the buckets were filled with mess and the sheets were in a terrible state . . .'

'I know, it was all that afterbirth. There's a reason why so many people have their babies in hospitals, so they don't have to do the clearing-up afterwards. Goodness, is that the time? I've got to get on with all of this.' Coco stands up with a rush of short-lived panic, before sitting down again.

'But Mum, what has that got to do with what you were saying?'

'What was I saying? Some days I think I've put my brain into the Magimix along with the mayonnaise!'

'*Uch*!'

'About babies coming at the right time and Joan. Remember?'

'Oh yes. Well, Joan was supposed, according to the doctors, to be a Capricorn and be born in January, but Joan decided she'd rather be an Aquarian and refused to come out for another two weeks. Maybe she decided she just didn't want to be a goat. Now you go upstairs and play.' Coco strokes her daughter's head on her belly, straightens the strands of her hair away from Mary's sweet, calm face. If that moment could be held and glass-domed, like a snowstorm, and then sprinkled across the earth with a shakerful of Jesus' icing sugar, there would be gentle perfect peace everywhere, thought Coco. Not ecstasy or soaring jubilation but quiet and filled and eternally sweet.

Mary gets up and moves away as easily as she came to Coco. Coco goes back to whipping the large bowl of stiffening cream and the only clear noise is the last of the summer bees sliding under the window, drawn by the colour and warmth of the kitchen like a giant sunflower, buzzzzzzzz. Coco looks at Mary trailing her finger over the cupboard surfaces, the light blue eyes, like large sapphires set in the snow of her pale, thin-skinned face, the juniper stain of her mouth never quite closed and the adult slim, straight nose that she so badly wanted to be pugged.

Mary, her firstborn, was really growing up, thought Coco again. She was never quite sure of where those years in between went, of her being a baby one minute – warm, soft and helpless, ceaselessly hungry, crying or sleeping – and now this big independent thing.

'I don't want to play really. I've got a book I want to finish.'

'What's the book?'

'*Swallows and Amazons* by Arthur Ransome. Dad got it for me last week. Did you ever read it? It's quite good and exciting, but old-fashioned, but far better than the Enid Blyton, I don't believe those. Which were your favourites?'

'No, I never did either. I think my favourites were *The Secret Garden* and *The Lion, the Witch and the Wardrobe*, and *The Phoenix and the Fire*. Let's go to the library tomorrow in town and I'll show them to you.'

'I've read *The Secret Garden*, remember, Mummy, you gave it to me last Christmas, silly, and we went to the film with Granny.'

'Of course. While you're here, can you pass the vanilla sugar over, from the bottom cupboard?'

'Hmmm. What are you making? This is the best smell in the world.'

'Do you think you can tear your nose out of the jar for long enough to let me pour some into the ice cream? There, now you can sniff it for as long as you like. Not for ever, I don't want to have to be saving up to send you to a vanilla-sugar rehabilitation centre. Is Carol upstairs with Joan?'

'Oh Mum! Yes. They're making the beds together. Just one more sniff. Carol is probably making them and Joan is jumping on top of them. You know Joan, maybe she is a goat really.'

'Is she still running about in her Cinderella dress? If she is, can you make sure she puts a cardi on top, or a vest underneath or something. I'm surprised she doesn't freeze to death sometimes, she hardly wears any clothes even in winter.'

'Dad said it was something to do with her metabolt rate, I think, being higher, that means she gets hotter than us and that's why she eats so much, so that she keeps warm, you see. But I'll try and put something on her. When you hear the screams, you'll know I'm doing it.

'OK, see ya, can I take a biscuit or four, thanks.'

And she was off, thumping the floorboards with her sure-footed step, not waiting for the reply. Up to the old servants' quarters where they all slept and played, or pretended to; the reality was more that they spread themselves over the house like a shaken trail of flour.

★ ★ ★

Coco got up and arched her back, stretching and pulling her shoulders against the knuckles of her hands, her ever-swelling breasts to the fore. Why did she go on having children when she couldn't stand the heaviness of her breasts that seemed to grow at a faster rate than the baby, or the backaches, or her water-retaining legs that became so tender she couldn't bear to scrape a razor across them to remove the stubble? Now her legs looked more like fir trees than fillings for silk stockings, and the baby would be here just after Christmas, the real stocking filler.

Optimistically, she thought, at least there wouldn't be the heavy clot of periods for the next year and a half, a saving on Tampax, to be spent on nappies.

The first time Coco started having her periods after Mary, she'd so forgotten what it was like that she'd end up changing her clothes five times a day, like an inexperienced teenager leaking over everything. She humiliated herself in public more than once in a pair of white trousers that soon developed a tell-tale scarlet streak. What do you do when you're out at the shops in the middle of summer with nothing to hide it with? Just keep on walking and pretend you don't know it's there. What else can you do? Pray that somebody doesn't kindly stop to tell you.

Finishing her stretch, Coco got the lemons and steel grater and started to grate their skins roughly away. Once white and soft, she deftly sliced the fruit in two, a fork inserted into the middle of the flesh. Her fingers squeezed the pith against the steel hardness releasing the juice over the cream and sugar, like pee over snow which doesn't melt, forming its river of connecting pools, then settling like rain on the rocks.

One, two, three, four, five and done. Ouch, a little of the acid had seeped on to her bandaged finger. She waved her finger in the air as if it was a wand to magic the sharp pain away, before stirring all the ingredients together.

Two-thirds of the grated lemon skins were stirred in, melting together, the thin strands of yellow obliterated by the buttery-coloured cream. She dipped a finger into one of the peaks and wiped the syllabub across her tongue, and then added the Madeira.

'Hmm, just right. Delicious, just the right measure of lemon to sherry to cream,' Coco talked to herself across the room.

It'll be something near perfection when it's served tonight, ice cream cold on top of the warm treacle tart, she thought, carrying it to the ice-cream machine in the cupboard, pouring it in, setting the machine in motion and closing the door on it so she didn't have to hear the irritating whir. She turned to the cassette player and put on some Debussy, humming and gently sailing her arms and legs across the kitchen in an Isadora Duncan-style dance. That's what she liked to think, though when the children caught her at it, they always laughed and pointed. Even Joan, wanting to be the same as her siblings, though she loved to dance would point and giggle, and Bill would say his usual 'Too much peppermint tea, if you ask me, she's gone mad as a parrot again.'

CHAPTER SEVEN

'Whooa with that gin! Is there any tonic?'

'I think there was some, it's got the yellow label. Here,' I pour a dash in to be swallowed by the gin occupying most of the glass. 'If you want ice, Barbara's gone to get some from the bath.'

'Thank you, that'll be fine.'

I am behind the drinks table set up as a bar tall enough, just, for the job of serving the drinks. Barbara is helping me but has gone to fill the plastic pineapple with ice. Thomas, Wanda and Mary are supposed to be serving the crisps and Twiglets and emptying ashtrays.

Mummy had said Barbara, Mary, Thomas and Wanda, who were staying the night, and I, could be the barmen and butlers until bedtime, keep us out of trouble. We saw it as a way to stay up late. How would any of the grown-ups remember when bedtime was, once the party had got going, but there's always one that spoils the fun.

'Aren't you a little small to still be up, young lady? It is gone ten.'

'Can I get you a drink? You see, we're being the butlers, aren't we, Mummy?'

'Yes chicken, you've been fabulous barmen,' she says with a glazed smile of acceptance.

Looking around at the results, I suppose we have. Everybody is careering around the room dancing to Tom Jones's, 'It's Not Unusual', or doing a standing stagger trying to have conversations.

Looking at drunk grown-ups is funny at first, but loses its

appeal once they start falling over you and laughing too loudly, shouting at your face as though you were deaf, talking too slowly or repeating everything. We're tired, it's hard work pouring gin, Scotch and vodka all night, remembering the ice, the lemon, the tonic. I never seem to be able to get the measures right, though nobody ever complains. But are you supposed to put more tonic in, or more vodka?

'I'll have whatever they're drinking. Looks like a crazy party!' a newly arrived guest exclaims.

'I'm afraid you'll have to get it yourself. We're going to bed,' we say, taking the bowls of crisps with us, forgetting the overflowing ashtrays and refill duty. The room is dark, smoky and crowded, spilling into the hallway and downstairs to the kitchen. In the full throb of the party nobody notices our departure.

'Night, Mummy,' I say, trotting off with the others. Upstairs we cram into our warm clean beds to fall asleep head to toe, to the sounds of the Beach Boys.

In the morning we creep downstairs to view the remains, slippers on, minding the broken green glass. The smell of stale smoke and gin permeates everything. Sniffed on waking, it had seeped through the floorboards to our room, curled its way up the staircase to our nostrils and pulled us out of bed.

If we tidy up the mess from the party Mummy will give us five pounds to share between us. If we don't some student hippy will get the money, while we watch him swallowing the leftovers. If we take on the job, it means washing and hoovering the floors, not our favourite thing, and doing the washing-up, but then we could spend the rest of the day eating Chocolate Éclair toffees that can remove a filling in a chew, Peanut Crunch that can splinter and crack your teeth in two, and Sherbet Lemons that give you the excruciating pleasure-filled pain of scratching the roof of your mouth, letting the acid of the sherbet seep its way through to the cut, on the very first sweet. We can buy a whole bunch of American horror comics and sit in the square reading them until Dr Who is on the telly and we can hide behind the sofa watching it. After, we'll still have money left over for a choc ice when the ice-cream van tinkles around the square.

On Saturdays, we might walk up and down the King's Road, Barbara, Wanda, Hillary and me, in a gang. We pretend we're very rich customers, daring each other into the shops with the snootiest shop assistants, browsing until we collapse giggling. Sometimes we sneak through the magic den of jewelled stalls in the Chelsea antique market, looking for an enamelled art nouveau butterfly brooch for Mummy's birthday or Christmas present. Through the smoke-filled passages of sickly incense and upstairs, there's a café where we once saw Jimi Hendrix puffing on an ornate pipe, lying on purple velvet rugs and against mirrored, sequinned cushions like our waistcoats.

We do it; the clearing-up. Mummy is delighted and even helps us do the floor. She never snitches on a deal or tries to get it cheaper, like some adults, because we're children. All she wants is the Alka Seltzer and a cup of tea. Poor Mummy, she's always got a hangover at the weekends and now that Richard lives with us they seem to be worse. When they've got really bad hangovers, Richard and Mummy go to the pub for lunch and drink Bloody Marys until they feel better. Richard's always getting into arguments. Mummy's friends don't like him. Daddy doesn't either. Sometimes I do, sometimes I don't. It's difficult, isn't it, when people are so sorry afterwards for what they've done when they've been drunk. The thing is, Mummy seems to think it's all right and soon forgets about whatever happened or makes it into a joke, as if that's what you get when you go out, or that's what being in love is about. Being drunk and shouting and fighting, then making up and being friends again, all sickly gooey, lovey-dovey.

Being eight I still don't understand. Why did Mummy give up all her boyfriends, from before and after Cecil, and choose just to be with Richard, who she's just met and who can't even ride a bicycle or a horse? He's a Scottish piano player, but he says 'I'm a Celt composer', and twirls the ends of the orange moustache he's so proud of.

Which is much grander. He doesn't like any of Mummy's old records around and says he wants to make her study his own, and put a piano in it too. One day he clears it out and puts all her things by the side of the house for the rubbish men to collect, so I ring up Barbara and we hide it all, including her Cilla Black records in the garden shed to be played with on rainy days.

'It was only junk, and a composer needs his space!' says Mr Richard Jones.

Mummy smiles back soppily at her new live-in lover.

'Well, I do most of my rehearsing and learning lines in the sitting room,' she says. 'It was all old rubbish anyway.'

That is that.

Things change.

Mummy's changed from going out by herself all the time. Every evening soaking in a bath, dolling herself up or out working every night for months in some play or other. I would sit in my bed, with a glass of warm milk and honey, comfort, and a packet of nuts and raisins after I've brushed my teeth, bribery, the babysitter in front of the new round red hanging telly, downstairs. Mummy's still in the bathroom, 'doing her eyes', splashing on Brut for men, wearing her Ozzie Clark leather jacket.

The deal was, I was allowed to have a good time as long as I allowed her to; I could have friends come over to stay or go over to them, just as Mummy could.

All that's gone.

I'm still not allowed to moan or say I'm bored. Ever. It is worse than swearing, Mummy says, we have so much in that all our faculties work, how can anyone ever be bored. Sometimes I test for effect: 'Boring!' or, 'But it's so boring there, Mummy.' Emblazons a calculated rage. I hadn't tried swearing until I was about six, there was no need, so much of it being said about the house, 'Sodding this', 'Bugger off', 'Cock and balls', 'Little prick', 'Bloody hell', 'Fucking fabulous', or the simple but effective 'Cunt', were the regular expletives ricocheting around the house. One day I try.

'Coco, can you go downstairs and fetch my coat.'

'Fuck off,' I smartly reply, rather pleased at getting it right.

I feel the sharp swipe across the side of my head by her hand, full of knuckleduster rings. I crash to the floor in defeat.

I had taken Mummy off guard, the remorse came in as large a portion as the hit. I didn't say it again; I prefer the consequences of whining, 'I'm bored'. Easy to do now Richard and Mummy stay home.

Daddy has girlfriends, too; some of them turn magically into wives, or disappear as quickly as they arrive, some do both. Perhaps I will wake up one morning and Richard will have gone . . .

Daddy invites me to his wedding parties. The first is to Sonny who is beautiful and kind and sweet. I didn't know her long before the wedding and not very long afterwards, and pretty quickly she was gone. It's a pity, I always liked her, but I never saw her again, don't know why. I can't ask, 'What happened to Sonny?' And it had been such a big party.

Marguerite was the next time Daddy got married. Barbara and I were fitted with burgundy velvet dresses from Harrods and even got sent to a hairdresser's on the day of the wedding for our hair to be curled and ribboned for the reception at the Ritz.

Marguerite has a halo of dark brown backcombed hair, like Bobby Gentry the singer, but the similarities end at the shoulders. From there Marguerite is long-backed and flat-bottomed, which fascinates me as I've got a curvy back and a sticky-out bum and I hadn't thought they made them flat, like boys' bottoms. She has long thin legs and a constant all-over tan, like she's been dipped in Bisto. She has a loud, posh, deep voice and calls everybody 'darling', while waving her jewelled hands about.

'Why doesn't she have any bosoms, Daddy?'

'Sshh, sweetheart,' Daddy replies, when she's sunbathing in the garden, topless.

She is very rich but nothing ever seems to be quite right for her. I have a soft spot for Marguerite, even though she is rather hard. Maybe because she always looks so perfect, like a dummy in a shop window: patent-leather boots, bag and minidress always matching, immaculately painted pink-pearled lips and solid-blue eyelids, hair like black-inked Js on either side of her suntanned face.

It's how I like to remember her best, but things change and mostly I think of her with her mouth wide and shouting.

They bought a house and Daddy gave Marguerite a cat called Tom, instead of any babies. Daddy always said he'd had his one, I was enough. They even decorated a room with bunk beds and Tom and Jerry wallpaper for me and allowed me to have friends to stay. I didn't stay many weekends there, in the house with furry white carpets, clear glass coffee tables layered with magazines and a massage table for Marguerite's daily attendant.

I think Daddy and Marguerite tried to play families together, I even had my sixth birthday party there, but she got very cross at all the mess. She was always getting cross. They were always having rows. Once Daddy and Marguerite got divorced they got on much better. They just shouldn't have got married. It certainly put Daddy off marrying – now he just has girlfriends and things are much better.

That's why the whole thing of Mummy getting married to Richard has got us all upset. Mummy tries to convince us that marriage won't change a thing to Richard living with us, but even I know that that isn't true. Marriage does change things, they get better for a bit and then they just get worse. Like with her and Cecil. Mummy starts telling me about the big party they'll have, how we'll both have new dresses, that I can choose anything I like from the whole of Biba. The excitement of the preparation sweeps us all up and even if responses are negative, I remember Mummy's reply to my reaction after asking me about Richard moving in.

Mummy, Richard and I are on a train going back to London from the seaside, where Granny lives, where Mummy has been in the musical, *The King and I*, all summer, where she met Richard. Richard was accompanying her on the piano. 'Love at first note,' she claims, constantly retelling the tale of their meeting. They've known each other for a couple of weeks, they have become inseparable. Why?

'There's a red long haired Jerry Brigg in bed with Mummy, who has sugar in his tea!' I shout out to Barbara (staying with us for the week), down the hall of Granny's house. I had taken her the usual cup of tea in the morning and been asked to bring another, and not to tell Granny.

Now we are sitting in a train with him and he is trying hard, trying to beguile me with jokes that adults think children will think are funny. I laugh, a willing audience, make him feel better. Make us all feel better.

There is something different about Richard to Mummy's other boyfriends, he is the same age as her but his hair's much longer, and I suppose it's his lack of sophistication that endears him to me. His voice is so different, but that's because he's Scottish.

Richard is sent to the buffet car.

'What do you think about Richard coming to live with us? Wouldn't it be fun! We'll do lots of things together and you know, Richard has two sons, and one of them is the same age as you, Coco.'

I want to make everything nice, take away the feelings of war that well in the pit of my stomach, the cannon of rebellion that I want to start in this small carriage. Do what Mummy wants, she seems to want it so bad. If I can pretend for long enough . . . If I can think of one thing, 'I think it will be all right, he tells funny jokes,' I say, but I can't stop myself there, my words and fears are running out of my mouth. 'He won't ruin everything, will he? It's nice just the two of us, do we have to have him, will it change everything?'

'Well, I've decided and I want him to, whether you like it or not. Richard's coming to live with us. He's moving in, in two weeks.'

That was the ultimatum, so anything I could've said would've made no difference.

I was right, it did change everything.

I am wearing a pale satin and chiffon medieval dress and match-ing floor-length jacket with pointed trailing sleeves. Around my neck is a matching beaded satin choker, and a wimple of a hat is pulled forward over my hair down to my charcoal-ringed eyes, my red-painted mouth and cheeks below. From the knees down, my legs are laced up in ribbons from embroidered Turkish slippers. Barbara is rather more tastefully subdued as the other bridesmaid in a pale beige silk trouser suit with matching stacked suede boots; a scarf casually tied around her curly hair hangs down to her shoulders. We are perfectly dressed for my mother's wedding, we've chosen the outfits ourselves, hitting the heights of sophisti-cation at nine and eleven.

High Street Kensington that Saturday was jam-packed to bursting, hooting, screeching, whooping standstill of traffic, as my mother and now stepfather descended the steps of the Registry office. Nothing quiet and dignified about this ceremony, it is a barefaced, boastful rant of their love. Mummy could hardly say 'I do' because she was laughing so much, but Richard's dour

Scottish tone is sternly audible. This is *the* wedding, nothing like
the one to Cecil; this is love. This was not an orthodox registry
wedding. No pretence there in the bride's clothes, floating in
fuchsia pink and orange silk-chiffon layers, her face demurely
hidden by a beaded web, the Chelsea harem-look circa 1970. The
groom wore a jolly kilt and a red and yellow fish tie and jacket;
everything clashes beautifully with his beard. On those steps
sophistication stops, enhanced by the dandruff-white and petal-
pink confetti, thrown in bucketfuls, covering everything, High
Street Kensington becoming a shaken snowstorm in March.

Off we troop, leading the parade, family first to the reception
at our house. I skip ahead to the car, pretending to be the Pied
Piper of Hamlyn, as everybody follows.

Champagne corks are exploding and we are guzzling the
contents along with all the other guests in the garden, living room,
kitchen and dining room of our house. I spy the French gourmet
buffet, the glistening strawberry cream tarts and relocate four
immediately into my stomach. The heady mixture of cream,
strawberries and champagne brings a rising nausea to my throat
and I run up to the bathroom with expectations of fast relief.
There is a queue of people and an irate barman banging on the
door, shouting.

'Can't you hurry up with that fuck, all the champagne's in the
bath.'

I giggle.

''Scuse the French.'

Out of the scuffling and from behind the locked door a
flushed-faced couple emerges: the man hides his face, the other, a
famous dancer, beams her way proudly out.

'It's all yours, darling,' she delivers with aplomb. A cat
stealing the cream.

'Sod it!' I think about these crowds of grown-ups, Barbara's
somewhere but it's not a children's party, or not as much of one as

I'd have liked. I go out to the garden and sit on the swing, to be alone. A photographer appears from nowhere and starts taking pictures, there is no escape from people today, they're in every crevice of the house, so I go to sit in my space at the bottom of the garden. But what on earth is Granny doing there with the spade under the rubber plant?

'Granny, what are you doing?' I ask, simply curious, not interrogating. Then I hear the familiar clink, clink of bottles, that sounds my approach disturbing her.

'Never you mind,' she says covetously. 'I'm just hiding a few bottles of this expensive champagne, it'll only be wasted, drunk by the rabble in there. This way there'll be some left for your mother when she comes back from honeymoon. No need to tell anyone, Jenny, I mean Barbara.' Granny's always getting our names muddled.

'It's Coco, Granny.'

'Mama, you don't need to go hiding champagne. Mama, there's more than enough for everyone. Come on back to the party, Cecil's asking after you.' Mummy's soft, cajoling voice, special for Granny, steers her away from her intentions.

The next-door neighbour, Eva, having witnessed it all asks, concerned, who is going to be looking after me during the honeymoon. It really doesn't matter, I have been self-sufficient for a long time now.

Suddenly Barbara's there, pulling me inside.

'Coco, Coco come with me, we're all upstairs in your room looking through the floorboards at this man doing a striptease!' she says.

Giggling, we race up the stairs, not sure if we want to look once he's got no clothes on, only to make the disappointing discovery that he's only taken his jacket and tie off.

CHAPTER EIGHT

DINNER – Sat 15 October.

❖

Gazpacho caliente with garlic olive bread croutons
Hors d'oeuvres:
Sherry marinated fresh anchovies
Tomato and fennel salad dotted with black chilli olives
French beans with pine nuts
Bruschetta with salsa, verde agrodolce

❖

Melanzane Parmigiana
Mustard coated leg of lamb, roasted on a bed of vegetables
Creamed potatoes with leeks and nutmeg

❖

Old-fashioned treacle tart with lemon syllabub ice cream
Warm marmalade bread and butter pudding with crème fraîche.

❖

Cheeseboard and fruit
Coffee or herbal teas with cantuccinis

The white, bright, autumn sun beckoned Coco outside. She picked up her special pen and wedge of paper from the drawer and went through the french windows to the wooden bench and table under the arbour. Sitting with a direct hit of sunshine upon her closed eyelids, she basked in the moment of quiet calm and the cool air that stroked the back of her exposed neck, vulnerable with her hair up in a pleat. Coco breathed in through her nose the rain-soaked earth, the winter roses, the warm, comforting kitchen smells of baking bread and browning pastry. Heard the bubbling on the cooker, the birds tweeting, the leaves being blown from the trees and somewhere from an open window upstairs, the familiar tone of Woman's Hour, and she was lost, melted into the universe; she could feel what it was like to be a blade of grass growing, a cloud forming.

The baby inside her kicked and she sat up with a start. The moment was gone, but not before she pocketed it completely and fastened it away in a time capsule to be brought out, examined and played with whenever she wanted to. Coco had always done that, consciously sealed little pockets of time, dated and preserved them, just like they had showed you how to do in a Blue Peter special on archaeology. She'd dug up half the garden burying packages to be found by ancestors or dogs in the future, full of 'symbols of our time'. For months after her enthusiasm had passed, her mother still moaned and questioned her about losing eyebrow tweezers, can-openers, false nails and eyelash curlers. If she had only looked in the garden, dug behind the ferns, loosened the stone in the corner of the shed, she might have found one of the shortbread-biscuit tins, the pictures spoilt by Coco's haphazard compass-point engraving that read: 'This tin is from the year AD 1970, put here by Coco Johnson, aged seven, human being, London, England, Planet Earth, The Universe. Not to be opened until the year AD 2000.' You could never be too sure who would be leading the expeditions in the future. It was sealed with two rolls of Sellotape, because after she'd finished the first roll, Coco realised she'd left out the halfpenny coin, an essential part of the collection. So the whole thing had to be cut through with the kitchen knife, the coin put in place and then resealed and buried.

One of the thoughts she liked to have was that somebody would discover it, just like Anne Frank's diary, and wonder who this Coco Johnson was and what she was like. Inside she had written a description of herself and stuck in a photo. The only one she could find was one of her on holiday with Barbara, holding hands. She didn't like Barbara at that moment and so she cut her off, even if it did mean losing one hand. Later when they made it up and Barbara had let her have all the green triangles out of the Quality Street box of chocolates she had got for her birthday, Coco had weakened and admitted what she had done: shown her, her secrets, the bit of the photo. Barbara had made her dig the box up straight away, cut open the tape and put in the missing bit of the photo plus a full description of who Barbara was: 'Beautiful, intelligent, star of her time with a rare wisdom for her age, twelve. Child of royalty from a love-torn union, secretly adopted by ordinary (very) parents. Misunderstood but courageous cousin to Coco.'

That box was dug up and hidden so often, that even the cats had started to suspect that a dog had buried its favourite bone there, and now they chose to go around the garden via the wall rather than cross the fern patch.

Coco unscrewed the cap of her italic pen and started to write the menu out in a *fin de siècle* manner, all swirls and fanciness. When she'd finished writing out the list of food, a spring of saliva jumped through her tongue, and she knew she'd made the right choices. Yummy-yum, yum, her greedy little voice agreed.

She was just about to get up and go back into the kitchen when she felt a soft tickle on her neck. She knew it was one of the children. She had pretended not to notice the rustling in the bushes and was half expecting a commando-style attack from Bill or the squeaks of Joan turned into a guinea pig.

Instead, it was the feel of tiny fingers or softly tapping feathers that disturbed the hairs on her neck.

'Hello, is that my Squirrel Nutkin! Or is it Mrs Tiggy-winkle?' She slowly turned about, her hand protectively reaching around her neck to stop the excruciating tickles. She smiled at her children's sweet gentleness, tender fingers.

'Mum, don't! Get your hand away, you'll kill or squash Terry.'

'Terry? Who is Terry, and what is he doing on my neck?' her controlled tone asked.

'He's my new friend. I found him in the tool shed. Terry is a spider.'

'Bill! Get him off me before you're roasted for dinner, you little animal,' Coco's voice rose with serious intention.

'Stop moving, Mum. Now he's gone up inside your hair. Now look what you've done, I can't get him, I'll have to wait until he comes out. Terry, Terry, don't be frightened.'

'Bill!'

'What? It's only a spider and you're bigger than him, think how frightened Terry is.'

What was I thinking of, my children's sweet gentleness? Her skin shivered with each twitch of her scalp as she imagined whole families of spiders had moved into her bun. She shrugged her shoulders and waited for Terry, watching Bill's cross face twisted in concentration before her. The tranquillity was splintered – she couldn't help but laugh.

'Mummy, it's not funny, stop it! Stop . . .' Bill was smiling, contorting his face trying not to laugh, cross at giving in, his dark brown eyes twinkled anyway and his body soon creased to their laughter. Soon neither Coco nor Bill knew what they were laughing about except from the sound that geed the other on, the kind that was good for you, that shook your stomach and shoulders. The kind of laughter that wipes away the nasty parts of a day and disappears as you get older, more cynical to those who can only comment 'How droll', with a raised eyebrow. People immune to tickling. The kind of laughter that scares spiders to death with its noise.

'Monster!' Coco lunged at her son, her belly toppling her to the warm, damp grass, and tickled him remorselessly.

'No Mummy, no Mummy. You're the best Mummy in the world, Mummy *please*, honestly.'

CHAPTER NINE

I'm hiding the sleek, green Gordon's gin bottle in the cupboard where the gas meter is kept, before Mummy gets home. I'll put it back in its place in the kitchen if Mummy hasn't been drinking, otherwise I'm keeping it hid. I'm not taking the chance. I know she'll be annoyed when she can't find it, but it'll be worse if she's had a head start on Richard and they get drunk. That's when the fights start.

Of course, the worst fights are when they've gone out to parties or dinners and Mummy has usually behaved outrageously, taking her clothes off or saying the wrong things. Then they wake me up with their shouting and screaming and slamming the front door. One night it got so bad and Richard was so angry he tore all the banisters down with one arm, as effortlessly as pushing over a set of dominoes. Hiding terrified under my blankets, frightened dumb, my ears were alert as rabbits for the next onslaught.

Mummy began throwing bottles out of the bathroom, down the stairs towards Richard's head.

'Coming to get you, bitch, I'll beat some sense into you,' he shouts back in retaliation. Smash, goes the bottle of Chanel No. 5, staining the wallpaper, making sure of a permanently perfumed hallway.

All I could do was lie there and listen to the cries for help, immobilised with fear. I suppose we're all frightened in this house.

Later, Mummy crept into my bed, the top bunk, like a wounded animal snuffling with pain, but what could I do to make things better? I cuddled her to sleep, hoping it was a nightmare. Hoping the next day Richard would be gone; but it was like an

Etch-A-Sketch or a blackboard, the mess wiped clean, all gleaming with daylight.

Mummy was gone the next morning as I got up for school, but broken and smashed on the floor was the fire, Mummy's favourite Magicoal.

The honeymoon is over with Richard and Mummy's return and family life starts in earnest. Jim, one of Mummy's best friends and favourite photographer ('Always shoots her best side'), gave them as a wedding present a year's supply of Alka Seltzer, but I shouldn't think it will last them that long.

It's not really that much different to before they were married, but it's a lot different to her being married to Cecil. Sometimes I wish we were back in Brockingford, but we're banned from going there. Cecil keeps inviting us and Richard says *no*. My pony's been sold, Cecil told Mummy, there was nobody to ride him.

Mummy still goes to work on the TV series she's in every week where she plays a nurse, and she's stopped taking work on films away, so she can earn regular money to keep the home going.

Richard goes up to his locked and bolted studio; he and his friends have started a band, and spend hours rehearsing. It sounds more to me like the kind of music I used to make on my xylophone when I was three. Plink, plonk, plink, bong, bong, bong, goes the piano. It is made more than clear to me and my friends that there are to be no demands made upon Richard, not for any reason. In case we forget, there is a big 'Do Not Disturb' sign on his studio door.

I must see to myself when I come home from school, make sure the food is there, ready to be cooked for dinner, that my homework is done and that I keep myself quietly occupied until Mummy returns at six-thirty or seven o'clock. We have steak and salad for dinner most nights, sometimes chicken. We must be there for dinner around the dining table, a modern, bleached varnished oblong table with benches either side, at seven-thirty. I must be in bed by nine.

We keep out of the house, Barbara and I, rather than tiptoe around it. Sometimes we go to Barbara's house and tiptoe around there because Auntie Anna has one migraine after the other, she says, she always has to sleep after lunch. Barbara's dad is never home. Uncle Ian has to work late and go away on business trips a lot, that's why Barbara likes coming around to our house, because it's so dark and quiet in theirs, with nothing out of place. At least in our house when Richard's out we can run around screaming and turn the living room into an adventure playground, magic castle or special den.

Barbara doesn't like talking about her mum and dad, some-times she pretends that mine are hers. She says they are too embarrassing to talk about. If I stay over at her house, dinners are never properly cooked – the vegetables are hard and the chicken's all bloody with veiny, stringy bits. Barbara pleads with me not to complain. We eat it whilst Auntie Anna lies on her velvet sofa with a bottle of wine by her side telling us tales of her and her brothers and sisters when they were children in India and never even had to dress themselves because there were so many serv-ants. The jungle was their garden and they had real pet monkeys to play with. Her daddy was right, she always says, she was silly and headstrong, she married beneath her.

I ask Barbara what she means, but she won't talk about it and starts to sulk.

I've given up asking Mummy about Auntie Anna, there's always the same reply.

'Yes, poor Anna, she was so beautiful when she married your uncle.'

I go to friends' houses, some days play in the square, go to the library a lot – I spend hours in the library until they tell me to go home. Richard sometimes talks to me about books, about music when we watch Top of the Pops together, and tells me stories. This is nice because he seems to know a lot and he did buy me *The Lion, the Witch and the Wardrobe* which has started me off on C.S. Lewis. The librarian tells me I should slow down otherwise I will have read all the books in the children's library before I'm allowed in the adults'. I'm not going to read all the books in the children's, I say, some I wouldn't touch with a bargepole, like Enid Blyton.

Richard sometimes jocularly complains of the pressure of being the only man in this once girl-only house, the only Celt in this English home, and I suppose he must find it difficult being in London England, instead of Scotland, in a different house in a different life. He makes it known that he does not like to be called Mr Johnson, not even by the postman, let alone *plus one* on all the invitations that arrive for Mummy for parties and premières, but he could hardly expect her to change her name to Mrs Ricky Jones. Nobody would know who she was.

When you are married to the kind of actress my mother is, you can't wear any old jeans, any old clothes. Poor Richard is patiently dragged around clothes shops until something that's fashionable fits him. He hasn't the model's figure for tight-thigh trousers and skinny-sleeved suits in bright-coloured cottons from Stirling Cooper, he's neither tall nor thin, but thick-set and stocky. Mummy makes it quite clear that he cannot go around in his old tweed jacket and comfortable corduroys or kilts all the time. Mummy likes us all to look nice. I am dressed in Biba or Mr Freedom, Mummy has clothes from St Laurent, Ozzie Clark, Quorum, Bus Stop. I hate the endless dragging around looking in shops for hours, I suppose Richard does too, but he doesn't complain, sweetly docile and smitten with Mummy when sober. That's Mummy's job, she says, looking good, and sometimes we have to come along. 'I'm never going shopping when I grow up,' I tell Mummy.

Barbara says, 'I will. Can I come next time? I'm going to go shopping all the time when I'm a movie star.'

Barbara says I don't know how lucky I am to have Ricky as a mother.

The three of us are off to America. Suddenly we are flying to California, Mummy says it's wonderful, sea, sun and oranges. Richard has got a job teaching music arranging at a university for the four-month-long summer sabbatical. Everybody is greatly relieved that Richard, self-appointed head of the house, is going to earn some money.

It's all very well marrying a man the same age as her, but one without money or position, in the world that we inhabit, makes it difficult. We have to work very hard to make him feel at ease. Richard calls anyone posh or English 'an upper class prick'; worse, when he really doesn't like them. Daddy doesn't like him, and he doesn't like Daddy. Which is almost enough of a reason to go away, now that Daddy is back in Europe. At least in America Richard won't be able to tell someone's class by their accent.

Barney is the opera-singer friend of Mummy's, who has secured this job for Richard. 'Easy as piss, and you get to screw all the students if you want.' Barney helpfully explains the job, laughing raucously through his black beard, his thin face peeking out from his dark curls; he should have been fat!

He teaches singing out there permanently in California, living with his wife and daughter in a dreamy beach house surrounded by fields and trees, looking out on to the sea with a little path that leads down to their private beach.

Our apartment here in California is a suburban condo, on the edge of town, but it's got a swimming pool where I go every day and train in life-saving with the other kids. Surrounded by steady roads to ride my bicycle on, there is no need to think of things for me to do. Mostly I am captivated by the TV that continues all night and day with an endless stream of old Hollywood movies and musicals, Mum's and my favourites. Starting the day at seven a.m. with *Here's Lucy* is enough to convert us to the American way of life, along with my new diet of butterscotch swirl ice cream, hot dogs, fresh orange juice and red liquorice shoelaces. I practise my American accent in the mirror at night, but during the day my new friends only want to hear me speak English. 'Say "pavement" again', they laughingly encourage, but what they really want to know is whether I've met The Beatles. I wear my hair like the other girls', in pigtails, with sneakers on my feet, Bermuda-short cut-offs and a T-shirt, nothing with a label on here. I ride my bike around the neighbourhood and climb the cherry tree in the garden.

The weekends are often spent on Barney's beach with other lecturers and their families, having barbecues, playing and swimming. The adults get so drunk on beer and whisky they can't swim, but they can crawl back up to the house to drink some more. That's when Sara, Barney's wife, always goes for a swim, to get away from 'my ugly bastard of a husband'. Everybody tries to stop her except Barney, but she violently reels off into the sea saying she's heading for Australia or Yugoslavia, never to return.

'Here's hoping!' Barney crosses his fingers above his head for everyone to see, and winks at his favourite student, Kam-Li, who always seems to be with him.

You can watch Sara swim out until she disappears from the horizon: it's always an inevitable surprise when she returns, staggering, dripping, her blonde hair worn like seaweed, and shouting like the Creature from the Black Lagoon: 'Somebody get me a fucking drink!' and somebody does because she quietens down for that minute.

The evening party is well under way by then, nobody gives up until the last beer is drunk and all the drive-in off-licences are closed. The kids play, ride in our jeans and bare, brown-skinned unisex uniforms, biking around the lanes, climbing astride un-saddled horses in the field to pick all the plums on the trees. When our faces are full and our bellies and hands stained red with the juice, we watch TV, snack popcorn for dinner as the clear dark sky fills with stars. Falling asleep on other people's beds, we are woken to stumble into the car and sleep the bumpy ride home.

Georgia (Sara and Barney's daughter) and I are lying on these enormous rug-covered sofas in the living room. We've been on the beach all day and we're tired and meant to be asleep, so we're not. We're watching the Late, Late Horror Movie Special. Next door are the rowdy drunken grown-ups in the kitchen, their noise growing more hysterical by the minute.

'Hey! Pipe down! Quiet!' we shout from where we lie, obnoxious children to the last.

'God! Aren't grown-ups the pits! They think just because they own the goddamn house they can make as much noise as they fuckin' well like.' At eight, Georgia holds a healthy disdain for her parents' behaviour, drunk or sober. I suppose I just put up with it, accept it as the way it is, now that I am nine and a half, and older than her.

When the shrieks and laughter from next door override the volume of the TV, I drag myself off the sofa to turn it up, but once up and on two feet I decide to go and investigate the cause of all the hilarity. I'm walking through the front door towards the warm, windless evening to the window at the side of the house to peek. I'm shocked. I call for reinforcements.

'Georgia!' I shout hoarsely. 'Come and see this! All the men are lined up, naked, measuring their cocks on the kitchen table. *Uch*! It's disgusting.'

Something tells me this family sabbatical we have taken in the land of the brave and the free hasn't been a complete success. Richard and Mummy have started to argue, again.

Rattling at each other's cages, I keep well away. Even the sweetness of the Shirley Temple cocktails he buys us at the faculty dining club can't take the edge off it. Mummy had taken the time out to write her first play, much against her agent's advice, and it hasn't got written, the socialising has seen to that. Nothing like an excess of a good time to make you feel really bad.

'It was an accident,' says Richard deadpan to Mummy, after spilling a cup of coffee over her white silk dress in the airport coffee shop.

We're boarding the plane home.

'You and Freud say there's no such thing as an accident,' Mummy replies with lip-protruding petulance.

I raise my eyes and sigh, digging into another pancake smothered in maple syrup and melting butter, go back to my *Tales from the Dead* comic, sneer at them and the prospect of the twelve-hour flight back; I feel sick.

We're back in England, just settling into our old pink house again when it's all change. The house is too small for our new family; Richard wants a recording studio; Mummy needs a room to write her play and I have new stepbrothers, Ian thirteen, Tim ten, who come to stay from Glasgow every school holiday.

The house is certainly not big enough for these boys, who seem to fight all the time about Action Men. Even the kitchen cupboards aren't large enough to hold the amount of food needed to feed them. OK, Barbara and I fight, but not about boy dolls! We fight about important things, like who gets to win Monopoly or Cluedo, comics, sweets and books.

Boys are strange, foreign things, I'm discovering now, having these stepbrothers live in our house. I've always had boys as friends but it's not the same as living with them, always having to flush the loo after them, wipe the seat or put it down again. They don't change their clothes or decide to have baths and their feet smell. I like Tim because he's only a week older than me and we like the same things and I've always been a tomboy, climbing trees, happier on my bike or a horse than off. Boys are more fearless of adventures and most of the time that fearlessness protects you. I've never thought I was going to break an arm/leg, and never have and I've only ever fallen off a horse a couple of times. If you think bad things are going to happen to you, then in a way you've already decided, and it's no surprise when they do. Besides, I know I'm being protected.

'Told you so, told you so,' chants are almost worse than taunts of 'Scaredy cat, scaredy cat, sitting on a doormat.'

I've been brought up in our family as an atheist, especially with Richard and the boys ranting and raving about there not being Anything, that this is it and at the end, there's nothing else. God is a capitalist invention, stopping the poor from rebelling, 'Religion is the opium of the masses', they say. They come out with cheery mottoes like, 'This is the first day of the rest of your life', and any disaster is always 'Part of life's rich pattern', followed by a shriek of sick laughter.

Secretly, I've always had something there to pray to, to help me find my other shoe, Barbara's lost signet ring, for them to stop shouting, to bring Mary safely down from the woods . . .

But I wouldn't tell anybody – I can imagine what they'd say.

We'd gone on a picnic, Mary, her mother, twin brothers and me, to Hampstead Heath for the afternoon. It is summer and sunny across the blue skies and green parkland and the woods seem the only place to hold a cool shade.

'Where are you all off to? If you must climb trees, take your school dresses off and change into your shorts and T-shirts,' says Mary's mother, sensibly.

'I haven't got any with me.'

'Well, you wear Mary's shorts and she can wear the T-shirt, and you two don't let your brothers get lost, play together. I'll be here reading, come back when you're hungry.'

She was nice, Mary's mother, she always cooked the best food, like macaroni cheese made with crispy bacon and chunks of boiled egg suspended with the pasta in lots of cheesy sauce, and always asked if I wanted seconds before anyone else. I was probably at her house two or three times a week and sometimes I'd stay for weekends too. She never got cross and she always thought of good things for us to do, cooking, papier mâché, pottery. She was always at home, a warm cake cooking, steaming and delicious out of the oven.

So off we go to the woods. Of course, Mary's brothers are off and running away without us, but we've only just got to the top of our first tree before they return.

'There's a man here who says he'll show us where all the rabbit burrows are. Are you two coming?' they say in Tweedledum and Tweedledee unison.

'Oh alright, I suppose we have to keep an eye on them,' says Mary, though neither of us are that interested in rabbit burrows.

We follow them deep into the wood.

'So where are they? We've been walking for ages and they don't seem to be around here,' I complain, bored.

'We're nearly there, little girl,' says the grey-skinned old man leading the expedition. Maybe he's not that old but he's bent and weathered and reminds me of Mr Bader, the school bus driver. Faded and crinkle-faced when he talked, with leather-patched elbows on his tweed jacket and a tie-less, chequered Viyella shirt.

'Let's go back,' I say. 'They're not here.'

I feel edgy and see that the boys have wandered off in boredom. We've been left alone. He stops us in a glade. The man is now holding Mary tightly by the hand, wriggling the fingers of his other hand up the leg of her knickers.

'Do you like this, little girl? You do, don't you.' He takes his fingers out and returns them covered in a white cream, smiling. 'You like this, don't you?' he seems to be saying to himself.

I am struck dumb. I know that it is wrong. How many times have I been told not to talk to strangers, but it hasn't seemed important until now. I can't leave Mary there alone and in that minute that I am frightened frozen he grabs my wrist and holds it tightly in the same hand as Mary's. Mary stands there like one of the rabbits we never saw, affixed unblinking by the headlights of oncoming danger.

'Your friend likes it, let's see if you do too, little girl.'

He forces his rough bony hand down the front of my shorts. The touch of his fingers is hard, pressing into my softness, the cream is cold.

'Oh you do like it, don't you, I can tell.'

'No! No! I don't, *no!*' I scream and tear his hand away. I run and run and run, until I have reached the sunlight and I'm out of the woods. Escaping the magic of the fairy glade.

I'm at the top of the hill looking down, frantically searching around. All I can see is The Mother lying out on the rug under a tree, sunbathing, a book over her face. Full speed ahead, I run down to her, and I'm praying that Mary is running after me, that she has got away too – I can't look back. Out of breath I collapse on the blanket beside her mother.

'Where's Mary?' she murmurs sleepily.

Why did she have to ask that question? Any other I could've answered, algebra, Greek, the mystery of the Holy Grail, I don't know.

'Actually, I left your daughter with some strange man having horrible things done to her. It's alright, I managed to escape and I've left her there alone.'

I'm so wrapped in guilt and shame I hug my knees to my chest and bury my head, praying.

Please let her be all right. I concentrate the prayer hard, harder, hardest. All my muscles tensed in concentration, holding round my legs with all my strength, my knees indenting my forehead.

I should have rescued her; now it's too late, but I can't speak of this.

'She's coming back soon, I think she's with her brothers.' I cross fingers, half knowing it to be true, but I can't tell her the truth, it is too bad, I am too shy, too scared and ashamed. Then, like the final beacon, Mary appears on the top of the hill, running back and over, collapsing into her mother's arms, crying and telling what I could not.

'Coco, why didn't you tell me!'

'I don't know, I couldn't.' I hang my head, disgraced, and think I can feel her silent hot rage shouting through my shamed skin, all the way to the police, all the way back home.

What happened was nasty and horrible and we're not to tell anyone, the grown-ups say. I am told off for not telling. Mary was the victim and I, the holder of the dirty secret. We are not allowed to mention it. It was bad, dirty, disgusting. Are we too? Nobody says. Now none of the children dare tell the grown-ups of the man in our local square who appears with his pork-pie hat, tweed coat, briefcase and magazines full of naked bodies.

Mummy's found a new house, a five-bedroomed one and there is a junior school just five minutes away. We're leaving Chelsea, moving house and I'm moving school, but we'll be closer to the comprehensive, where I'll join Barbara next year. Mummy says everybody is sending their children there, the embodiment of socialist education, and it's free.

Maybe I won't be going after all. Barbara has started to mature nicely in her thirteenth year into a skinhead, covered in Ben Sherman, two-tone trews and heavy tasselled loafers. She is almost complete in her disguise away from Auntie Anna's daughter, with an attractive line in shrugs and mute moods.

Auntie Anna isn't very impressed. I'm not sure I even want her as my cousin any more, which is just as well as she's not too keen on me either. She says I'm a baby. She hangs out with her gang on the dodgems in Battersea Park trying to lose her accent and pick up black fairground boys. Her haircut is the one give-away as to her origins – the careful skinhead layering has been feathered into place at Auntie Anna's Mayfair hairdresser's. 'Ah well, we can but try. Until we can send her somewhere else at the end of the year,' I overhear Auntie Anna saying in resignation to Mummy.

I hardly have a chance to mock my cousin's transformation, too busy trying to chameleonise myself from Chelsea public-school girl into rough west Londoner.

'It's only for two terms, chicken, and then you'll be going on to grammar school and that is supposed to be awfully good. It's just too far to travel to Chelsea every day, at least here you don't have to wear school uniform.'

'But Mummy, you don't have to wear it in seniors anyway, at school!'

'Good. Well you don't have to wear it at this school either. How about we go out and buy you a new outfit, or shoes, for the start of term, eh?'

I think this is taking a few things for granted after my first day, like passing my eleven-plus and surviving the next two terms.

'We've got a new girl in our class this term and her name is Coco. I'm just going to run through some of the things we'll be doing this term. Mondays, music and maths, Tuesdays, art and English . . . Any questions? Yes, Coco?'

'Miss Taylor, when do we have French?' I innocently inquire.

Why's everybody laughing, including my teacher?

'Miss, Miss, what's French, is that why she's got a funny name?' asks one of the kids, genuinely ignorant.

'And a funny voice, like the queen, posh.' Sniggering asides.

'It's the language people in France talk. Why Coco, can you speak any French?'

'Of course I can.'

'Would you like to say something for us in French?'

With the howling laughter and pigtail-pulling and the hard

gazes of resentment, I quickly learn to keep my mouth shut and not rise to being called any list of bedtime beverages and clowns.

'No,' I firmly reply, and don't open my expensively educated, middle-class mouth for the other kids to mimic. Not for the rest of the day. Not until I've learnt the new language, the one that they all speak.

'Mum, please can't I leave,' I beg her, sobbing.

'It's only another two months until the end of the term, I can't take you away. I'll go and speak to the headmaster, alright?'

'But he'll only smack their bums and all the boys know he likes it. It never stops them from smokin' or stealin' or nickin' uvver kids' fings, not nofink, honest Mum.'

I have crawled my way home on the pavement, shocked and pained and bruised. I can hardly speak to Richard when he opens the door. Cross at being disturbed, Why haven't I used my key? He stops, realising my state, and leads me into the kitchen to make me a cup of tea.

I am being blackmailed for money and beaten up every day after school by the boys, my classmates. They don't touch me in the playground, because I have made sure that my best friend is Steph, the toughest girl in the school, whose speciality is grabbing girls by their ear lobes, knee-butting them in the nose and pulling their earrings out, all in one movement. You can't tell if there's more blood from their shredded ears or their broken noses. She's a clever girl, Steph, she even knows that however well she passes her exams she won't make it to the grammar. ''Cos I can't speak aw' lardy-da, lark you can, Miss Poncey.'

All niceties had been wiped clear off my lips by the time I had my interview at Daneston. I'd learnt new things and coveted new toys — records were the things to want, not chessboards and backgammon sets. In the playground we didn't sit and talk or turn the climbing frame into a spaceship. There was no

80

climbing frame. I learnt hopscotch with the squares drawn across the rough tarmac ground with a piece of chalk nicked from the classroom, juggling balls against the wall, What's On Telly At Four-forty-five On ITV? I'd never watched television that much before, now I memorised the *TV Times* and *Radio Times* as soon as it came through the door and determinedly found out what was happening to Meg and Jill Richardson on Crossroads. I never mentioned the ballet, theatre or time spent in museums, I didn't tell of the parties I went to, the Oscar nomination my mother almost got. I stopped going to the library. I pretended Barbara was my sister, 'and she's the leader of the biggest, most vicious Paki-bashing gang, and they carry razors', I boasted around the playground.

My teddy bears are hidden on top of my wardrobe and at night I secretly knit them warm jackets and sing them songs under my bedcovers. On Sunday nights when the theatre is closed, I can hear my mother playing Billie Holiday's last recordings: her voice, torn and sad, wails through my floorboards and sends me to sleep with the clickety-clack of the train that echoes away across the garden walls into the purple street-lit night.

'I'd like to accept your daughter into our school, she is bright and intelligent, but where on earth did she get her appalling accent from? What is it that you do that you allow your daughter to talk like this, do you work?' asks the headmistress of Daneston Grammar School for girls.

I had remembered enough of my past education to pass entry.

'Yes, I do actually. I'm an actress at the National Theatre and Coco's accent has purely temporarily changed itself into the accent of the local school she has been attending since we moved here from Chelsea. That's all. Of course you know Bernard Shaw, and how easily accents can be changed.'

I leave Daneston just after turning thirteen. My last report has shown my progression from As to Fs. The only subjects apart from art that I maintain scrupulously high marks in are bullying and religious knowledge, 'and me an atheist', I protest, outraged, crossing fingers and hoping God isn't listening.

Nobody understands where I could have learnt my bullying from. I could tell them, but I don't want to unbuckle my armour.

I have already been expelled from the church choir for reading *Candy* by Terry Southern. They hadn't caught me reading Nabokov's *Lolita* the week before, during the sermon. Mum is delighted, something to boast of proudly to her other enlightened friends. I'm not too cross about it, you get better-looking boys down the youth club on the Harrow Road than you ever do at church and you can smoke there, too, Players No. 6, just like Granny.

Mum's started having affairs again. I should have known from the records she's been playing. Once Ella's voice started to fill the house with 'Don't Fence Me In', swiftly followed by Mitzi's 'I'm Gonna Wash That Man Right Out Of My Hair', something's out. She's regaining some of her old spirit. I think the penny finally dropped that if she'd wanted to be a mother to three boys (Richard being the eldest of them), she would've had them herself. That's what I hear her shouting to Richard. That and, 'Don't expect me to be a hausfrau! Do your own bloody washing!'

Mum starts taking me out to the theatre. I sit and read in the green room while she's working, then we go out to dinners and parties. Now I'm *plus one* and Richard's in the pub. It's like being girls out together, my mum, my best friend, me and mine. We giggle in restaurants at the men who send notes over to our tables or gloat, leering. We link arms as we walk down the street, share cigarettes and sing songs from *West Side Story*, and *Singing in the Rain*, dancing around like Gene Kelly.

Mum's just finished her run. 'Hurrah! No more boring theatre, saying the same thing night after night, even Shakespeare starts to get dull, let alone Ibsen.' She always says that until she does a film and then says she can't wait to get back in front of live humans again who give a reaction. In the autumn she starts in a big series, so she's happy that something is in the offing, and it's like her allergy to rejection has been swept clean away.

'Neurotic? Me? Never. Of course I knew I'd get another job. I'm looking better now than I did ten years ago, why shouldn't I be working? I'm one of the best actresses working today!'

I wake up one morning and know what it is. She's happy; life is fun.

At the weekends we lie around to Richard's disgust watching black and white movies, legs slouched across the sofas. I love these times, when she paints my toenails, teaches me how to put make-up on and shows me what tweezers and eyebrow curlers are for. In between the beauty-parlour routine when we're lying still and rigid with face masks, trying not to speak, she tells me snippets of Hollywood gossip, old and modern, that make my mask crack up and crumble. We coin names after the tales: 'In-like-Flynn', 'Cola Arbuckle'. 'Gay-boy Gable'.

One day we're watching *Platinum Blonde* with Jean Harlow, 'sex in a satin slip'.

'You know she hasn't got any knickers on, or bra.'

Mum always wears a bra, 'cantilevering necessity'.

'In fact, she even shaved her pubic hair off so there wouldn't be any disturbance of that dress to her smooth lines. Harlow was famous for never wearing underwear and marrying gay men, pass me the chocs.'

'Never? Here.'

'Yes. Have you eaten all the caramels?'

'Yes, but I left the Brazil nuts.'

'No wonder she died of pneumonia, no knickers, she must have been freezing. Didn't her granny warn her to always wear clean knickers in case you're run over by a bus?'

'That and marrying a heterosexual.'

Mum starts gauging me as to whether I'd miss the family home and whether I love my stepfather, like she doesn't. Finally she breaks down and it all pops out with the champagne cork.

'It's over between Richard and me. I'm sorry, Coco, I tried to find a good father for you . . .'

'But Mum, I've already got a father, you don't have to find me one.'

'I know, I know, darling, I'm sorry. He called me yesterday. How do you feel about going to stay with him over in Spain? While I get everything sorted out here?'

'Of course I want to, Mum. If you came too we could go riding along the beaches.'

'I think I'd better deal with Richard before I give myself a holiday, darling. But thank you for inviting me. I'm not sure how thrilled your father's girlfriend would be if I turned up.'

When I get back from the holidays, Richard is gone. Four years and the marriage is over. I run up and down the stairs shouting, just to make sure. The emptiness echoes back at me.

'Yippee, yippee, yippee!'

Dad comes with me to England to try and find a boarding school for me now, somewhere posh where I'll talk properly again, call him Daddy instead of Dad, where I'll get an education in something more than religion. Thank God, he's decided on a coed: I'd go mad shut up with a load of girls, like Daneston, but twenty-hours a day.

Barbara's so grown-up now she can hardly speak to me. She has parties on Saturday nights when her and her friends snog all night with the lights off, smoking 'herbal' cigarettes and drinking cheap wine and cider. Terribly sophisticated, I don't think! Auntie Anna had to take her away from her school after they got to read all the reports that she'd never passed on, mostly about her habitual bunking off. She never invites me to meet any of her friends now she's not a skinhead any more. She's at a school for young ladies learning how to be a snob, or, as she puts it, a model.

In the middle of her parties, in our house while Mum's away, I'll charge in playing my saxophone, manoeuvre an anglepoise lamp into her doorway and then suddenly turn it on and laugh at everybody furiously putting themselves in order, unplugging themselves from each other, the boys wiping brown lipstick snogs off their mouths. So what if I'm jealous.

Such things alleviate the boredom before being sent away, and I have to have some time off to act as a child. I'm glad I'm going, all my friend Liza thinks of is David Cassidy, Mary is obsessed with Donny Osmond and I can't bring myself to have dreamy thoughts, age twelve, about either Stevie Wonder or David Bowie, my favourites. There's also this annoying boy who's tall, black and sixteen! Called Clinton, who won't stop following me about. I know I look older than I am, with make-up, my Oxford bags, stack-heeled shoes and Consulate cigarettes nicked from my mum, but honestly.

My dad has chosen the school, with my help, and we go to lunch with a friend of his, the daughter's already at the same school. We sit in a corner, Harri and I, and she tells me about snogging boys and unbuttoning shirts, about sex in swimming pools, where the nearest shop is to the school to buy alcohol, who's nice and who's nasty, about lumps in boys' trousers and how she got 'gated' ('almost expelled, except you're not allowed to leave the school grounds for a whole term so you have to get others to buy you your fags and drink'), during her initiation into the girls' gang, for setting the fire alarm off at night. Harri twitched through lunch, said she was dying for a fag, only because of her hangover from last night's school disco. We excuse ourselves to go to the loos, lock ourselves into the cubicle, stand on the seat, open the diamond-paned window and chain-share a St Moritz gold-tip menthol strand of sophistication down to the stump. Each puff of smoke I try to keep down, but the coughing gets me in the end. Harri, practised smoking starlet, inhales deeply and blows smoke rings around the loo and out of the window. She lifts her eyebrows in disbelief at my cough.

'Haven't you ever done this before, Coco?'

'Of course I have. All the time.' But not under an interrogative stare of competition, I think. 'It just went down the wrong way.'

I take another drag, close my eyes as Harri does and pretend, holding the smoke in my mouth letting it out only in small drabs. My head is dizzy with it, either from holding my breath – or did I inhale?

That night Liza came to stay over. I told her that I had to practise smoking and drinking spirits, so we crept down to the bar in the middle of the night and mixed exotic cocktails from the drinks cabinet, downing them in one, holding our nose to dull the taste and filling our mouths with Tic Tacs.

We climb the walls, the garden walls, in search of adventure. We creep out the back door, climb over barbed wire and broken-glass-topped walls, poor-man's security, to the local bowling green. We dodge the barking dogs tied in the backyards, freeing ourselves from bushes to reach the excelsior of excitement, a black and empty playground with broken swings and a wobbly see-saw. We light up our machine-bought Players No. 6, sit down on the roundabout, lungs at the ready to practise, three cigs each. After a gutful of Tia Maria mixed with some gin, vodka and a trickle of Dubonnet, a few rides on the roundabout signal the night's doomed end of sick and tears. We leave our liquid stamp sprayed across the tarmac, 'Coco and Liza were here'. But what is excitement after five years of furniture-throwing with Richard and Ricky? Liza and I use the street route home and my front-door key on a ribbon round my neck to return to our prison of comfort, resigned to having missed the fun of nicotine and alcohol for that night. But we're stickers, none of us gives up too easily, like they're always telling us at school: 'Girls, if you don't succeed at once, try and try again.'

'Yes, Miss.'

Boarding school seems more fun than this, corridors full of boys and experience, none of them relations and I'll be thirteen years old next week. Old, older. Well, old enough.

CHAPTER TEN

'The spider eggs might have fallen in the soup. You might have infected everybody's dinner. I'll have a frozen pizza tonight, if you don't mind,' was Mary's retort after Coco had told her about the spider trials.

Terry the spider had been retrieved to Bill's delight but Coco had insisted that if he was to be an indoor pet he had to be in a controlled environment, unlike the rest of the household. So they'd found him an old fishbowl, the last resident having died of overfeeding. Bill now had the serious occupation of finding more insects so that Terry could follow the same route and not starve to death.

'Mind? Eat whatever you like as long as you're making it. As long as you don't start worrying about my head being burrowed into by brain-eating spiders nibbling through my skull.'

'Oh, I won't worry, is there anything I can eat now?'

'Sure you can help, what would you like to do?'

'OK, what would you like me to do, Mum, but is there anything I can eat?'

'There's tuna salad in the fridge or yesterday's pizza you could heat up and bread in the bin. Those biscuits didn't last you long, wasn't the book any good? Mary, sweet, do you think you could slice the leeks on the chopping board there?'

'I've almost finished the book and I had to give a biscuit to Joan before she'd put a jumper on and another one after, besides it's lunchtime. What are you doing Mum?' Mary asked, her head in the fridge bobbing from one shelf to another.

'I'm rinsing the salt off the aubergines before I fry them for the *Melanzane Parmigiana*.'

'The what? What's that?'

'The thing that you like with aubergines and tomato sauce and mozzarella cheese all melted together in layers.'

'Like lasagne without the pasta?' Mary asked, setting quickly to work on the leeks.

'And without the meat.'

Coco looked back to her task of rinsing the ingrained salt, put there to bleed the bitter juices from the vegetable. It had streaked the white flesh with dirty browns as though she'd just used them as a J Cloth for mopping the floor, but the purple skins still glistened smooth and dark. In the cookery books it said the aubergines should be dried by laying them on a tray and putting them out in the sun, not much of a handy tip for autumn England. Coco pressed them dry with kitchen paper before putting them to fry in the hot, green bubbling olive oil. It spat back in excitement as each piece of flesh hit the cast-iron pan. When the oil started to seep through to the top of each aubergine slice, their colour turned again to an olive ochre and then it was time to turn them over and fry them golden on the other side.

The shallow round earthenware dish sat, oiled and rubbed with garlic, on the side, next to a plate of sliced mozzarella and the pan of tomato, onion and basil sauce from the cooker. Coco placed a ladle into its thick redness. As each set of aubergines was fried, she blanketed them over with the rich sauce and covered them with cheese, again and again and again, until the sauce, cheese and aubergine were finished and the dish was full. Pepper and nutmeg were grated across the pale bumps of cheese, spoiling the pureness like a bucket of soot thrown in the wind across freshly fallen snow. Then lastly, before entering the oven, crumbling, yellowing, curving Parmesan was scraped from a block to fall on the top. In the heat it would melt and bubble, each layer seeping into the other, the juices mingling to be mopped up with thick chunks of rough white bread that would absorb its pinkness. A warm comfort of a food, like linguine *carbonara*, good cassoulet or the very best steaming, creamy mashed potato with thick yellow butter rolling down its peppered slopes. The taste in your mouth of calorific comfort as it slides with each swallow across your tongue and settles down into your stomach; filling company. The problems start once you've polished off four helpings and you feel like a lead-bellied pig, lying stuffed and bloated on the sofa. Or like being nine months pregnant, uncomfortably virtuous, because at least you haven't eaten a box of chocolate truffles.

The leeks were sizzling now, in yellow-river ease. Mary was julienning the carrots, courgettes and parsnips as an absorbing mattress for the lamb and its juices. Coco, by the sink, took the spatula once more around the ice-cream machine and cleaned it off into the container bound for the freezer. As she heard the trotting steps on the stairs overhead and the loud *jump thud* of Bill's Red Beret landing, she took the lid back off and scooped a large portion back into the machine. Carol came in with Joan and Bill to give them lunch.

'Ah, you're just in time to help clean out the ice-cream machine – want a spoon?'

Coco held out two teaspoons, one for Bill and one for Joan.

'Is it chocolate?'

'No, it's lemon syllabub.'

'Ucky, what's that?'

'Hmm, it's lovely, Mummy. I like you,' said Joan with conviction, between mouthfuls.

'Give us a try, then. Leave some for me, greedy pig,' said Bill to Joan.

'Ballerina.'

'What? Budge over.' And Bill hooked himself on to the seat next to her.

'You can't sit here until you call me Princess Ballerina.'

'Princess Ballerina Greedy Pig, give me some ice cream.' Bill saw his mother giving him one of those evil-eye looks, so he added, 'Please.'

'OK, brother. Are you the handsome prince I saw riding in the forest?' Joan half sung to herself, and Mary signalled, smiling, half laughing to Coco that Joan was from another planet, or going loco.

Bill scowled.

'Girls!' he said. Then almost in the same breath he jumped from his seat on to Coco's lap.

'Hug Mama, hug.'

As she reached her arms around the top of his big back, hugging him over her ballooning stomach, he kissed her cheek and nuzzled his nose to her neck.

'I love you too much,' he said.

'No such thing as too much love,' she replied, kissing him back.

This is real mashed-potato warmth, Coco thought, and held him in open, relaxed arms before he slid off and was on his way again.

CHAPTER ELEVEN

'No, no! You can't put that out, that's my bra and pants drawer! Oh, God!'

'That's it! Your duvet's going out now!'

'What exactly are you doing, Margi, holding Sara-Jane's duvet out of the window? I hope it's only a polite airing you're giving it?'

'Of course, Mrs Grey. I mean, Vivien.'

Reluctantly Margi pulls in the duvet, throwing it at Sara-Jane, along with a creased, braced smile of resentment, and closes the window, trying not to look after what has already gone, half the dormitory and all her underwear, new bras and everything.

The rest of us in the dorm are trying desperately to strait-lace our faces into bedtime conformity, lights-out routine.

'Good. I'm glad you're settling in nicely and all getting on. Sleep well, girls.'

'Goodnight Mrs Grey,' we uniformly chorus.

'How many times have I got to say it – call me Vivien.'

'Goodnight, Vivien.'

'Goodnight girls.'

Our housemistress turns; her tight, beige-tweeded bottom and prim flowered shirt bursting at the bust tell of her at a different size. Her face is sharp and her short-cut hair grows untidily grey (do we all grow to resemble our names?) Vivien isn't like the other teachers, cool and laid-back. With her yappy terrier called Tobemory, she looks, as Jason the art teacher says, 'as though she's got a rod stuck up her arse'. We think she's creepy, the way she stands at the bathroom door staring in at us in the open showers. Poor Mr Grey, the geography teacher.

The lights are out and all five of us lie stiff and silent, listening for the footsteps that carry her away down the hall to her next call of duty.

'OK, anyone got any ideas on how we get all the stuff back?'

'You've only got your dirty washbag out there, douche bag, I've got my entire collection of underwear draped on the trailing rosebushes.'

'Douche bag yourself! Can't we fish anything back from out the window?'

'Somebody hold on to my legs. I think I can just about reach my coat and Coco's hockey stick and then maybe with that a few other things. Most of it's landed on the path. Turn the light back on and I might be able to see what I'm doing.'

'It's no good, we're going to have to creep out and retrieve the rest of the stuff after everyone's gone to bed.'

'But all the doors are locked in Main House, aren't they? We're sure to get caught.'

'Oh, come on scaredy cat, the back staircase door is only bolted.'

'And how do you know that? Don't tell me big-boy Billy has told you all the doors to unlock to get to his dormitory.'

'If you're so interested, he's coming up here on Saturday night,' Margi boasts, her perfect teeth gleaming through her smug smile, a child with her scrubbed freckled face and Pippi Longstocking-style pyjamas.

'Saturday night, he's not! You've only been going out with him for three weeks.'

'So? We develop faster in the outback. It's the retarded in you English, that's the problem. Retentive and retarded, that's what my dad says.'

'But Margi, you're only twelve, you're not actually going to do *it* with him, are you?'

'It's none of your business whether I do or not, but let's say it's not as though it's the first time, so I don't see why not.

'What? Don't look at me like that. Don't worry, he's not coming – no pun intended – until three in the morning, so you'll all be tucked up and fast asleep. You won't hear a thing. Anyway, I'm thirteen next month.'

'Margi! Is that you again? I thought we already had lights out in this dormitory.'

'Sorry Vivien, but I had to find a Tampax to go to the bathroom, otherwise I would have leaked all over the sheets and the blood never comes out properly in the laundry.'

We stuff our own sheets in our mouths to gag us from laughing at Margi's brash Australian daring. I haven't even started my periods yet, but it's no big deal, I mean, you just stuff a tampon up, none of this trauma of ripping sheets up and boiling them clean again in the stewpot, like my mum had to do – she revels in telling me the gory details. Disgusting.

What can the poor woman do? It's not as though she's going to ask for the used Tampax, as proof.

Mrs Grey tightens her facial muscles to a shrew and says, 'Alright, I don't need to hear the details, be quick about it.'

Later that night we collect the results of our mucking about from the gravel path that runs outside Mr Rumbridge's (the headmaster's) office. There is only one detail we cannot retrieve, a bra that hangs provocatively in front of his window, the one his desk faces out to. There's nothing to be done but forget about it and our fate until morning. We renegotiate the creakiest staircase in the world, pushing, hushing and giggling, trying to climb the walls back, in our efforts to be quiet, to the dorm and our beds.

'Biba-freak, Biba-freak.'

'Aren't we calling her Coca-Cola, Coco the Clown, Hot Chocolate, any more?'

'No! Look at her, covered head to foot in Biba clothes, I suppose she thinks it's smart not to wear jeans. Let's get her tonight and dump her in the drains.'

'Biba-freak, you haven't had the Abdamians' initiation yet, we think it's about time you did. Rheiner, Brownson and I will meet you after prep, show you what it's all about.'

'Thank you, but I'd rather not. I didn't like the way Sara-Jane stank up the dormitory for two weeks after her ritualistic dumping in the drains. Sorry, it's not a surprise, and that's the whole point, isn't it?'

'No need to be so high and mighty, Miss Trendy, Sara-Jane saw it as an honour.'

'Poor her, that's what being brought up by the swamps in Orlando did for her, she's always trying to return.'

I've managed to escape any nasty rituals so far, apart from the obvious and agreed-upon snogging competitions in Pets' Corner, the disused hut where pupils were once allowed to keep animals and where now they go to behave like them. Then there's the necessary drags of fags, after breakfast and breaktime in the boys' bogs, behind the shed and in the woods. The surge of nicotine through your veins makes sure your heart is racing and your hair and clothes are stinking before assembly, making sure you're *in* for the day, a walking, smelling advert for Camel or Marlboro cigarettes. Our mouths aren't just like ashtrays, our bodies are trough-trays full of them.

From the day I arrived and saw the train of boys stationary along the surrounding wall, met the girls in my dormitory, boarding school has been like a dream come true. A teenage Disneyland. Maybe that's overstating it a little, but it is really fun. I never have to think about home. It isn't quite so easy as I'd heard, you do have to go to classes, even if you don't want to. You used to be able to smoke in class – now if you get caught you're fined fifty pence for Cancer Research. Those were the days when the school trip to India never returned because they set up an ashram, and when the rugby pitch was turned into an impromptu pop festival by an invasion of rock bands, incense and tie-dye.

The kids regularly slept with the teachers, and each other if they wanted – and not because they were homesick or looking for teddy replacements. Sex was the thing.

Now there's a reformed accountant running the place who's discovered Buddha, Allah and a variety of wood spirits, he says, but I think he only said it to get elected. I can't believe the pupils at the time voted him in, but then God knows what drugs were going round.

Abdam Hall, Devon is a pretty hippy place. Everybody wears shredded jeans, desert or monkey boots and great big baggy dirty old jumpers, a unisex uniform. I'm not the only 'new bug', that's what they call us, to arrive for the Third Year. All five of us are new in our dormitory, and three of us are a lot more clothes-conscious than everyone else. Rainbow is all Peruvian Inca brightly knitted skirts and jumpers, Louise is terribly French, tight jumpers, coloured shirts and bum-hugging cords, and I am all Biba and Bus Stop. Dark, flowing re-creations of Hollywood's golden era: satin dresses, velvet coats and high-waited, full-bagged, turned-up trousers. Dollies of our parents' tastes.

To me, Biba seems to be five storeys of everything I've ever wanted. From the pop-art display food hall, with Warhol baked-bean can towers, to the 1930s dining nightclub elegance of the Rainbow Room. We're teenage counter-slouchers from one floor to the next. Lost in the dream of make-up displays with black and green and blue lipsticks, accessory counters full of extraordinary hats, ostrich feathers of every colour, scarves and bags of chiffons and velvets and . . . the clothes. Well, the clothes. Maxis and midis galore in every style of Hollywood glamour from slinky, slippy satins à la Harlow, to Crawford and Davies small-waisted, large-shouldered fun-fur coats and tailored trouser suits. Colours are everywhere, on everything, Matisse-blue glittering wellies, yellow ochre mackintoshes, rose madder mascara, crimson lake Carmen Miranda peep-toe stacks. And those are just a few of the things I've got in my school wardrobe.

In the holidays Mum takes me to the concerts held upstairs at the top of Biba's, in the Rainbow Room: Bill Haley And His Comets, the Pointer Sisters, the New York Dolls, Ian Dury and the Blockheads. We go to see them all, glam London dolled up for these starry events.

However incongruous lying around Biba all day seems to the louche-looking boys of my boarding school, they copy too, once the school holidays are out and most of us are relocated back to London, spending all our Saturdays in High Street Kensington. Carnaby Street, King's Road? Wouldn't be seen dead there.

Back home, and Ricky's on the phone telling me the gossip, hers, she's going to write her play properly, now the last series of her playing a women's lib/lobbying housewife has come to an end. This is good news, she's been going on about it for so long I'd started to think it might be a cover for something else. She says she's shown it to her friend David the director, and he's encouraging her. 'It might even make a movie, David says,' she tells me.

Now Richard has gone, she has her own workroom, which looks more like a drag queen's dressing room, wigs and hats and shoes hung all over the fluorescent-pink walls. Neon lights glow around the mirrors, every surface is covered in make-up or loose pages of writing. Nothing as sluttish as the way false eyelashes used to be stuck to the rims of old tea mugs by her bedside in the old single and fancy-free days, or fished hurriedly out of ashtrays to be reapplied the next morning. That's married life for you. Everything of Mum's is still shut into this little room; neither of us can quite believe Richard isn't going to come stomping in at any moment, telling us off for our mess or noise.

Richard's large white, white, white studio next door stands empty. I trespass in sometimes to cartwheel across the floor, when I come home for a weekend, and still feel villainous for no good reason. Their bedroom and bathroom was all dark purple, depressing in winter, depressing in summer, not a room to be ill in. Now Mum says she's going to paint it all reds and pinks, more foetal than mine. My room and all my furniture are all my favourite colours: orange, red and yellow, warm, sunshine colours that feel glorious to come home to after the pale sludge-brown of the dormitory.

I was worried first of all about leaving Mum in the house on her own, with no Richard. I was worried she would get lonely and maudlin, reclusive; drink, spend her time sleeping and waking with pills. I shouldn't have worried: parents have a way of looking after themselves. She must have got busy on the phone, got her social diary out because she's all over the gossip columns, it's pointed out to me at school. 'Married movie director David Simpson, seen here with the recently separated Ricky Johnson, is currently directing her in Jimmy Bott's new comedy *Women's Army*.'

So the play she's writing goes on hold.

Mum is being interviewed in all the papers, on prime-time chat shows: the play is a success and she is the lead. Shopping with Mum is worse than ever because now she's stopped to ask if that really was her on the telly last night. I die with embarrassment, spotted in the crowd.

'. . . This must be your daughter, you must be really proud of your mum. What's it like? To have such a famous mum?'

'No, actually, we're sisters appearing on a Palmolive soap ad, you nosy old cow,' I feel like sarcastically saying to yet another accosting stranger. Instead I smile and nod, or sulk and sneer, whatever seems more appropriate to the occasion.

The problem with Ricky is she doesn't seem to realise that forty is old and that she should be retiring, not getting shorter skirts. I love her, but it's embarrassing. Whenever I mention, hint about, other friends' parents, she trills out 'Life Begins At Forty' by Sophie Tucker, and that chronic singing really isn't worth staying around for while she covers herself in the latest plastic peel-off face mask and colours her hair for another role.

Ricky says I can have my fourteenth birthday party for all my new friends at Abdam's.

'But Mum, why can't you go out when I'm having my party? You go out all the rest of the time.'

'Coco! Do we have to go through this again! I said you could only have it if I was here. I don't want to come back and find the Cocteau gone or worse, coloured in.'

'Oh Mum, don't be silly, we're not children! Besides, what if any of my friends see you? It's going to be so embarrassing. At all the other parties their parents have gone out,' I say straight-faced, fingers crossed behind my back to her inquiring, suspicious look.

'More fool them! Nobody will see David and me, we don't want to be at your party. We'll be in the front room reading or watching the telly. Don't worry, Coco, I'm sure it'll be a great success.'

'OK, I s'pose it'll have to be alright. You won't start talking to them or anything? Promise?' I cringe at the thought of her being friendly with them, trying to be in with them, getting it wrong, being laughed at. Why I should think that when she never is, my friends always love her, our house is the one where we can do anything.

'No chicken, not if you don't want us to. I'll leave plenty of condoms in the bathroom just in case anybody needs them. Alright?'

'Mum!' I say in indignation at her mentioning the subject of sex, and then I retreat.

'Thanks, Mum, for everything. I love you.' And I give her a big hug, and leave a maroon kiss mark on her cheek.

The rules are only wine and beer, no spirits allowed and smoking is obligatory. The girls are dressed to kill in sequins and lurex with tight satin bottoms. The boys are automatically in dirty flared jeans, clean rugby shirts, fags at the ready, proudly displaying their manly bum fluff on their chins. We're all bundled into the back of the house, Richard's son's room is now my sitting room, all that boy's stuff repainted new. We drink until the lights are extinguished, darkly groping anonymous flesh to the pounding music of David Bowie's *Aladdin Sane*. Snogging till your lips are invisible, ears soggy with saliva, sucked and blown like Louis Armstrong's trumpet, and covered in a necklace of bruises.

Now I know I've had a good time.

Oh, William Mead, Mead, nectar of the gods that night, sweetly dribbled across my flesh. His hands upon my skin, my breasts squeezed like market fruit, groans suppressed and bodies rubbed in an innocent confusion of warmth.

I dream of William, a pillow hugged close to my body and cheek. So these were the feelings my friends felt when they gazed dreamy-eyed at teen idol posters. But I have a real live one, to exchange tongues and cigarette-smoke kisses with. Will Mead. I will. Mead. Coco Mead. Sounds like a new fizzy drink instead of conjuring realms of my romance.

'Coco, have you got any nutmeg?'

'Why do you want nutmeg, Ariel?'

'Didn't you know, it gets you really high if you smoke it in roll-ups. You have to grate it first, but then it's just like dope, like dope and acid. You can get really psychedelic experiences, man. My cousin told me.'

Ariel's an older, more experienced drug taker than the rest of us. When he's at home in Suffolk he says he has his own motorbike and is an honorary member of the Hell's Angels gang. I believe him – he looks like one, except for the gold-rimmed glasses.

'I think we've got a lump in the drawer, in the kitchen. We can go and have a look if you like. One thing, remember to put it back afterwards, otherwise my mother will go mad.'

'Thanks a lot, sure thing. I'll give you a drag on the spliff once I've got it going, see what it's like.'

'Man, Coco, that nutmeg, like it's really crazy stuff. I had a joint of it and I thought it wasn't working so I put it back in the kitchen and then I met this woman with bright purple hair and this red dress, I mean, like, it's something else, like wow, fantasy!'

'I don't know about the nutmeg, but that was my mother, Ariel, and I'm afraid she has got purple hair.'

The secret was out. Now that everybody knew, she'd be able to take me out at school, though what they'd do at the local hotel at teatime, God knows.

Ricky always says as long as she knows where I am and I've got my cab fare home and no school the next day and I've done my homework, I can stay out or up as long as I like. It's as much my right to have fun as it is hers. She even gives me her taxi account number, better a taxi bill than funeral expenses, she says. There is no way of stopping teenage girls going out, it's best just to make it as safe as possible. Limit the damage.

Her idea of fun seems decidedly warped to me, at the moment. David is a bit of a health freak ('I used to run for my county, I could've won gold at the Olympics if my tendon hadn't given in! You should do more sport, Coco'), and has convinced Mum to have the back garden tarmacked over and made into a badminton court, where they spend the weekends with friends having badminton parties and contests. One game is quite fun, but a whole day spent drinking and jumping up and down! I think it's just another excuse to get drunk, but then that's all adults ever seem to want to do.

In the evenings when she isn't at the theatre, she puts on other performances with full audience participation. Ricky has such drunken dinner parties that it's hard ever to feel outrageous even at school; it's just doing it somewhere different. It'll start in the bar in their living room. Painters and poets and writers and actors are the usual mix who come to dinner, never any other directors (David is the only one in this house), unless there's some poor businessman interested in maybe investing in one of David's productions. Then he'll be invited, or worse, him and his wife, sitting among the bohemian rabble where nothing is taboo: outraged but enchanted, they sit strangely surreal, like fish on bicycles.

The living room is where it formally starts, barred to the children – unless specially invited we won't see the beginning. After a few drinks the troupe progresses into the apple-green dining room/kitchen for dinner and copious amounts of wine and cigarettes for everyone, including us. I like the odd menthol cigarette that Mum smokes, and at that point nobody seems to mind us smoking or drinking. Not even the poor bastard being press-ganged into signing on the dotted line to fund the play, so that he can leave our house. Then they all fall back into the living room with its bar, dispensing brandy and ports, celebrations in order until the early hours of the morning. If I have a friend over we never stay the distance, and are asleep in bed oblivious of anything else that's going on downstairs – for all we know it's an orgy. The only noise that wakes us is somebody scratching over another cheery Billie Holiday record at top volume, the record player's arm for ever stuck on automatic.

It's strange, this thing with Ricky and David. They've only been seeing each other publicly for three months and already he's in the house every night. Every weekend that I'm back, there's David. A Richard replacement but posh, older, darker, tall and wiry. In fact, nothing like him really. More sensitive, with his hairlines running away from his face, but jollier, tries harder, except when he's got a hangover and you have to tiptoe around the house on a Sunday, just like old times, really. When I'm back in the holidays I sneak out to the cinema, spend the afternoons submerged among the mackintosh men watching X-rated avant-garde Andy Warhol movies. I try to concentrate against the soft clapping of rustling cloth and exaggerated breathing about me, every time Joe D'Allesandro takes his clothes off, a needle in his arm. It quite puts me off from being an intellectual.

Barbara says what do I expect of the Era, a fleapit and full of pervies on piss-stained seats. 'I'd take a disposable seat cover in there with me if I was forced to go.'

After that I take to going to the Gate and watching all the old movies. *Gilda, Gentlemen Prefer Blondes . . . But They Marry Brunettes* (Thank God for that, I think. 'No they don't,' says Barbara tossing her blonded locks), *Notorious, Mildred Pierce, Little Foxes.* Anything deeply involved and seriously escapist. For a moment I become Rita Hayworth singing 'Mame'.

Within the hour I'm Bette Davis wielding a whip. The next day Joan Crawford lipstick scales up to my painted eyebrows, after the interval I'm a drunk Ingrid Bergman having Cary Grant tie a handkerchief around my tummy to stop me catching cold. I willingly suspend my disbelief each time I buy a ticket. Mum reimburses me; well, it's culture, innit.

Roll on term-time, at least at school there's only serious drinking on Saturday, disco/movie night, and I'm as drunk as they are. As irresponsible as my other pissed peers on half a bottle of vodka each. We sit in a circle, each with a bottle in hand, a giant Coke doing the rounds, passed on to swig down the taste of the lethal spirit. Once standing up, we're tumbling down the leaf-strewn embankments of the woods, the familiar Saturday-night stagger to cross Main Lawn. Once there, keep going, do not stop and pee on the grass, do not rest on flagpole and crumple vomiting to the ground: that has already been done over some poor unsuspecting admirer who only tried to kiss me – I rewarded him with a faceful of sick. Poor old Tim, but there's no going back to help him wipe it off. Keep going through the car park, do not even think of walking over the staff cars into Main House. That would not be sensible. Once inside the tricky part begins: collect yourself or go straight to jail if caught. Try to dance until lights-out in the disco snogging through the slow dance with some boy whose name and memory will make you wince and blush for days to come. Or if too drunk for that, sneak up to your dorm early, get ready for bed and pretend to read, only remember to keep the book right way up, to avoid being spotted. Unfortunately I am spotted, fortunately I am spared the usual retribution of expulsion or suspension, and only have to fetch the junior housemistress's Sunday papers every week by nine a.m. for my sins. This is quite a good way to curtail excessive drinking on Saturday night at school, but is useless in affecting my habits when off to London for Mum's first-night parties.

Now that Ricky and David are all settled, what have they decided to do? Only up and leave it all to go and live in the wilds of Cornwall. What am I supposed to do for a social life in the holidays? That's when all the real good parties happen. What about Barbara? I'd never see Barbara, Barbara hates Cornwall, it's full of old yokels and nothing to do. Translate as: when we go there on holiday we end up in deserted coves, not lying buttock-to-bosom on a surfers' paradise beach – I know how she feels, I feel the same. I wonder seriously as to the point of traipsing miles down some cliff so that you can be naked on your own – you can do that at home in the garden.

Ricky makes her feelings quite clear, that is what David and she want to do. They have found the house, one bedroom with a converted cow-shed round the back for the children to share during the holidays. David has two younger sons – why do they always have boys? Why doesn't Mum at least get someone with daughters! I don't care about her being with David as long as we don't move. That way I'd still know where I was.

Besides, I'm at school most of the time, she says. I ask her how she expects to be on the stage or ever get famous, and that always annoys her.

'There's a wonderful theatre near to us, open-air on top of a cliff . . .' she says, trying to keep her cool.

'And the only way you'd get famous from it is dropping over the side in mid-performance. I can see the headlines now: "Little-known Actress Finally Gives Performance Of A Lifetime",' I retort spitefully, but for once she won't rise to my bait. 'Do parents ever think about anything other than themselves, Mother? How am I supposed to keep any of my friends during the holidays?'

I leave the question open on the other side of the slammed door and stomp off to my room. My bedroom. I try to hug it to me by lying spreadeagled across the carpet, eyes to the ceiling, sweeping it all closer to me. Squeezing it down into a warm cell of security to pack around my heart.

Barbara is the sister I never had; my love–hate relationship with Barbara continues. I miss her when I'm away but when I visit her in the hallowed halls of RADA, her control mechanisms full on, I inwardly sneer in rebellion.

The prospect of Barbara reaching major stage fame and fortune fills me with dread, as she has mapped out my own career ahead of me. She has always promised me from a small child, because of my precocious sewing and ironing abilities, that I would be her chief dresser/wardrobe girl, the lot! At six, she made it an exciting, glamorous and honourable profession; by fourteen I was beginning to wonder if the world held something more entrancing than the smell of greasepaint and windowless rooms, just like so many of my mother's dressing rooms.

Barbara will have to see to herself for the time being, sew her own hems. I'm at school and in the holidays I'm now in Cornwall, sleeping on the sofa of a tiny cottage in the middle of nowhere until the spare room gets done up. It makes school seem luxurious, exciting. I suppose it is a glamorous school. Some days I sit sipping large G and T's, smoking gold-tipped Sobranie cigarettes in the sixth-form studies, decorated in Versailles style by some friendly Arab parent for his student son, or lounging, drinking

Beaujolais among the American girls, riveted, listening to their tales of basketball-team sex on long-haul flights back to England.

Can you really have sex with somebody seven foot tall in an aeroplane seat without anybody seeing? I start to have nightmares about the problems, the possibilities, the pain; Harlem Globetrotters invade my dreams.

Sex is everything. It preoccupies us day and night. Jim Packett has already offered me the use of him and his Durex, which he keeps secured in the top pocket of his jean jacket. I asked Ricky what she thought I should do.

'If you feel like doing it, we'll get you on the pill.'

'But that's not the problem, I like snogging him, but I'm not sure I'd actually want to do *it* with him.'

'Well don't chicken, there's no pressure. You have sex when you feel it to be right. Don't be steamrollered into it. You'll know when it's right, and if you're happy at the moment, then there's nothing to worry about.'

Ben is different, he's also in the fifth form, like Billy who Louise my best friend is now going out with, the one who used to have actual sex with twelve-year-old Margi, so she said. I don't think Louise has sex with him, I'm sure she'd tell me if she had.

In the middle of Saturday nights, Louise and I steal out of our dormitory and sneak through the woods to the boys' house. Luckily they've a room on the ground floor, so it's easy to slip in through the window, otherwise we'd be scaling the drainpipes, breaking limbs and spraining ankles. We spend the hours until dawn lying on top of each other snogging tightly on the top bunk, Louise and Billy, me and Ben suckered together, bodies glued in bliss. Sometimes I even take my bra off, but I don't tell Louise.

Sundays are spent, these summer-sunshine hours before the holidays, helping Billy and Ben to revise for their O levels, by providing picnics and portable cassette players playing Santana, *Black Magic Woman*, lying bikinied beside them and their books, and snogging. Revising. More snogging, not much revising, until dark.

I've invited Ben down to Cornwall for two weeks of the holidays. We have not actually done anything that involves making you pregnant, but talking in the common rooms with the older girls about oral sex almost puts me off kissing.

'Sucking dick is just something girls have to get used to. It's disgusting, it's vile, but men love it and that's the truth.'

'Yes, but have you done it on a boy who hasn't washed properly?'

'You mean on a boy who isn't circumcised and you can taste the smegma?'

'The what? Smegma, what's that? On the other hand don't answer, I think the word is gross enough to imagine.'

'You're so prudish! It's the stuff, Coco, like ear wax which smells and covers their things when they don't wash.' Big guffaws of laughter and giggling erupt across the room.

'Smeggy, smeggy smegma. Sounds good. Or if you're really familiar you would say, "Sweetheart, I wish you'd do something about your sm".'

'*Uch*! I don't know if this French guy had it or not, but the first time I had to do *it*, was on a life-guard in St Tropez last summer. On the beach, and I'd only finished having dinner with my parents about an hour before. There we were, totally immersed, paradise almost reached, half my clothes off, when he suddenly comes out with it! In more ways than one!

' "My darling Susie, you are the most beautiful girl in the world and I would like to make our lurve, 'ow you say, complete, but I 'ave no rubber. Make me the 'appiest Pierre".'

'Oh my God, no! I don't believe it, you didn't fall for that corn!'

'Did I hear "'appiest" or "a penis", then?'

'Very funny, Cathy.'

'Wait, the worst is yet to come! He then grabs my head and

stuffs his thing into my mouth. I mean, I'm used to sticking my fingers down my throat after dinner anyway, so you can imagine what happened next! Lobster thermidor and crème brûlée all over his lap. I almost pissed myself at the same time! I mean, puking's something you do in private.'

'You didn't, Susie! What did he say! What did you do!?'

'Nothing. I just ran home and didn't speak to him again. I was in hiding for the next two weeks. I had to pretend I'd come down with Spanish flu. It completely ruined my tan, I had to book up for two weeks of sunbed when I got home!'

The thought of sharing a double bed with Ben expecting his conjugal rights for two weeks terrified me (I knew Mum would provide us with only one room, the shed). I had to think of something. Meanwhile, there was the end of term, exams over and Founder's Day. I am performing in the play, the dance, the recital and I have my new Stirling Cooper outfit to show off. Dad, Uncle Ian and Barbara are coming down. Cream teas are served, only for the guests and parents, along the green-rolled lawns beside the trellised roses. Here was the day of proof that the school fees were worth the parental investment, that high art was being executed amid the Devon countryside. That the children attending this rare intellectual place of study (ha, ha), were discovering about life through art, drama and literature. The first play we put on was *Who's Afraid of Virginia Woolf?*, followed by the semi-clothed version of *Hair*. Choosing our own O-Level books for English, because of our teacher being on the Oxbridge board, meant that I could revel in Joe Orton, Evelyn Waugh and Stevie Smith for two whole years. However it was happening, we were getting educated in some kind of life.

'You there. The one in the clown's suit, what's your name?'

'Coco, Mr Rumbridge, Coco Johnson.'

'What on earth do you think you look like! This is not a

circus you're performing in. Is this supposed to be some sort of joke on your name? Go and change immediately. This is Founder's Day, the most important day in the school year, and you dress up like Coco the clown.'

'But Mr Rumbridge, it's new and it's not a clown's outfit, thank you. It's by Stirling Cooper and it's the latest fashion.'

'I had to speak to you last week about wearing make-up and intentionally showing your petticoats from beneath your skirt, didn't I? I believe you gave your excuse as fashion then. Well I'd call it old hat, following the dictates of magazine clothing obsession. Go and change into something more respectable!'

'Yes, Headmaster!'

'Louise, didn't our parents put us in this school because it was meant to be liberal?' I sniff back, upset, to my friend.

'Hardly very Zen, his attitude!'

We dart up the main staircase and down the side to the back loos to share a quick Marlboro before our parents arrive. Only the night before we were locked in one of the cubicles pushing the cork of a wine bottle in with a stiletto heel, no corkscrew available. A drag of nicotine supplies me with Dutch courage.

'I don't see why I should change, I look a damn sight more attractive than him in his humongous, moth-eaten, mouldy old suit. Miserable git!'

'Get ye to a monastery, you harlot! Don't worry, he's only jealous that he hasn't got any decent clothes.'

'Monastery? Isn't it s'posed to be nunnery? Get ye to a nunnery?'

'I don't know and I'm doing *Hamlet* at the moment, but I'd rather go to a monastery. Give us another drag.'

'One more puff each, then down to the circus. Your mum and stepdad will probably be looking for you, Louise.'

'More like looking for Mr Rumbridge to ask him interesting questions about the school and who I'm mixing with. Parents! Have you read that Philip Larkin poem? "Parents, they really fuck you up, they don't mean to", it goes something like that. It's good. His novel *Jill* is a bit depressing, though.'

'Does it really say "fuck you up"?'

'Yeah.'

'God!'

I suck the last bit of tobacco from the cigarette, till it burns my finger on the filter and I drop it like a hot potato and stamp it out on the loo's wine-stained lino, with my suede, stacked, strapped sandals, blue toenails peek-a-booing out as I deftly kick the stub into the corner. We leave, clomping down the stairs, and get back to the school circus.

At the end of term, on the train back to Cornwall with Ben, I'm wearing his shirt like a ring and the problems of real sex chug ever closer. Suddenly the solution arrives and I gleefully spring upon it in the loos, placing a Tampax to stem the flow. That's it! I've got my period for two weeks, I tell him; how's a boy going to know how long they really last? After all, everybody knows you can't have sex when you've got your period.

Not only will I not sleep with Ben (forgivable as under-age sex), after a week I won't even speak to him. I leave him to talk with my stepbrothers-to-be who've now arrived, Mum, David, total strangers. I can't deal with him here. The games from school turn too serious in my own backyard; besides, he's left Abdam's now and I'd have to be faithful and write letters. So I blank him out, read another book, go rock-climbing alone. While Ben, the sweet, practical soul, fixes half the house, the wind generator, the bicycles. The creep can make everyone laugh but me, becomes everyone's best friend but mine. Mum doesn't stem her annoyance at me.

'If you're going to invite people to stay at least talk to them, Coco! And you could do with being a bit nicer to Charles and Henry (David's sons), it's strange for them here too! Ben's so nice as well, you really are a little shit!'

'Takes one to know one!' I snap back.

The change from London to Cornwall is extreme, but then that's Ricky, one giant extreme after another. From the opulence of town to the frugality of the countryside. No electricity, heating, neighbours, openings, parties. A lot of mice, pubs, Cornish cows, artists, brambles, home-made bread and growing your own vegetables. It seems as natural for Mum to be saying, 'Go and pick some lettuces from the garden, darling', as it used to be for her to say, 'Isn't it time you booked another appointment at Vidal's, Coco? The state of your hair!'

David is busy on some script that'll ensure our fortunes for life, Mum whispers to keep us children quiet. While Mum is back on the play and the beginnings of her autobiography, she also earns money that I am not to sneer or complain at, for 'adult entertainment' magazines, 'men's magazines', or sleazy sex rags: her stories, salacious pieces of titillation, slotted between the 'open beaver' shots of girls at their nubile best.

I can't say how embarrassing it is to have boys in my own form pleased as punch to report how they wanked their way through one of my mum's stories from these magazines. I'm sure there are parents with far worse jobs in my school, but on the embarrassment clapometer, I'm not so certain.

In Cornwall, Mum is no longer a celebrity. She moulds well into being another wife, for Men are the thing here. No sexual revolution among the tin mines, *Poldark* on telly is about the level. Every man a dark, brooding mystery; every woman happy to be an extension of his appendage. Every Friday night it's down to the pub. Along the road from us it's darts night, the all-male teams challenging and playing other all-male teams. The women, including – and I can hardly believe it – my mum, sit in the shadows on the sidelines, cheering their men on to victory, making sure they're well supplied with beer. Onlookers, gossiping, knitting like *les tricoteuses*, all perms and handmade jumpers. I try to shift Mum by telling her about my project on the women's suffrage movement.

'That sounds interesting,' the women all agree, nodding their heads.

'David knows a lot about that, Coco, you should ask him. He did a film all about it. I think it had Vanessa Redgrave in it, somebody like that.'

'Yeah, sure, Mum. Of course it would be a man who'd know all about it.'

No sense of irony, the older generation, these days. I can't believe they were around through the so-called Sixties revolution.

There are no rules on under-age drinking here in the wilds, no packet of crisps and a shandy on the doorstep, children are included as though it were a French bar. I slope next door to the Young Farmers Club and fantasise a bit of glamour into the situation. They may all be young farmers barn-dancing, but at least I can see myself as Jane Russell lying in a haystack, poured into her cleavaged coned bra especially invented for her by Howard Hughes. You have to learn to make the best of a bad situation, and a bit of fantasy never did anyone any harm. I go to the loo and reapply my carmine-red Rimmel lipstick, curving my bows to my pout, I hope. The mirror's cracked and the light doesn't work so it's all a bit of guesswork. I chance that the room won't turn around and laugh when I go back. The truth is, they don't even seem to notice the lipstick or me, except one boy who looks like the scarecrow in the *Wizard of Oz*.

There's fantasy and fantasy.

The beginning of the new year at school is getting rather too fantastical for my liking. It's the acid. And the dope. The Mogadons don't help.

It started badly when a new bod OD'd on acid, totally freaked out and tried to attack another sixth-former. He had to be physically restrained and force-fed vitamin C tablets until he'd calmed down enough to be returned to his parents. Then a friend sends an envoy to fetch me one night from my dormitory – he's stuck in the woods and can't get out. I go to him, staying until almost lights-out, when I can cajole and coax him back from his drug-induced paranoia to his dormitory. He has told me his bad acid-trip story. He is not the only one: at the weekends children from twelve years up can be seen staggering through their nightmares, lost in the woods around the school, collapsed in the common room, splayed out over the hockey pitch. I'm waiting for a formal announcement at assembly. I'm wide-eyed at the teachers' incomprehension – it's all put down to wild teenage behaviour.

Dope, to those in the know, in the right gang, is the thing. We sprinkle it on to our food, into our coffee. Teachers are on the next table, we're mad with bravado, slurred and sleepy through double English. We smoke it in the library after prep, whilst revising for our mock O-level exams.

It's all getting a bit too much. The Mogadons have taken over. My friends are comatose and I am alienated. I'll try dope, that's one thing, but not acid, not downers and here I can't see the point in taking speed. Speed up for what? We're in the middle of the goddamn countryside. What's there to stay up for?

Some parents go away and leave their son in charge of their beautiful house and garden. One girl on Mogadons is shagged by a few of the boys, one after the other, and is left like a disused wrapper behind the hedge. One of the boys passes out on their manicured lawn in a pool of his own vomit. Another girl drinks so much vodka she had to be admitted to hospital for alcohol poisoning. Kids will be kids!

It is hard sometimes to remember that we are still children. When parents say it we don't believe it: 'We're teenagers, but more sophisticated.' We'll fight our side, the right to smoke, drink and stay up till twelve strikes and fades. Inside we know, however many times we are able to fool the local off-licence with our demands for alcohol and cigarettes, that we are children playing with adult games and grown-up sweets.

'Have you tried dissolving ten aspirin in a can of Coke yet? Gives you a real buzz and it's not illegal.'

I call Mum, reverse-charge.

After I've told her about it all, I don't know what I expect her to do but I know it feels better not sharing the full responsibility of illicit knowledge. I feel I'm the only one walking normal in the wonderland, like Alice, or Patrick McGoohan in *The Prisoner*.

I'm hauled out of bed with an anglepoise lamp to my face. Allowed enough time to stumble into my dressing gown, not to find my slippers. Sleep-sodden, I glance past the hall clock; I register it is one o'clock as I'm marched down to the headmaster's office and asked to sit. I've no time to get my head straight, or to worry whether my parents have been killed in a car crash, this is a part of my dream.

'So you've been telling stories to your parents about drugs, have you? What kind of drugs, are we talking about hashish, prescription, hard-core heroin? What?'

The smooth-faced headmaster towers above me, reminding me of Peter Lorre in *M*, haunted and hollow-eyed.

'It's the acid and Mogadon I'm worried about, Mr Rumbridge,' I squeal back, frightened by the nightmarish scenario.

'What acid, Mogadon? I want facts, girl! Names, an incident, not snivelling on about what worries you. Are you trying to tell me that pupils in this school are taking them on school grounds without us knowing? I find that very hard to believe.'

'Yes, Mr Rumbridge.'

'Well, who? Come on, out with it. You can't go around making insinuations without proof!'

I can't look at him. I fix my stare upon his slippered feet, then the hole by his big toe, then the sock beneath. I'm concentrating so hard I can almost see the bone.

'I don't want to say, I don't think it's right. I mean, what would happen to them? It's not their fault. I just don't like seeing the effect. I don't think it's fair to offer it to the first-and second-formers.'

'Is it a boarder who's bringing it in? We're not going to be able to help if you don't tell us who,' he softens his voice to a collaborative tone that attracts trust.

'No, it's a day-boy.'

'Coco, these are very serious accusations that you are making here, and if there are no foundations to them you realise that even going this far with them will get you into real trouble. So who is it? I want names, facts!'

'Jacob Stanley. He's selling acid for fifty pence a tab. Angelina has the Mogadon and she's giving it away. I don't think she's very happy, her parents are getting divor—'

'Happy? She certainly won't be once I've got through to her parents. Who's been taking it with her? If you don't tell me I'll find out anyway, you realise. I think we all have a fairly good idea, don't you? Rheiner, Tring, Titus, Mead. The Rabelasian retrogrades of the school. Now perhaps, Missy, you will think rather more seriously about the kind of effect telling tales has. Don't be surprised if you're not as popular as you once were. You can go now.'

'Yes, Mr Rumbridge.' Oh fuck! Oh fuck! Oh fuck!

Mr Rumbridge was right. Mysteriously, I don't have as many friends, and I'm excluded from most of my previous social activities once the drugs squad's called in. Expulsions and suspensions fly like midges around a stagnant pool.

For my last year, aged fifteen, I am staying mostly sober, making friends with the square gang, who aren't as exciting and don't have the boys flocking around, but survival's this year's fashion. Other girls this last term have taught me a different bodily abuse; the rudiments of bulimia. But I'm too greedy, I'd rather keep the warm bulk in the pit of my stomach that half a loaf of Mother's Pride, toasted, with Marmite and hot butter, eaten just after prep, gives just before bed. Caroline has shown me the alternative diet – it comes in pill form and you get to eat nothing except black coffee and cigarettes. I think it's a little too sophisticated even for me, but then she does live in Monte Carlo with her twenty-seven-year-old boyfriend during the holidays.

As she says, 'You never know what lithe competition is creeping around the next spin of a roulette wheel, darling. I have to keep myself in trim.'

Caroline is a year older than me and is the only sixteen-year-old girl I can laugh with about the drug bust.

'I can't believe they'd take prescription drugs for fun! Bolivian cocaine and American Martinis, now that's a different matter,' she says.

'As opposed to Kent cocaine and Hounslow Martinis, Caroline?'

We laugh at the simple inelegance of my clumsy, drunken, final deflowering. The night before term ended, squashed down among the forest bushes, with a boy not of my choice was hardly picturesque. As I came to and he simply came and pulled out, all I could think to ask him was, 'John, what have you been doing with that Durex?' I can't think what all the fuss was about. I can console myself with my O levels, but hell knows what will console my parents with the likely results. At least I've managed to persuade Mum and Daddy to let me escape the social pressures of boarding school. I'd rather go to the local tech to do my A levels, the local comprehensive, anywhere.

Anywhere it is, then. So for the duration of my A levels I am to be rusticated to the Cornish Riviera. Just sixteen.

When things get tough, I like to think I steal all of Bette Davis's best lines.

'Watch out, you're in for a bumpy ride.' Or is it me I'm talking about?

CHAPTER TWELVE

'Oh, thank you so much for my pasta, Mummy, it's beautiful. Even fairies have to eat sometime,' said Joan with a three-year-old's staged graciousness and some batted eyelashes directed at Coco.

'You're welcome, sweetheart, I'm glad you're enjoying it.'

'She's had two bowls, Mum! She's hardly going to be a fairy after all that. I shouldn't much think you'd ever be able to fly again, and if you did you'd probably come crashing down on somebody's head like a bomber plane,' said Bill, imitating the crash landing, whirring down to an exploding climax through his lips.

Joan giggled in reply, her hand daintily over her mouth, shoulders shrugged into her ears; her response pleased Bill, though he wasn't meaning to be funny.

'Isn't it, Mum?' he said, through a mouthful of hand-held pizza.

'Wait till you've finished that mouthful before you ask me the rest of the question please, Bill.'

'Too late – chew and show, Mum.'

Coco smiled back unimpressed, trying not to encourage him in opening his mouth full of half-chewed food.

'You're going to have to improve your table manners if you're going to work for the Queen as her helper.' Coco reminded Bill of last week's career ambitions.

Munch, munch, munch, munch. Swallow, gulp.

'Isn't it, Mum? Isn't it, Mum, that Japanese war men used to have to crash-die in their planes and weren't allowed back alive? Isn't that true, Mum?'

'Almost. Only at the end of the Second World War when they knew they were being defeated by the Americans. Honour was more important to them than their lives. Their bodies are only vehicles for this life, their spirits are more important to preserve so that they can graduate spiritually in their next life.'

'Like cats having nine lives? How many do we get?'

'Hindus think that the same spirits just keep on returning, dying then being reborn, working through the lessons of past lives.'

'Yippee! So I could be a pirate in my next life.'

'I think you've already been one in your last,' said Mary. 'I think I shall be in my next life an inventor of miracle cures against all the diseases in the world, then nobody would have to die of cancer again.'

'Why wait until your next life? You could do it in this.'

'You know why, Mummy, because I'm going to be a marine biologist and save dolphins and whales. There's only so many things you can do well at once. You say that.'

'If you think you can only do one thing then you only can, that's right Mummy, isn't it? I'm going to do ten but I'm not quite sure which yet, apart from dinosaur-digger and a king's or queen's best friend,' said Bill.

'Well I'm going to be a singer and a ballerina and a fairy and a Sleeping Beauty, and only ever wear pink and always be happy. Would you like to hear my new song?

'Oh, I am a fairy queen, living in a castle where I dance, dance, dance,
I am a sleeping beauty wearing beautiful pink dresses and I sing, sing, sing,
I dance and I sing, sing, dance, dance . . .'

'Joan!' Mary and Bill chorused against their younger sister, who sounded like she was doing an audition for the Beijing Opera, terrible to their untrained ears.

'I haven't finished so don't interrupt, it's rude!

'Sing, sing, sing, dance, dance, dance, wearing pink Sleeping Beauty clothes!

'Do you like my new song?'

'Bravo, bravo,' applauded Coco, the doting mother, to her daughter's curtseying approval.

'Thank God that's over, you little minx, were you really trying to kill our ears?' said Bill, smiling and teasing and tickling his youngest sister as she laughed her dimpled smile in reply, happy with her brother's attention, which she knew would only be there for a moment.

'When's Granny coming, tonight? And can we stay up and will there be bread and butter pudding? You said there would because we don't like treacle tart.'

'One thing at a time. Yes, Granny's coming tonight, at about six-thirty so you can see her after you've finished your bread and butter pudding and before you go to bed. Maybe if she's not too tired she'll read you a bedtime story, otherwise Daddy will. OK?'

'Can't we have dinner in the dining room with the grown-ups? Please Mum, please.'

'No, it's too late, you'll get too tired and so will I carrying you upstairs to bed.'

'Spoilsport. We'd let you stay up. Now I'm not so sure I'll let you into my room any more and you're banned from my den!'

'Poor Mummy. Horrid boy. We love you.' Her daughters' conciliatory arms wove around her neck. Bill scowled at them from beneath his fringe and dug into the table with his stick. Just as suddenly as his brow had knitted into disapproval, the board of his face was wiped clean and a smile of an idea lit up in its place.

'I know, why don't we do a play, something like *Peter Pan*, and I can be Peter and we can show it to Granny when she arrives. That's a good idea, isn't it?'

'A very good idea.'

'Come on, Mary, Joan, we'll raid the dressing-up box and one of you can be Wendy or Captain Hook and I'll have to fight you . . .'

Coco stood up, clearing the plates and listening to the children's voices trailing up the stairs for the great production and Joan's little voice piping up as ever, 'Wait for me,' and then to slow them down, 'Bill, Mary, do you want one of my plums?'

'Is there one for me?' She could hear Carol joining Joan on the stairs.

And she had just been about to say it was time for her to get on with the bread and butter pudding, and now there were no volunteers to help with the buttering or stir the vanilla-milk custard to its sweet, pale conclusion.

Coco got to work, out with the breadboard and the day-old white crusty loaves. She sliced away at their coats until every bit of crust was removed and all that was left was an irregular white sponge square. Just as well Bill was upstairs, she smiled to herself, remembering how she'd prepared five loaves like this one day, had turned her back searching for something in the larder for just one moment and had turned round again to see Bill stuffing the remains of a loaf into his mouth, whole.

At least he'd stopped picking out the insides of fresh bread and leaving its husk in the bread bin for whoever wanted to make toast next. Infuriating child.

And she wondered again if this child inside her would be a boy, to join him. There seemed no way she ever predicted correctly, even with a fifty per cent chance of being right.

Coco sliced easily through the bread and then thickly buttered each slice and the inside of a deep, round glass dish with the local farm's fresh-churned butter. She glazed each slice with her sweet spiced marmalade before cutting them into triangles and covering the base of the dish with them; marmalade side up. Then came a sprinkle of crumbled walnuts followed by the chopped candied peel and raisins, to make sure nobody was in doubt of its sweet pudding-ness. A large tablespoon or two of golden syrup was laced and trickled across the first layer of the bed. The second, third and fourth layers followed the first routine until all the bread, butter, marmalade and syrup were finished and the dish full and lined to the top. On top of the stove she stirred the black bobbing pod around the pan of milk, sugar and eggs. Carefully Coco took the custard and poured the steaming vanilla liquid gently, so as not to spill it over anything other than the glistening black raisin-buttoned bread. She pulled out the vanilla pods and rinsed them under the tap and laid them to dry by the window, and greedily went for the half-glass she'd kept back as a treat for herself.

'Good for the baby, all that milk and egg, calcium and protein,' she murmured in self-justification, when the sweet creamy liquid hit her tongue and the strong smell of vanilla filled her nose. Like coffee, more than half the delight was in the smell. And she had been telling Mary to watch out for her vanilla-sniffing habits! But then don't we always foist upon others the worry of our own obsessions?

Now Coco could joke with her mother about her obsession with her exam results, as though without top grades you couldn't gain entry to the human race. Without grade As, her mother had tried to have her believe that life's eternity would be spent in a high-street shoe shop, examining people's corns, verrucas and smelly toes.

'Well,' she now said. 'That's what my mother and father always taught me. If you didn't get the grades, you couldn't escape to the professions.'

The sins of the fathers . . .

Coco picked up the dish and pushed it into the waiting oven and thought, 'And Mum could never cook, could that be considered a sin? Then, neither could Granny.'

A lot of things had stopped at Coco, only to be replaced by others. Still, she could see what might have been repeated in her but she'd stopped, or been given the grace to change. Pregnancy makes you more reflective.

Is one life just held on repeat from the last?

How much of our lives do we own? Even consciously?

Hasn't everything always been done by somebody else before us?

What can we hope to add, leave our print upon, apart from our children who can repeat our mistakes as surely as we did our parents'?

The futility of life, or its grand hope.

But you can't entertain these thoughts long when pregnant: fleeting answers appear and then scramble to be lost among the trivia all in the same box. Faith and belief are the only things to hold on to – the belief that only good awaits the contents of your burgeoning womb.

'I know I should have a rest,' she said out loud to drown her good sense that was protecting the baby inside her. 'But I've just got to do the beans . . . OK bugger the beans, they'll wait until I'm ready and they only take five minutes in the microwave. Don't push yourself.'

She pulled herself forcibly away from her warm cave of a kitchen, taking an alarm clock with her to make sure she'd be back before the pudding burnt.

Up to bed like a good girl. Already she couldn't wait for her feet to be off the ground and her body to be resting horizontal and snuggled warm in her white fluffy feathered duvet. She'd draw the curtains all around her nest of a bed and be asleep in seconds.

CHAPTER THIRTEEN

This is the long hot summer of 1977 and all around Cornwall the sea is rolling over the long, pale sand of beaches. The sun shines, no matter what I shout at it. The wind softly blows the steam-white clouds across the watercolour blue wash of a sky. Each day is a photocopy of the one before. Each morning my new step-brothers (David's sons), Charlie, Henry and I, wake late, have breakfast, and walk down to the beach. We lie on the sand fully clothed, hair carefully styled in ice-cream peaks, reading *New Musical Express*, until our street cred evaporates with the sun and we tear off our clothes to run laughing into the cold green waves.

In London there are riots in the street. The King's Road is overtaken by warring factions: anarchist punks and Teddy-boy rockers. Luxury-living Chelsea, London SW3, is flooded with suburban rebels. This year's youth are anti-heroes entering the Establishment's gates, vomiting over their nicely raked gravelled paths, and cheering. Vivienne Westwood, Malcolm McClaren, Johnny Rotten, the Sex Pistols, The Clash, The Damned, The Stranglers. Everything seems to be happening that I could possibly wish for in my sixteenth rebellious, white middle-class year.

And where the hell am I? I'll tell you where!

In the back of beyond, on the ice-cream-drenched beaches of Cornwall.

My boyfriend Tom is my compensation. He is eighteen, too short but Italian, (once you can see past his spots), and he plays in a real punk band, The Beasts.

On the train coming down together, I am already uncomfortable, memories of the holiday with Ben and Mum's resulting disapproval shadowing the journey. Can I stick with it? Why did I ask him if I didn't want to watch a repeat? Fear of being alone in Cornwall, trapped inside my own greying walls. I do want the relationship, but I can't bear to hear the intimacy of his sickly shared childhood secrets. This boy turns into a baby, with my myopic vision.

After the first week, I can feel the removal men arriving as I distance myself, retreating into a silent disdain that I used to reserve solely for adults. Tom tries to be outrageous, to hold my attention: smoking drugs and snorting lines of sulphate on the beach only triggers my sneers. He rolls a joint the size of a cigar and gives it to poor Charlie before dinner, who turns green and vomits all his sausage and mash back on to his plate, to Mum and David's surprise, but not ours. Charlie's sick is the last straw. I want Tom on a train home. I can't stand this drugs thing, I probably take it too seriously after what happened at school. Maybe I'm using it as an excuse for what really gets on my nerves – the way Tom always wants to have sex in public places. I'm not sure I like sex; sex or Tom.

Once Tom goes life seems more fun. Maybe it was just Tom I didn't like having sex with, because once he's gone I'm more than eager to experiment with a whole string of boys. Partners with no past, and definitely no future, none of the obligations or rules. Just disco dates, snogs in dark doorways that thrill zings up your spine. Holidaymakers I say I'll write to, boys from inland villages with no direct bus route, I never call. I make it easy on myself.

Now that we live in Falmouth, in a flat above the Golden Egg, everything is easier. In one leap, San Lorenzo's to the Golden Egg. This is Mum and David's concession to living with a teenager, me. I thought complaining enough would get us out of the country and back to London, but at least we're near some sort of civilisation. You can tell by the smell. The first thing you notice about the place is the constant reek of week-old fry-up and every time we open the window to get the glorious sea's ozone the contents of their air vents fly in. On top of that, the flat is small and ugly in a yellow modern bathroom-suite way, carpeted throughout in a sick-swirl mélange of buff, orange and lime green. Mum moves in and cheerily renovates the place with rugs and mirrors, paintings and chairs, but there's still no way to camouflage the size of the place once we are all at home. The flat is rented. Mum says we've living off the profits of the house sale, short-term stringency for long-term profits, the big investment is David's manuscript, masterpiece of western screenplays, eighteenth draft. When I ask why can't we afford a house, something bigger, David says, 'First families don't come cheap.'

'Anyway it's fine, we've still got the money from my last two films,' says Mum, ever cheery. I'm sure some mothers marry men with money and don't have to use all theirs, but that's Mum pushing women's lib to an extreme, along with everything else – they aren't even married.

Lucky there is still some money, somebody has to pay the grocer's bill, my stepbrothers eat like animals; loaves of bread there one minute are gone the next. Massive bags of potatoes that I've heaved home from the greengrocer's are consumed in a single meal. No wonder families turn vegetarian, economic necessity. Mum takes to the lentils, making everlasting bean soups that we all complain about. It's not just the taste but the unbearable after-effects in the small, confined space of this flat.

All teenagers stink, but boys must be the worst. Their festering feet and dirty clothes, repeatedly strewn around the room, or re-worn until holes appear to let the smell escape. It's just like being with Tim and Ian, my last stepbrothers, who I don't see any more. Charlie and Henry are just posher cricket-obsessed replacements also with no knowledge of deodorant, or those finer points of hygiene the rest of us like to call washing. Nothing stops the sickly sour odours that run screaming from their armpits.

If personal hygiene was taught at school before sex educa-tion, it could revolutionise the teenage approach to sex. You might want to spend longer than the regulation four minutes wrapped in another's skin and we'd never find our way back to class. How are Charlie and Henry in their single-sex boarding schools ever going to find out with anyone that sex can take hours, like in the Kama Sutra?

Ahh, sweet brotherly love.

I can hear them wanking at night, *yuch*! Henry's the worst at rattling magazines, their pages left stuck and scattered across the floor. Hallelujah to the sea, a ready-made bath on the doorstep to wash away all our blemishes.

Somewhere in London my friends from Abdam's are doing their A levels in sixth-form colleges and going to the Roxy, the Vortex, the Marquee; seeing Siouxsie and the Banshees, The Slits, X-Ray Spex, Generation X and The Adverts. Like me they wear dark glasses, black lipstick and cool sneers, leaning against jukeboxes, but their jukeboxes are in the Roebuck or the Man in the Moon, World's End, London, punk Mecca, playing 'Peaches' by The Stranglers, 'Police and Thieves' by The Clash. My jukeboxes are in Falmouth or Penzance and are playing Status Quo or '*Saturday Night Fever*'. At night I grind my teeth and pray to a God that doesn't exist for a black leather jacket and release from my Cornish exile. I get neither.

I must bide my time, knowing that the jumble sales down here are better for stiletto shoes, tartan clothing, ski pants and diamante or enamel brooches that I cover Mum's St Laurent black drape jacket with, requisitioned to my wardrobe. Wearing it every day has redefined it as mine – undrycleanable and unrecog-nisable as couture's finest; punk perfection achieved. I have my hair cut into a fine crew, wear too-tight trews, too-large shirts, a tie and a kilt, to make up for the uniform I never had at school. So what if nobody appreciates it but me.

'How do you ever expect to get a boyfriend looking like that?' my mother asks, genuinely perplexed. 'You need some nice dresses, flowered cottons in this heat, that's what boys like,' she tells me.

'Now you tell me!' She doesn't get the joke even with the metal-plated irony; I have to explain. 'I don't want a boyfriend, Mother, who likes nice flowered cotton dresses. I'd rather not have one at all than one who wants me different to the way I am,' and I turn my back and skulk out of the door.

My father is one of them; he doesn't like the attention safety pins and zips bring. He tells me to bring some nice dresses with me on holiday in his house in Spain. He says Barbara might come, so I pack my case and wait for the ticket. When I call her, Barbara says no way would she be seen dead in Spain, that she's going to Greece to study the origins of theatre. If you ask me, she's studying a case of ouzo and as many waiters as she can wrap around her pale anorexic English body. I'm jealous. Why didn't she ask me?

David says, 'Why do you need a holiday, we live a holiday.' But holidays are only times to get away from the common routine whether you live at the seaside or not, I argue. Times to escape the people you live with. I could never understand going on holiday with your family.

This holiday it's me and Pa, plus a few of his close friends. The English abroad must be held in some time warp, or maybe they change into a prescribed style as soon as they enter a hacienda. Dolly-birds in their cotton flares and halter-neck bikinis fresh from a Martini commercial casting, hair curled and eyes as big as saucers, lie around the pool with gay swingers in seersucker suits, receding hairlines or bad implants, hey baby! Kerchiefs knotted around their necks.

When not buried in a book, I lie floating in the pool, the

ninety-degree heat making the safety pins in my T-shirt unbearable, but I will not give in to topless bathing and polite conversation. Not with the elderly MP and his Chinese friend that nobody is supposed to know creeps across the hallway into his room each night. I suppose he thinks it is better than sweeping the streets of Westminster, which was what he was doing before kind Mr Brockles found him and brought him on holiday. 'It's different here, from Streatham, where I live,' he tells me.

'Yes,' I said. It's different from many places.

The American heiress on her sunlounger glistens in the sun, coconut-greased for fast frying. If you get close enough I swear you can hear her brown breasts sizzling upon the folds of her skin. Sunglasses as big as darkened windscreens saddle her nose, occasionally to be lifted to ride like a hair band across her head, making her smiling, smouldering winks at José the gardener a little more obvious.

To relieve my boredom, I dress and undress with the curtain open, knowing José's watching from the orange tree. I tease him blatantly, the power of youth versus the power of wealth; she takes to wearing all her diamonds, a large G and T cemented in her hand. My, how cross she gets at such a little game, small excitements to shift the inevitability of the days. I drink and smoke too much. Poor José is torn with confusion, but in the end his loins rather than any sense guide him. I spend a couple of siestas snogging dark-eyed, brown-haired José behind the changing huts, his hard body pushing mine, grinding groins against the white-peak plaster until it hurts. His hands mindlessly grasp at my flesh, I don't care, until he begins to dig inside me with his dirty nails, rubbing my unmoved skin sore, then I'm fed up. I refuse to speak to him again, I wish he'd go away. The American harridan can have him, probably does.

It serves me right, really. I was greedy, finished all my books in the first four days and all I'm left with is other people's leftovers, a glut of holiday novels soaked in Ambre Solaire. I reread my Dorothy Parker and start on Heinreich the Austrian. His wife lies ill in bed most days, surfacing for the occasional dinner, suffering from too much or too little medication, to stop some pain. 'Heinie baby,' I tease him, sit on his lap after dinner, stroking his forty-year-old hair. I push it further, I agree to an assignation under the bougainvillea at the bottom of the garden, when the night sky is at its wide, dark blue best, full of clicking cicadas jostling with the stars and heavy jasmine scents. Heinreich grows too hot, too serious – the only escape is to run and lock myself in my bedroom. Doesn't he understand it's only a game?

Apparently not. Pa has words with me; Heinreich has been declaring his love for me to my father. Pa never seems to notice anything unless shown to him, and he doesn't believe any of this nonsense.

'You're quite right, Pa,' I say, backing him to the hilt. 'I'm afraid it might just be Heinreich's wishful thinking. I mean, it's hardly likely anything would happen, is it Pa, I mean, he's ancient.'

'Less of the ancient if you please. Coco. A case of too much sun, brandy and an ill wife. All I hope is that it's not affecting his work too, I've got a job with the bugger next week.'

It might have been fun with Barbara around to talk it all through with, instead I just feel grubby on the flight home for giving myself away, too cheap for the tease.

From the airport to a hotel; from teen teases to adult games. I am meeting Mum and David in London for the first night of Mum's play: the Royal Court Upstairs are actually putting on one of her plays. Celebrations. I know how much this means to Mum, so I congratulate her behind David's back so she can't keep one eye on his expression, to be felled from her deserved happiness. Competition isn't a game.

'We have to be sensitive about David's professional pride,' says Mum.

'But what about you, Mum? I'm so proud of you,' I say.

'Thank you darling,' she kisses my cheek and gives me a splendid old-fashioned hug that reminds me of some time in the past. 'I'm all right. Poor David.'

'Poor old David,' I sympathetically say to him, because he is looking so glum. 'What's the matter?'

'Less of the old, thank you Coco. Nothing's "the matter", as you so sweetly phrase it. I think it's time for a fresh drink.' He turns his fifty-five year old grey-suited back to me and walks to the bar, to be followed by a sycophantic theatrical entourage talking of past successes.

I think I can guess what the matter is. David is so tight-lipped in his congratulations for her success, I think Mum's almost hoping she'll get bad reviews; she's worked in the theatre long enough to understand the frailty of this man's ego.

Since I had declared I was willing to do my A levels anywhere rather than board again, I am enrolled at the local tech. The night before, I start to question my sanity. By seven-thirty the next morning I am scrubbed, ironed, dressed and appetite-less.

First day at college and something tells me it's going to be like this for the duration, the next two years. I've arrived for the first day dressed down: didn't want to be spotted in the crowd and start a reputation too soon, but I have and everything is wrong about me. I can tell at the way the staring starts when I go into assembly. I spot immediately what is substantially different about my clothes, the sniggering and pointing by the other girls makes me sure. It's my jeans, those universal classless standards, have let me down – they are too tight because they don't have sails of denim flapping about my ankles; they are drainpipes. I know fashion isn't that important if you're training to be a farmer, engineer or miner but here they are still, all in baggies and A-line midi skirts! I might have been more sympathetic a few years back when I got my first pair of spray-ons from an antique shop, proudly strutting down Portobello Road with my three-inch suede stacks, a Hawaiian shirt knotted beneath my breasts – sneaking a triangle of bare flesh seemed outrageous.

Nobody could contemplate that drainpipes would ever catch on again, like they still can't in Cornwall. I suppose the tightness causes some of the stares. To get them on this morning I had to lie flat on my bed to squeeze them over my bum but when the zip failed to meet it had to be a shoulder-stand job. Bum and legs against the wall, head almost angled off with the pressure, it always works – the fat must drain into the shoulders till you stand back up again.

There's only one way to be – proud and aloof. Give the signal out. All who know the reasoning of stilettos, drainpipes and bright yellow knotted silk shirts, this way. The rest of you can bugger off!

'Have you been to London?' a voice behind me enthusiastically calls. 'I've been too. It's brilliant down there.'

'Yes, I've been to London,' I reply, turning to smile. 'A few times.'

'Oh you, your 'avin' me on now. You're from there, you are. I can tell by your accent – pure London. Or are you American?'

'Yes. London. No, American.'

'I thought so. What are you doing here? I'm doing business studies, well, you never know when it might come in handy, do you?'

Yes, what am I doing here? I'm talking to an ironed-into-place Teddy Boy and finding him cute with his black greased hair, chipped front tooth and enthusiastically nervous chatter. The opposite of punk, and yet I fancy him, well, well, more things in heaven and hell . . . When you can't have dreams, reality fits in.

'I'm doing my A levels at the sixth-form college. Do you know which building I'm supposed to be in?'

He points in the direction of another architect-grey building.

'You want to go and ask in there. I've got to be off too, maybe see you at lunch in the common room? I'm Joe by the way, nice meeting you.'

We go our separate ways, meeting regularly at lunch and weekend discos. His parents live in a bungalow on a housing estate which some weekends I stay at, if we go out near him. Then we conduct furtive sex against a brown Bri-Nylon, broderie-flowery-anglaise sofa and matching armchair. Like Tom he enjoys the risk of being caught. I lie detached, slightly nervous in this strange house and think of *The Joy of Sex*, *Candy* and *Myra Breckinridge* where sex becomes something other than what I'm doing. I find it amazing that he is able to come, I certainly can't, not that that is of any interest to adolescent boys. The only question they seem to ask in retrospect is, 'So you are on the pill, aren't you?' the strain of anxious hope pulling in the last two words until the reply is affirmative.

'Of course I am, you stupid dickhead, I wouldn't be doing this otherwise.'

Sometimes I wonder why I am doing it. I imagine it will satisfy some kind of craving, fill a hole (and not the one between my legs), the one that exists in my solar plexus, the empty, dark, black space. Hangovers don't help, I know that. Going out, getting drunk and sleeping with a boy is not an answer, I know but . . . Sometimes for a split second after the fuck, the warmth and comfort of lying in a boy's arms, does. Is this a love thing?

Love is a weird thing. What is it?

Only ever walking together holding hands, attached at the hips, not a night apart, sex three times a day. Living, sleeping and working together. Having your bottom drawer overflowing with luridly coloured nylon underwear . . .

At home, true love seems to be more frequently creeping around the flat because David is in a 'bad mood' again. Always let him have the last word, control yours and your actions, never speak to other men. True love has no trust in our house. This love is there if dinner is ready and the Scotch is on the table at six o'clock precisely.

'I hope you've done a good day's work. Well, I'll be the judge of that . . .'

Tender love is getting drunk on a Friday night, is shouting and slapping around the flat before noisy sex because, because of the wrong remark.

Love is competitive, jealous, cruel, aggressive, conditional on giving yourself away to another's whims, completely selfless.

Things have changed since the play and Mum's success, so she feels guilty and responsible for his upsets. And he is upset. She cosies and cossets, breakfast-in-beds him and makes such an effort to bandage his wounded pride with her fur-lined love; she wants so much for this to work. I watch her picking up and staring at glamorous photos of them together, smiling at some gala, and I can almost see a comic-book bubble appear with her resolution. She must turn to David and say, 'I love you!' at least twenty times a day. Who's she saying it for, him or her, I don't need to hear it. Maybe vows would make it better but still they stay unmarried.

I needed to get an understanding outside of our family, so I asked some twenty-eight-year-old friends who'd been in love since they were fourteen – surely they should know.

'How can you tell if you're in love?' I start with the simple basics.

'You just know, it's a feeling,' they inconclusively reply.

'How do you know it's not just lust? That's a feeling.'

'It's a different feeling, believe me Coco; you'll know when it comes along.'

'Will I, are you sure?'

They nodded their heads in complicit agreement, but it wasn't enough. I wanted an insurance policy. I was lost and supposed to stay here and wait for a 'feeling' to descend upon my head and mark me with grace. The grace that my mother and David hold?

If that's love, fuck it!

Lust seems a more honest emotion. No Cinderella syndrome for me, thank you very much. Melting into some surfer's armpits until I'm willing to wear rubber. To lie always in a bikini waiting for his return, on whatever beach the surf feels best for him. Consoling him on 'bad surf' days, stroking his matted, salt-bleached hair and listening interminably to The Eagles, 'Hotel California'. Forget it.

I'd rather shag in a field behind the disco in Helston (No Casual Dressers), with a soul boy. If I'm being truthful I prefer any soul to the screeching hardness of punk, but I wouldn't be caught dead admitting it. I hide my George Benson records behind my cupboard and play them when everyone's out, singing along to 'Nature Boy'.

I make fun of Joe and his rockabilly dancing in his brothel-creepers and drapes, but secretly I'm rather impressed.

I'm not going out with Joe, he has a girlfriend he's been seeing since he was fourteen. Her name is Margaret and she's training to be a hairdresser, she's a fifties rocker in white ankle socks, petticoats and ponytail; they'll get married. Being seen with Joe does my street cred no good, so mostly I hang out with my new friend Katherine – she comes and stays over.

I prefer her place near the art school with real art students and they're different, they don't mind what you look like, they're interested, they talk to you. In the pubs in Penzance, Mousehole, Truro, Newlyn, they're rude to anyone who doesn't look the same as them. In St Ives, the council knocked down the sea wall to get rid of the hippies in the Sixties – they thought no wall, no hippies. The pubs still have 'No Beatnik' signs in the windows, and notices at the bar saying 'Beards, long hair and sandals will not be served'. Funny, since in the summer that seems to be a description of the fishermen. How the artistic community ever thrived there is a miracle, unless they all looked like Magritte, the be-suited bank clerk.

ALL GROWN-UP

★ ★ ★

The White Club, Thursday night, is my salve, the excitement that makes the rest of the week bearable. If a band makes it to Exeter University they might as well come here; at least they'll be sure of enthusiasm, from this excitement-starved audience. Kathy and I are out on the town, 999 are playing tonight. Katherine is borrowing my silver lurex Marilyn Monroe dress (five pence from last week's Operatic Society jumble sale), identical to Swanky Modes' latest collection, high stilettos and fishnet stockings. At the end of the night the fishnets have to be picked out of the balls of your feet with tweezers, cemented there from pogoing in the angle of those shoes. Strapped into place on my ankles are similar four-inch heels but my legs are encased in 1950s black and gold threads tight to my thighs, hips, knees and ankles. Diamante is liberally sprinkled over my ears, neck, fingers and descending into my black satin cleavage. Our dead-white complexions are blood-ied with scarlet lipstick, our eyes stretch to our hairlines, while brown shader digs beneath our puppy-fat cheeks in a desperate attempt to define bones that might never appear.

Our hair is stuck up with sugar solution, perfect in cold weather, but with the lights, dancing and the heat of other bodies packed close, the stuff melts off your hair like golden syrup with a steady, sticky trickle down your neck.

We get off the bus, queue, pay our two pounds, check our fake leopard-skin coats in and make our entrance across an empty, dark floor towards the brightly lit, more promising bar. Here you can browse, spot a good thing, see your quarry, follow it to the next room and in the blackness lean close to . . . If there's a note of rejection, you can silently slip away to nobody's embar-rassment, it was an accidental touching of the flesh, bodies rubbed the wrong way up.

Right way, and *Bingo*.

'A vodka and lime for me, please. Then I think I'll go on to tequilas and lager,' declares grown-up Katherine. At seventeen we're not even old enough to be allowed in.

'I think I'll just stick to Pernod and lemonade. Don't look like that, it's delicious, I tried it down at Purgatory's disco the other night. It's just like a Barrett's lemon sherbet sucked through the liquorice stick. Have a taste?' I offer enthusiastically, still a child.

There's some sad support on, a whining geek in glasses that nobody's watching, not even the lost hippies. They always come to the gigs, though what punk has got in common with the Sixties I can't understand. They try to explain the similarities in their time-warp, dope-slowed speech but it takes too long, and anyway the band's on. We're crowding in, bodies tightly crammed, pushing towards the stage.

Kathy and I are trying to keep our space, remain unruffled and aloof to glow pure beauty, sophistication and simple lust to this week's heroes on centre stage.

See Us, Notice Us, We are Different from These Oiks. We could be up on stage.

'Can I have your autograph?' I ask the lead singer at the end of the gig. 'I've got a pen.'

'Sure darlin', no problem for a lovely of your calibre,' he says, looking me up and down again.

'Got any paper? What d'ya want me to write?'

'Do you think you could do it here?' I innocently suggest, pulling my shirt away from my shoulder, leaving a pale, bare plain for the marker to trail across my breast.

'So, no paper, eh! I suppose this will 'ave to make do,' he says, bemused, his face grinning as he tackles the task. It tickles, I try hard to keep still and not laugh. 'Anywhere else you'd like me to autograph?'

'My dick!' shouts the drummer from the back of the dressing room.

'I wouldn't know where to find it, where'd you last leave it, Mick?'

'Could you do me too?' says Katherine, in her sweetest dark-honey voice.

Her eyes are azure blue, peeking through her cloud of auburn curls. Never let it be said that I choose plain companions to make myself shine brighter, I sometimes wonder if I shouldn't with Katherine. She is so overtly sexual I suspect she wears suspenders under her jeans. Katherine widens my horizons. One night she says Why not? To sleeping with the whole of a visiting punk band, so we do. Nothing happens; we're all so drunk they give us separate beds and a cup of tea the next morning. We stagger home on the bus, dirty stop-outs, in last night's stained and stinking clothes. On another night in Falmouth we go and visit a painter she sits for at the college, who suggests we all go to bed. The problem is I don't fancy him (I don't know how she can), I feel awkward undressing, cold in his damp sheets and bored as he tries and fails to make love to first one and then the other of us, but can't make it with either. None of us knows the roles we are supposed to play and it's almost a relief to get back to Kathy's house. Her parents are sitting up waiting for us with hot chocolate, keen to know all about the film we said we were going to see. We make up a plot on the spot and then escape to her room and play our favourite record, Bill Withers's, 'Lovely Day', crossing our fingers and hiding our giggles.

The day after the 999 gig we're back at college in the canteen opening our shirts to show our night-out medals. We will never wash again – well, not until the weekend. We go down to the pub at lunchtime to celebrate our hangovers with the gang of boys we hang out with from our English A-level class. Sebastian, a mad taxidermist who shoots anything that moves to stuff it, Jim the mod, ugly and funny and only there for the grant, and morose, mooching Malcolm sunk deep in *Melody Maker*. Poor Malcolm, we say, us *NME* followers of Julie Burchill's amphetamine-induced vitriol, but we play him at pool anyway. Somewhere in between we herd into classes, the library, revise and pass exams to cross into a different pasture.

'Art school's just the place for you!' David says to my delight. 'I can't see you making it to Oxbridge in that get-up,' he kindly laughs.

I am busy filling up sketchbooks, I've had inside information from some of my old schoolfriends who've gone on to art college that the thing they like best is sketchbooks. I have two weeks before my interview to complete the fifteen sketchbooks I have laid out before me. I am ageing them with coffee stains, stubbing cigarettes out on them, sandpapering their covers and filling them with cut-outs, collages, paint, ideas, designs, postcards, photo-booth leftovers, sketches, ticket stubs and poetry. But for the last year I have kept one, a dress diary, each day drawing the outfit I'm wearing, to spur me on to dress up even more.

'Why's art school just the place for me?' I ask innocently back. I am longing to go to art school, I dream about it at night, I want to talk about it all the time. I am obsessed.

'Because art students never stop talking either. You'll be as cosy as a pig in shit. Chatter, chatter, chatter, pretending to work. At Cambridge where I went we were serious, engaged in real work. You couldn't get away with the buffoonery that goes on in drama and art schools, they're not like universities.'

'Good!' I laugh. He's joking, I think?

'You, you laugh too easily!' he sneers over his paper, spearing my joy.

'So why do you think nobody's bought your script yet?' I retaliate where I know it'll hurt most. He doesn't even get my jibe, but it makes me feel better.

'It's the state of the British film industry,' he cranks up the old excuses, 'that they can't appreciate a script that deals with more than just the surface inanities of life. Something with true intellectual content threatens them, they . . .' Dream on, old man, why is it always somebody else's fault?

I put on my finest new, second-hand RAF jacket, ribbons of diamante strung across it like awards of Tiffany bravery, hair bleached and set in Marilyn curls, make-up in place and a tight skirt and belt to keep it clinched in place. I am off to London this afternoon for my interview at art school in London. Hobbling up the hill in my pencil skirt and too-high stilettos to catch the coach to college this morning, portfolio in one hand, suitcase in the other, I stop every five minutes to gather my breath, swop hands and start again. Two policemen come towards me. 'How sweet,' I think, 'they're probably going to offer to help me.'

'What do you think you look like!'

'Very nice, thank you,' I reply sweetly.

One steps close, helmet to my forehead. He says, 'Do you realise we could do you for impersonating an RAF officer?'

'I'm sorry? I must be quite out of date, I didn't realise they were wearing lipstick, diamante and fishnets these days.'

He lays a hand on my shoulder. 'You could also be done for disrespect towards a police officer, so watch it.' He jerks his face towards mine like a turkey. 'Gottit!

'Where you goin' anyway, what are you up to?'

'To catch my bus to college, and if it's all the same to you, officer, I can't stand here gossiping all day otherwise I'm going to miss it.'

'Well on your way, and don't let us catch you with your cheek or that jacket on again round 'ere, or we'll 'ave you under arrest, see!' and he pushes me hard against the wall to nail his point home.

I'm shocked. I pick up my stuff and turn to go, biting at my lip, tongue, anything to stop me from crying, anything . . . If they think they're going to have me showing my vulnerability to them, they must be fucking joking. The wind blows against my face,

141

forcing the water out of my eyes; it must be the wind.

I make it to the top of the hill without stopping; no turning back.

'It's true, that's what they said, Louise. Can you believe, I almost didn't make my interview because I was too busy in police questioning! Cornwall is the pits!'

'Well, at least you had a good interview. I'm sure they loved the fact that you came from Cornwall, all ethnic and country-bumpkinish.'

'Oh yes, they loved that, but they couldn't understand why I didn't want to go to Foulmouth College. They obviously haven't been themselves. They said I probably wouldn't get a grant, but I said I wanted to come here so much I'd work my way through college. They seemed impressed. On the other hand they thought my black and white Warholesque Friesian cow on fluorescent-green paper was a study in abstract line design!'

'I'm sure you'll get in. The question is, will I get into the Fashion Department.'

'Yes, of course you will. It's going to be so much fun if Rainbow gets in too, when's her interview?'

'Tomorrow, and I think Harriet's is on the same day. It's going to be the big happy Abdam's family back together again.'

'More like The Addams Family.'

'We're all meeting up tomorrow night to go to the Blitz, rendezvous at my place, Sloane Square, nineish and we can have something to drink before we go. Sample the drinks cabinet. Mum and Peter are out and they won't mind, they won't know if we refill the vodka and gin bottles back up with water.'

'OK, Louise, see you tomorrow. Remember there's the party in the country on Saturday, as well as the warehouse thing on Friday night.'

'Speak to you tomorrow then, have a good day. I've got Barbara's number where you're staying.'

'Mum, I've got my mock A-levels results.'

'How did you do?'

'I got eighty-seven percent in English, seventy-eight per cent in art, seventy-two per cent in sociology, pretty good, eh!'

'Did you come top?'

'I think Kathy got more in English, I was fifth in sociology . . .'

'What are you going to the fancy-dress ball as tonight, a dunce?'

'What!'

'Well, you didn't come top, you won't get into college and you'll probably end up as a Woolworth's shop assistant, but then if that's what you want out of life . . .'

'What are you going as tonight? A shit? Because that's how you're behaving!'

Something tells me she must have had another great day with David, but that's her problem and I'm not going to let it spoil my joy. I have got into art school. Yippee!

I am going to leave Cornwall. Yippee!

I won't get a grant, a drag! But Louise and I have appeared, interviewed and photographed, in *Disco Dancing Weekly* after being spotted at the Blitz, Steve Strange night. I wrote to *Ritz* magazine and suggested I be interviewed or at least photographed in a column. They ask me to review Julie Burchill's first book, which I do. But *Disco Dancing Weekly* – and they don't even know who my mother is!

I was looking forward to a nice relaxed summer awaiting A-level results, working in Purgatory's disco, an art gallery, or the posh French restaurant, in the kitchen, like last summer. Collecting funds and suntans for my London onslaught, but that's it, isn't it? Just when you start to feel relaxed about life, the bombshell crashes. Mum and David have decided to up and opt for Los Angeles a week after my eighteenth birthday, so I've practically got to be packed off a week later. To move into Barbara's flat and up and find a job to support myself. Dad's paying my college fees and giving me forty pounds a month, Mum's the same. Rent's ten pounds a week, cheap without bills, but it's definitely a self-fulfilling prophecy. Work my way through college.

I know I'm eighteen but I feel too young for this responsibility. Too young to be alone in London with Barbara, whom I don't know any longer. Barbara's changed so much. Grown-up and working at twenty, she's part of the outside world.

My dad's in Spain and when he comes to London we'll have lunch, chattering for two hours and saying nothing. I'll walk away from the table with a tenner in my hand for a taxi fare when we both know I'll take the tube, yet it's never enough – I always feel cheated. I'll bury myself in the pictures for the afternoon or an Anita Brookner novel. Too suffocating, and I'll stand in the middle of the Italian rooms at the National Gallery and wait to be absorbed by some passing cerulean blue.

I feel estranged after five years away from London on my holiday visits: how am I going to cope there alone all the time?

It's the two years in Cornwall that has put everything out. Being in such close proximity to Ricky and David I don't think is healthy for a growing girl, and though I feel annoyed and deserted by them so quickly going off to Los Angeles, I'm glad I won't be living in that flat any more.

'Listening to rows and blocking my ears, seeing them angry . . . These are a few of my least favourite things,' I hum.

Bound for parochial Putney still seems like the vivacious lights of London to me; compared to the Cornish Peninsula, it would. How to get through the summer when I can't wait for college to start, with the parties, the clubs, the dressing up: I'm returning to my fold with a licence to Paradise. Let me in, let me in! Open the gates or give me the key around my neck, I'm arriving on the two o'clock train.

CHAPTER FOURTEEN

Up the stairs and to the left was a main door marked Private.

The children ignore the sign. The door leads to Coco and Ben's suite. A bathroom, a bedroom and a sitting room, all with connecting doors from one through to the others. The rooms were bright and warm, painted Mediterranean blue and Indian yellow with touches of ochre, burnt umber and raw sienna. Every time she walked into these rooms Coco's heart glowed and her face smiled like she was really coming home. She could quite happily have lived in just these three rooms and forgotten the rest of the house, been content with their smallness and gone to the studio each day that she and Ben shared in the grounds. But that was before babies and hotels and more babies came into the equation, and there was no way the children could ever be taken out.

Not that she would have wanted anything different to the peace and love she had now. Her family, her painting (when she did it), her food, the hotel, fell into a rhythm of harmony, a contentedness that she never even knew existed or thought was possible. Even the arguments that happened within the family appeared and left and flowed like a river on to somewhere else. This ease was happiness.

The rest of the house had been lovingly decorated too with colours and furniture that made you feel you were stepping into somebody's home as a privileged guest, a long-lost member of the family. That was the appeal, but just like staying in somebody's house you didn't ring for tea, you had meals at a set time, plenty of privacy and a roaring log fire and the countryside to be with. Some people were affronted, expecting more from a hotel, wanting constant attention and to be set apart as something extra special, to be treated differently, requiring VIP service. Either Ben or Coco would have to quietly, subtly hint that perhaps they were in the wrong place, that there were other hotels which provided those services. They had fun and laughed over it, but they were firmly set in their niche and it didn't happen so often now. However it appeared, it was still a hotel, a going concern that provided their home and kept them fed and stimulated, or bored by the ever-changing roll call. With rooms that had to be continually changed and remade, cleared and made fresh. The Moroccan and Indian rugs had to be hoovered or beaten, the Mexican bedspreads to be washed, the hand-painted tables, chairs and bedheads to be dusted and polished, paintings to be straightened and bathrooms to be cleaned and bubble bath replenished.

If any of the guests came back this afternoon, Julie and Martha, due to arrive within moments, would have to see to them. Make the tea and heat the scones.

Coco sat on the edge of the bright blue leather chair in the corner of her bedroom, and unlaced her shoes. Her feet had swollen from standing and pregnancy and she couldn't any longer simply kick them off. So many things became a palaver with pregnancy. Riding a bicycle signaled a miscarriage over the handlebars, running downstairs and jumping the last two steps was replaced by the steady gait of a gouty Victorian gentleman, getting out of the bath made you feel like installing a winch, while the lingerie industry confined you to white-only matron's bras, which cancelled out a half-black wardrobe.

For a moment Coco didn't know if she could move herself to the bed, thought she might just sleep there upright for the effort it took to move, but she felt the blood pump in her toes and she pulled herself up against gravity. Opening then closing the bed curtains, slipping between the warm eiderdown covers, smelling the comfort of the pillows, she let her body and brain slide into the oblivion of sleep. To dreams of comfort and warmth, an untroubled sleep that fed her body and her baby. Dreams of fresh yellow clotted cream sliding over piles of sugared strawberries, eaten on islands with pale soft sand lapped by mild turquoise oceans, a distant red sailing boat to separate the sea from the horizon. A warm sun benignly covers her back; a weightless existence. A boat docks in the untroubled water and a flood of children splash towards her while Ben moors the boat; her family, everything, safe, clear and warm. Untroubled dreams that aren't even remembered on waking.

CHAPTER FIFTEEN

The street is grey and every house looks the same; six, eight, ten, but still I'm excited. Twenty Cambridge Street, Putney and the cab screeches to a stop outside. I've made it to Cambridge in spite of David! I'm fumbling for that fiver in my pocket. I know I put it there, maybe it's in the other pocket – shit. I panic at not one light showing in the windows of my destination and no money to pay the cab. I know I put it somewhere safe – ah, found it, in my inside jacket pocket. I step out into the darkening, clouded sky of early London summer, handing over my last note.

'Well, take your bags then!' the cab driver shouts. I haul my life in three suitcases out and wish I had the guts to ask for the tip back.

I'm a grown-up and this is it, I'm eighteen. I have to get a job, I have to rely on me now, financially, emotionally. Forget about the parents; but Barbara's going to be here, almost a stepping stone. Barbara. I hope.

I ring the bell then hunt for the keys under the mat, unlocking the door on to an engulfing darkened silence. There's a hollow emptiness as my cheery 'hello' echoes a lonely retreat down the hall. I walk into the first open doorway straight ahead, where the last of the light bounces off the geometrically patterned black and white walls, table, chairs, duvet. I'm not quite sure if it's Barbara's room, it seems too hard for her with its gloss-painted floorboards. Where are the soft pile carpets for her 'purrfect pink'-painted toenails to sink and luxuriate in? I go back to the hall to open the next door, a roomful of dresses, a trick wardrobe. The last door opens to the scrunch of notepaper wrinkling under its push.

Dear Coco,

> *Welcome to your room!!!!*
>
> *HI! Sorry I can't be here for your first night but I'm working at the theatre.*
>
> *Will be back at 11.30 approx., so see you then or in the morning.*
>
> *Love Barbara* +++

The walls, high ceiling and bay windows are Venetian red. The floor is covered in greengrocer's grass and unceremoniously dumped upon it are my red wardrobe, a wooden curly hatstand and a new single bed, the mattress still shiny, wrapped in its plastic coat. Mickey's hand on my watch says seven forty-five and it feels too late to call any of my friends to do anything tonight, besides until I get a job I've got ten pounds a week to live on, and I've got to unpack. I want to say fuck it but what for, what else have I got waiting for me? I can't see a limo and an endless supply of hot dates appearing down the street, deafening me with their impatient horns. They must be late.

Sitting on the crackle of mattress plastic, gazing unblinking at the light from the uncovered bulb, I feel a new loneliness dribble upon me. Different from the escape of self-imposed solitudes of school and home, but then this isn't escape. I'm not cramming hard-pressed hands into my ears until I shut out the shouting, or transporting myself from a crowded reception, mind, body, soul, somewhere else. This is where my life begins and what happens is now up to me, my decision from now on and I can't think of one. Not one decision or resolution. I'm sure I had some somewhere, decisions, resolve, ideas – maybe I'll find them at the bottom of one of my cases, I hope I didn't leave them in Cornwall.

The house has a strange feel to it, no happy, bright warmth. The light doesn't work on the stairs, and the single forty-watt bulb that hangs in the cramped maisonette's hall shadows the steep stairs into the basement. I catch my heel, falling on to the banister.

'Bloody hell! I almost broke my fucking ankle. What a brilliant start that would have been as an entrée into London society!' I shout at nobody.

A warning to any burglars lurking in the bathroom before I enter to scent my new patch. This is the kind of dog they'd be dealing with! The Don't Mess With Me kind, even if I have got a limp and it's my first night away from home.

The basement is cold, damp, dark and wallpapered in Russian newspapers, not so the bathroom. That is just plain white with the odd crack and crumble that I notice as I cringe sitting on the hard, black, freezing, split loo seat which catches my soft thigh, ouch!

It may be slightly falling to pieces but at least it's arty, I couldn't have borne a velour sofa of a place. It's a friend of a friend of Barbara's place, who's moved to New York, and it's perfect. There's a refectory table and benches that almost take up the whole of the dining room, more of a corridor really, that leads to a scullery of a kitchen and a back door. An overgrown, muddy, mossy, grassy garden lurks on the other side.

'Brilliant.' I think. I shall sunbathe there, hidden among the weeds from the neighbours' prying eyes, and invite friends for picnics and dinner parties.

I shall like it here, I affirm. A resolve found in my back pocket, hidden there for this moment. It takes time to get used to freedom.

I have my home; I set my mind towards finding a job. The first ad I answer is in the back of the paper and asks the enticing question, 'Interested in fashion?' Who isn't; I pick up the phone and find myself walking the streets the next day with a bagful of mail-order shirts, knocking on people's doors. Hassling hairdressers and secretaries, accountants and newsagents. Hauling samples around in a suitcase until my shoulders fall off, I can't get used to the rejection of people saying, No thank you, they don't want to buy one of the hideous bargains I'm tempting them to. I take it personally that somebody won't buy the lime green and burgundy striped shirt in a specially created silk-sateen substitute, with washable broderie-anglaise collar.

'Would you wear it?' they ask.

'Well, it's not quite my style, but it would look great on you!'

'Match nicely with my eyes. Thanks, but no thanks. I'd rather wear my breakfast to work after I've eaten it, than that shirt. You expect some sucker to pay a tenner! Get real, you're in Brixton, not Mayfair, dumb cluck!'

'Well, thank you for your valuable advice and time. I'll call back next time I'm in the area, then?'

I chuck in my 'foot in the door' career. What next? A waiter, a cook, a shop assistant, chambermaid's job. I know all the stories from friends in Falmouth about the extras you can earn as a good chambermaid, just make the occupant as well as the bed. Mum would probably advocate a nice Mayfair hotel with a constant supply of hot running Arabs.

"You'd only have to work once a week, you'd probably get enough to see you all the way through college. Of course, if you pretended you were a virgin (you'd have to hide a sachet of ketchup on you), once a month would probably do it."

I get exhausted just leafing through the *Evening Standard* and *Time Out* job columns. I'm sure there's plenty of people who'd like to give me a job, I repeat twenty times a day until one appears.

'What experience have you had? Jim, my hairdresser, said you needed a summer job before you started at art school. Is he your sister's boyfriend, or something?'

'Just a friend. I've worked in three restaurants, and as a barmaid in a disco in Cornwall, where I come from.'

I want to lie and add some more references but I'm afraid I'll be found out. Discovered as a fake grown-up, incapable of being anything but a child. I want this job so much I'm wide-eyed and so eager I'm almost falling forward off my chair.

'Well, fill in this form. We might need somebody extra in the next few days. We'll probably ring on the off chance.'

Will, the manager, sweeps his fine blond public-schoolboy hair back with one hand, takes a drag on his cigarette, exhaling through his nose and rests his loafered foot upon the step. Smart but 'amusing' socks cover his neat ankles, a perfect match for his braces.

'OK, yah?'

'Yes, fine. Thank you.'

'Drop the form in here when you've finished. And when you turn up for work, clean that nail-polish muck off, make sure your nails are clean and don't forget there's a strict black and white dress code. Don't try to be fancy!'

And I'm dismissed with a half-grimace, half-smile.

I'm elated. A job at the Desert. The club we came to for Barbara's eighteenth birthday treat: pop stars, movie stars, West End stars, all come here after work.

Now that's what I call a summer job, even if he did sneer at my nails, half fuchsia, half crimson, painted with such loving care for an hour before the interview. I don't care, I'm in. I go straight home to sit by the phone, wait for my bidding. Any calls, I tell them 'Get off the line, I'm expecting an important call.'

'No, I can't possibly go out, you see the Desert might be calling me any minute to start work. That's right, the Desert.'

After three days of phone-watching, afraid even to go out for milk and bread, my doggedness is beginning to waver. Paranoia sets in. Did I even go for an interview? Maybe he just said that he'd give me a chance to fob me off. He didn't like me, I could tell by the way he sneered me up, then down. I haven't got a job, I haven't got any money. Help, Coco, what am I going to do? Now calm down, get yourself together. Phone them up. It's what a normal person would do. If you haven't got the job, it won't matter if you scream filthy abuse down the phone to some toffee-nosed receptionist and if you have, you can behave perfectly.

I behave perfectly. I have a job. I earn twenty quid my first night! Once I have this, everything seems to slot into place. I have a place to live, money in my pocket, friends, and I start college. Everything except a boyfriend. I seem to be very good at having other people's leftovers, ones they don't want to see for the time being, until now, unfaithful, they call them back. This is boring. I have too much time to spend pursuing the unattainable.

Louise and I go to clubs, OK so it's the Blitz, the Embassy, Legends, and usually end up chatting to gay boys. I go to the Tate Gallery (well-known singles pick-up spot on a Sunday) and try to look dreamily beautiful, intelligent yet approachable by Marcel Duchamps' *Pissoir*; to no avail. I walk the markets of Putney, Portobello, Camden Lock, interested, interesting, attractive. For God's sake I even sit in coffee bars and do I once get approached, not even a dirty old man on the horizon. I am following all the guidelines of every French romantic film, every American middle-class movie, and not even an inkling of 'Do you come here often', 'Oh, this is my favourite painting too'. 'Didn't we meet some-where . . .'

Something is wrong and needs changing, but I don't think for a minute that it might be me. Bugger it. I stay home and paint diagonal black and white stripes on my stilettos and concentrate on how to divert the Desert's dress code, make friends with my fellow workers and spend my proceeds in book shops, cinemas, and the green room (bar) of the theatre where Barbara works. 'Yes, actually, my cousin is in the play upstairs . . .' I have a little success here, but it doesn't count, they're only drunken actors wearing other people's characters that flirt briefly past my body.

'OK, OK. You can quieten down.

'You may all think you're special because you managed to get on this foundation course and maybe you were from your school, but you're all pretty ordinary put in one room. No special treatment here. You'll be divided into three groups alphabetically . . .'

Yeah, yeah, yeah. The tired old voice from a body of baggy old jeans and beer-bellied sweatshirt drains through the cigarette-grey skin and bitter, beer-wrinkled flesh.

Some students fuck their tutors. Sleep with them. Have affairs! I look with renewed horror at the specimen of advanced learning and ability before me. I think of him naked. Disgusting.

'Come on Coco, we're meant to be going downstairs to have our photographs taken for the school records,' says Rainbow, dragging me back to reality.

Rainbow and Harriet are in Foundation with me from Abdam's and Louise has got into the Fashion Department. Cruella (self-named after *One Hundred and One Dalmatians*) who I'd met when she was in Foundation, is now in the Painting Department. I am blissfully happy, apart from the non-boyfriend situation which I see as a lifetime project. The thing is, I'm now doing exactly what I want every day and it's not illegal or expensive and there are no exams. I'm meeting people in new departments, and apart from outraging my personal tutor by doing a portrait as my first oil painting, I'm getting along with everybody.

'Never did I imagine that I would see the day when figurative art would be being practised at a stalwart abstract college like this! I suggest, Miss Johnson, you find yourself another tutor. I don't see that we can possibly get along.' And with that, my first tutor purposefully strode out of the studio, hair flying, beard to the fore.

I didn't know what he was talking about. It was only a picture of my new friend Jester.

John Jester was a butler, a vagrant, a misfit who worked at the Naval Command Club. He cooked the breakfasts there, borrowing pornography from the officers' rooms hoping they would inquire with the manager about what happened to their copies of *Golden Showers with Susie*, *Correction for Adults* and *Fun with Animals*. They never did, so Jester took to borrowing other things from the kitchen instead. They never seemed to notice.

I met Jester at Cruella's Turkish tea party in her parents' house in Hampstead. A group of us went from college, the requisite hour being spent making up and changing into our best Ottoman Empire look in the ladies' loos, to be stared at on the tube all the way from Tottenham Court Road. Getting in the party mood we swigged at our bottles, cigarettes permanently fixed between our sateen-gloved fingers.

Cruella's mother is at the door of their large imposing Victorian-Gothic mansion, guest-greeting in an oil-smeared boiler suit, spanner in hand and a very determined look upon her face.

'You see it's this damned boiler, I'm trying to fix the thing. Do you know anything about boilers? I'm Cruella's mother, have you come to tea? Oh, don't you look nice. I'm afraid the blancmange got into rather a mess and seeped into the cucumber sandwiches, never mind, the jelly turned out splendidly. You do like jelly?'

I walked into the room and there was Jester, lying on the floor trying to lick chocolate blancmange from his belly button, digging out the mouth and eyes of a polystyrene wig head with his curved Turkish sultan's sword, filling the holes with caviar and delicately snogging the contents out of each orifice. Replete, he gives the rest of the jar to the dog and Cruella's equally vampy seven-year-old sister. Outside the window Catherine wheels burst, bang and spin a month before Guy Fawkes' night. 'Any excuse for fireworks!' the father beams to an inquiry. The family seemed so familiar, almost déjà vu, until I remembered the Frank Capra movie, *'You Can't Take It With You'*, that I'd watched the week before.

'Who is that?'

There was so much to take in, just on the walls of this

muddled bohemian home, let alone the people at the party. I wasn't sure who I was asking, a boy toking on an exotic pipe and guardedly swigging wine from the bottle by his side, replied, 'Oh, that's Jester. Don't you know Jester! Who are you anyway? Have I met you before . . . no, I would've remember that turban,' the chirpy, thickly Liverpudlian accent drawled.

'No, I haven't met you. Why aren't you wearing a turban, it is a Turkish tea party after all!'

'I suppose you're from The College,' he peered at me intently and said menacingly, 'Would you like this bottle? I'm Tony Hammer. But you can call me Sledge.'

'Oh, thank you Tony, yes.'

I thought, what a friendly boy, until he replied, 'Where'd you want it, smashed in your face! Ha, ha, ha . . .'

I missed the joke, but Tony seemed to find it funny; maybe it was just my face he was laughing at.

'So you've met Sledgehammer,' said the dark, mysterious voice of Jester, his lipstick smeared across one side of his face, his eye make-up going in the other direction. 'As in, "subtle as".'

'Yes, he's rather rude, isn't he? I'm Coco, you're Jester aren't you? I was watching you with the blancmange when I came in. Did you manage to get it all out of your belly button with your tongue?'

'Not quite. Look. Are you hot chocolate, or a clown? We could start a circus, pop group or coffee bar between us.' And he pushes each side of his tummy together, squidging his flesh until the residue of sweet, sticky chocolate jelly oozes out of his navel, dribbling on to the pale, hairy skin below.

'Do you want to lick it off?'

'No, thank you for asking, but I'm a bit full from the Marmite sandwiches, and I'm neither chocolate nor clown, it's worse. I was christened after a Paris fashion house by a mother who always wished she could afford more couture.'

'Oh, I was never christened, what's it like? My parents

thought it philosophically unsound and saved the money to send me to a psychiatrist instead, but it didn't help my handwriting one bit. I've still got some caviar left between my toes, if you'd like it.' With relish he lifts the dirty, overgrown nailed things to his mouth and sucks his toes with absolute delight, stops, smiles at me and finishes the job.

'What do you do at college all day?' asks Barbara, only half interested, while putting on her make-up in the bathroom mirror one morning.

'This morning I think we've got life drawing, painting naked women to you. This afternoon, graphics and free period, then I'm off to work at the Desert. Another wild Friday night.'

'Do the boys do it too?'

'Do what? The same lessons? Of course.'

'Drawing naked women? Don't they get embarrassed, get erections? I mean, they are only teenage boys.' I raise my eyebrows incredulously. 'Well, I shouldn't think they've had that much sex,' she reasons. 'Not as much as you, at any rate. And who was that boy you had in your room the other night?'

'None of your business, O big surrogate sister. Simeon from graphics, if you must know. You've got to be joking about college, haven't you? You don't think about sex just because there's a naked boy in front of you. It's work. It's "art". Even the young boys are too busy concentrating on portraying the figure correctly, besides, most of our models are over the age of seventy with nylon wigs that slip when they start to nod off. It's like action drawing, you have to start all over again because she's completely changed position from falling asleep. You see, life at college isn't all merry-go-rounds, there's pain and heartache as well . . .'

I'm joking, I love college, everything about it.

The conversation stayed with me at college that morning, and collecting my takeaway cappuccino and roll from the Italian café next door, five minutes late I walk into the awed silence of the Life Studio. I'm awkward, balancing my coffee and portfolio. Lying among the background of draped velvet curtains, piled sheets and pillows to be drawn is this gorgeous pre-Raphaelite model, voluptuously curved into her setting. Then I see the boys, all in the front row, sitting on their donkeys and steadfastly gawping. Not a pencil mark on their paper between them, their hands covering the fronts of their laps, their tongues covering their chins.

Busy studying the model.

Paris! Wonderful, beautiful Paris, home of my namesake, Chanel. My first college trip and we're over for the major Picasso exhibition at Le Grand Palais with two nights to hit the town with our glamour. Meet Claude Montana, hero of the padded-shoulder denim catwalks. Go to the Pompidou Centre, hanging out in the waste-pipe tribute to modern art. Stagger the clubbers at Le Bain Douche and Le Palais with our sophistication and art-school style (surely a contradiction in terms, when you see the frayed hemlines).

Paris, France and we've arrived. Too terrified to mumble our schoolgirl French, to sit luxuriously ordering Pernods in the 'Deux Magots'. Too money-conscious to enjoy anything other than the trip around the supermarket, for cheap wine to return home and get drunk with. We go round to see an old friend of my mother's, a famous French movie star, who I've always been in awe of. We walk into the high-ceilinged apartment block and I feel like subtitles should be appearing around my feet, it's so French. She is out, Victoria her daughter is in, comfortably ensconced with a Parisian boyfriend, lounging on a large enveloping sofa. French-style, clean jeans, T-shirts, no make-up, natural blonde hair swept into a ponytail on one side of her beautiful young face. Riveted with insecurity, and none of the style of her mother that I was expecting.

'Where are the cheekbones?' I keep thinking.

'We thought we'd come and see you before we go to Le Bain Douche. Do you want to come? We hear it's the only trendy place to go to in Paris. What's it like?'

'I don't know, I haven't been. You'll never get in, will they?' She shouts across to her boyfriend. He is disinterested and turns away. 'I wouldn't say there was much point in trying.'

Rainbow, Harriet and I look at each other. Me in a pink chiffon ball gown and bouffant hair, bejewelled, fur-wrapped and stilettos. Harriet shimmering in a 1920s (but it looks Sixties) up-and-down of silver and white beads and sequins, her beautiful heavy red hair cut just below her ears. Rainbow is the Courrèges princess in a space-age silver jacket with diamante buttons, moon-silver leather booties on her toes and a tiara on her head. These princesses will go to the ball, but certainty has been replaced with trepidation.

We arrive by taxi at the inconspicuous doorway, a large bruiser of a bouncer in full monkey suit barring our way. I head our troupe.

'Le Bain Douche, s'il vous plaît.'

'Oui! Cinquante francs!'

'Non, non, les pauvres étudiantes d'art à Londres?'

'OK, OK.'

He gives us three tickets and a pitying look at my painful French.

'Merci, monsieur. Merci,' I beam, as we sail down the stairs into this year's fashionable heaven. The club is tiled like an underground swimming pool. The air is damp and steamy, condensation running down the walls, while the fog of black tobacco smoke hangs waiting in the darkness. There's a spotlit pool in the corner with large chequered tiles. Divers play underwater chess for the disco-dancing patrons, further amusement. In true French style it is there only to look at. If anybody jumped in the water and used the facilities, it would be revolution and outrage. We go to the bar for a five-franc glass of beer, to find it costs us five pounds. So that's why everyone does their drinking in bars and then sobers up at the discos before they make their way home on the all-night metro.

A boy sidles up to me in the way I'm always imagining one will do in London, and never does.

'I see you are English, are you girls from London?' he asks, the best Alain Delon lookalike I've seen so far.

'Yes. Is it so obvious?'

'Why of course, you English always have the most original style,' he replied in his whipped-cream accent. Yum, yum.

'I guess it's art school that does it,' I say, quite perked up. I had started to feel slightly insecure at the tatty glam of my outfit. Could people tell that it was bought from the second-hand antique clothes shop in Putney High Street? The early elegance of Parisian girls is almost frightening, all so sure and chic. All their hemlines so straight, and no safety pins showing.

'I am coming to London as a student next month. Is this how all the girls are looking like there?'

'Oh, God yes. You can hardly get into a club unless you've got a long dress on.'

'In fact we got dressed like this for a tea date and haven't had time to go back to our hotel to change into disco gear.'

'Simply nobody wears jeans in London. You'll be a social misfit if you do.'

'Our advice to you is to take a three-piece suit and tie if you're going to London. You can't go wrong.'

This poor boy's eyes are darting first from Harriet, to Rainbow, to me in a pleading horror of disbelief. My how we enjoy ourselves at the expense of one poor unsuspecting male, making fun, playing games, too scared to join in life.

I've become quite friendly with Tony and his friend William. William used to go out with Vin in the Film Department. Together they ride about on William's ancient, roaring motorbike, fringed scarves flying in the wind, his gauntleted hands posed on the handlebars like a twenties' matinée idol. The boys are both at London University, but you wouldn't know it by their attendance levels. I think the tutors at college will be surprised that they haven't got end-of-year shows here. They only seem to attend college for concerts and parties and then we all go along too if there isn't a good club happening.

Jester seems to have disappeared, nobody seems to know where, perhaps to the Island. He comes from Hayling Island, which everybody says seems to explain his behaviour; the island mentality.

Gary Glitter comes on stage for his first revival concert from obscurity and from his bankruptcy of the Seventies. It's not so full that you can't shove yourself to the front and see the glistening tears of gratitude welling up in his eyes for an audience, even if it is mostly skinheads.

I'm dressed in tight silver 1950s glam-glitter lurex and diamante and sequin studded stripper's stilettos, sent from my mother for my first-Christmas-alone present.

Something damp and warm, soft and sticky lands on my neck and shoulder, it couldn't be gob, it feels too heavy and it smells. Then another, this time on my head. I reach with a dreading hand to look and see. I am being rained on by little slivers of fine-fleshed meat. They can't be falling from the rafters, but must be being thrown from the heaving balcony. I'm scouring the balcony, not too antagonistically in this environment, to see what, who. A figure in a flat-topped trilby and raincoat turns, then disappears upon my gaze.

'William, somebody keeps throwing lumps of meat at me, look.'

'Don't be ridiculous!' But he looks and agrees that they are lumps of meat. 'So who do you expect me to pick a fight with in here to protect you?'

It's not really a question, but he presents it with such charm, and a grin to forget it all.

William stands out in a crowd. He's a broad six-foot-two and dresses as a 1920s biker, complete with goggles, jodhpurs, lace-up knee-high boots and a wool-lined leather flying jacket. On his back he always carries a backpack – no ordinary one at that I'm made to recognise, as he proudly shows me the WWI insignia on the underside of the khaki canvas flap, he shows me with pride and brown leather. Rebellion takes all forms, not the uniform for a nineteen-year-old engineering student.

'Hello. Did you like the presents?' Jester's recognisable monotone slides up beside me.

'Oh, so it was you. It's not even cooked! How did you know I wasn't a vegetarian, I might never have spoken to you again.'

'Well give them back then. I'll 'ave 'em.'

Now even warmer from my hold, he slurps the greying meat back. Finished, he opens up one side of his mac and shows me his canvas rack of Sabatier knives pinned to the inside of his coat. He looks thoughtfully and pulls out a small slim one and, reaching with his other hand into a pocket, he produces a lump of fillet steak and stands casually slicing and swallowing his offcuts as if it was an apple.

'Yum, yum,' he said. 'If this was minced and had a raw egg on top and you was in a fancy restaurant, you'd eat it then and like it so much you'd pay the bill!' he explains to my bemusement.

Desmond Dekker is playing live upstairs. There are cult classic movies playing in the lecture theatres. This is all-night and the pills and joints are being passed around from William's sweetshop backpack. Thai sticks, black, Moroccan, black bombers, blues and the lines of student cocaine, speed and amyl nitrate. We all have to supplement our student income the best we can. I work in a club, William supplies a much-needed demand for students craving soft drugs. They've done the hippy trail before uni and can't settle back, or maybe they've never been and are pretending it now, swilling beer and puffing bongs in the uni bar. It never seems illegal or wrong, just forbidden.

It's a strange sight, all these skinheads in a place of learning. I don't think the organisers realised what could happen – they just thought it was a bit of kitsch camp, in the same way Sweet's 'Blockbuster' keeps on being played in the clubs.

Suddenly there's this giant rush, the National Front are raiding, but it's not for Gary Glitter, 'I'm The Leader', it's for Desmond Dekker's sweet ska singing, 'The Israelites'. There's this massive gang charging into the main hall, rumour has spread before action and we're following William up the back staircases, hearts pumping, running away from the roar of trouble, through to a secret room of libraries. I trip up the stairs catching my stripper's heel, torn from its moorings and I run barefooted the rest of the way. Once safe above the marauding hordes I'm bent over double with a stitch, panting my breath back and grieving for my beautiful shoes, the limp heel in my handbag, for the rest of the night until morning.

At least we didn't get beaten up, stuck with a blade, whatever Jester's suggestions about arming us up with Sabatiers in open combat, Michelin Star fighters. I have a spare pair of shoes in my suitcase in a locker downstairs. My outfit for my cousin's wedding in Wales – I'm off for the weekend.

'I'll see you downstairs,' says William.

'Thanks, I always get lost in this warren.'

'Coco.'

'Yes, William.'

'I've got something for you, for the weekend.'

And he holds my hands in his, making me feel vulnerable to his touch. I look into his eyes but he is shy and averts them. He presses the present into my palm. I look down to my hand, dazed from the moment of intimacy, and he has gone, purposefully striding down the corridor, away.

Five little pale blue pills covered in specks lie there like eggs about to hatch. They are old-style speed, strong and authentic, something for the weekend to keep me going, to tide me over or move me on. William's so kind and thoughtful, but I never take pills, unless for fun.

'Auntie? It's Coco here.'

'Where are you for goodness' sake, we'll be starting for the church in three-quarters of an hour.'

'Don't worry, I'm here at the station. I just need to know where the nearest Oxfam shop is.'

'Why do you need to know that?'

'I've broken the heel on my shoe and forgotten to bring my others.'

'Well surely you'll need a shoe shop, not an Oxfam shop.'

'I haven't time to explain, but I need a pair of stilettos and I don't think they'll have any in the local Barratt's. So if you could just tell me . . .'

'I'm pretty sure there's one in the high street. I'll send Thomas to pick you up from outside it in fifteen minutes, shall I?' says Auntie, incredulous.

I hobble the twenty yards from the station, one silver-sequinned diamante heel on, one off. I stride purposefully to the shoe counter and find Oxfam's finest. A neat pair of 1960s leather stilettos. So they're brown, my dress is black wool and velvet with matching hat – you can't have everything perfect for fifty pence.

'So when are you getting changed for the wedding? We'll be going soon.'

'This is it. This is what I'm wearing, Granny.'

'No! You must be joking, you can't wear black for a wedding. We're not going to their funeral for goodness' sake, child!'

It hadn't occurred to me for one minute, the tribal ritual of colours in Christian society. It was never a thing I thought about. All my clothes were black, unless they were full-length evening dresses to trail a blaze of silver, pink, gold or red with.

Poor old Granny, I don't think she understands about fashion. How could I be seen in anything but black?

The phone rings. Shall I answer it, shan't I? It might be Joe, yuck. I could answer it and pretend that I'm Barbara. I could answer it and pretend that I'm a foreign person and that he's got the wrong number.

'Hello,' I say, in what I think is a darkly mysterious manner.

'Coco, is that you? It's Mum. What's that strange voice? David and I have arrived from LA for a week. We're staying at Blakes.'

'Oh, hello Mum. How are you? I just thought it might be somebody else calling that I'm trying to avoid. When can I see you?'

'I'm afraid we're really busy this trip. But I'm doing a photo session around the corner from your college on Thursday morning. I could pop in and see you afterwards. I'd like to see what you're working at. And what's all this about you applying for fine art instead of the Fashion Department? I thought we'd decided upon your career. I'm sure you'd be making an awful mistake, but we'll talk about it on Thursday, OK?'

'Yes, all right. We can go to lunch in Soho, I know some great Italian cafés.'

'I'm afraid I'm a bit too busy to have lunch, I've got a meeting in Chelsea. Maybe we can squeeze in a cup of tea if there's time. Lots of love, from David too.'

I wish I hadn't picked up the phone. I'd rather it had been Joe, who's been dogging me since he's moved up to London.

Why did I say yes to Mum? Why can't I say, 'It's none of your business, no I can't possibly fit you in, my schedule's far too tight.'

But everything's about *her*, Ricky and David, the perfect couple. The universe in its entirety revolves around the star-studded duo. Why do I comply?

These phone calls always leave me feeling emptier than a derelict toilet. I fumble in my pocket for some money and slam out the door in the direction of the sweetshop. A couple of large Toblerones should see to it, and the afternoon black and white movie on my six-inch portable, *Red Dust* with Clark Gable, Mary Astor and Jean Harlow. Another cheery Saturday passes. Never mind, don't think about it.

I don't think about it. It just sits there like an undigested bagel in the pit of my stomach.

At least there's a party tonight and I'm going out on the town with Cruella. That's fun.

Take another bite.

I don't know why I had such a thing against Edwin Davie coming to my party, but it wasn't particularly him; I just didn't want huge numbers of gatecrashers appearing, drinking all our wine and buggering up the flat whilst Barbara was away on tour. I was only having the party because she was gone. Unfortunately it was Ed I told, as the leader of the group, to leave and I successfully made him keep to the boundaries, except for him pissing all over the garden. Git.

If I knew all this was going to happen, I probably would have let him in, not because of the violence, just all the emotional repercussions.

Hate. I can feel it welling up in my stomach. Shame and humiliation pricking the back of my eyes. Utter helplessness, as I sit in this basement pit of a party, my hands bloating and bruising the other side of the handcuffs. The bones of my wrists are hard-jarred against the metal. The cuffs couldn't get a millimetre tighter, without something cracking, breaking. Something's broken in me already, I feel like I've almost fallen into the black hole inside, with just my fingernails gripping on to the light and any small hope that is left outside.

My fault. I shouldn't have fought so hard, struggled so

successfully against the boys that jumped and handcuffed me, dragging me to this crumbling wall, attaching me to the bars. I am their male-ego prize displayed, hung for all to see. I got away for a minute then, almost escaped, managed to get back to Cruella waiting outside. I slipped the cuff, their grasp, wriggling my hand through and running. I didn't make it. Ed jumped me again, pulled me down and forced the cuffs on so tight he grimaced with the strain, his red face clashing horribly with his orange hair. Then, making a big thing of it, he found the key and flung it down into some unreachable darkness.

The rest of the party-goers are not quite sure what to make of this kind of human animal activity, drunk and stoned and removed. I can see them wondering if this is a performance, the only entertainment on offer. I cannot look at them. I am in shock.

I hear somebody mutter '... Is that all? What happens next?'

I see too many faces of people I know, that I thought would have helped me. They stand back embarrassed, not wanting to be involved. Somebody approaches me and I can only just hear through my tears and Ultravox playing too loud, droning through my head.

'Are you alright? Can I get you a drink?'

'Of course I'm not fucking alright. Look at me, look at me! Get me out of here. My wrist is fucking breaking, it hurts so much!' I bury my face in the curve of my elbow to cry and sink into the rubble of this 'fashionable' squat, scraping my shins. I'm trying to disappear, think me out of this nightmare. I can't. My victim role is complete. How easily human suffering is tolerated, but how embarrassing.

Cruella appears with her granny's next-door neighbour, a friendly biker, a knight in shining leathers, who dismantles the whole wall in minutes with a crowbar he happens to have on him. We begin a trail of the local hospital and police station, who haven't the keys but call the fire brigade to saw me out, and a doctor, in case my flesh is sliced too. I'm so happy to be free I'm almost up for celebrating but that's probably more to do with the half-bottle of brandy I've drunk in an effort to decrease the pain, the memory.

'So are you going to tell us where this so-called party was going on, that they'd handcuff you almost fracturing your wrist as entertainment?'

'No, I'm sorry. I can't.'

And I don't. I still see the police as the enemy. My guilt from the effect of the drug bust at school is still too close.

I walk away from the station keeping the hurt and hate – it's well labelled as mine – bundled close, sunk in my bile. Vitriol spread thickly over my tongue drips from my lips. I feel like an RSPCA poster of an abused dog. The next owner that comes near me, I'll bite.

Jester wants to slice Ed Davie's head off and keep it as a centrepiece for William's and my wedding. I wouldn't have any piece of him there. I wouldn't piss on him if he was on fire, I say.

William and I have been going out for two and a half brilliant months. I have had sex like I have never had, regular. William is moving to Brixton, sharing Tony Hammer's council flat, and I am moving there too. I am going to Los Angeles with William to visit Mum, Spain with William to be alone, and Hayling Island with William to visit Jester – hell! We might as well be living together. We've been down to Kent, I've met William's mum and stepdad in their bungalow. Dad's met William, he isn't impressed, but I'd like to know when he would be. I can't see him ever being satisfied with any of the beaux his one little princess offers up for his approval.

So we're going to get married. William is wonderful, he brings me roses and takes me to the local Indian or Italian, for dinner. Proffers lines of cocaine and bottles of champagne for my further amusement. He takes off his helmet and lets me wear it as

I ride pillion with him on his Brough Superior bike and opens doors for me. I've never been treated so well by a boy before. He even fills up my handbag with black bombers before I go to work at night, 'just in case you get tired'.

There is no end to his consideration.

'No, of course it's not a real marriage, do you think I'm completely mad, Barbara? Louise's playing the part of my mother, and Vernon my brother. Lizzie and Vernon's boyfriend Clive are playing William's parents, who have to hand over a cheque for a million pounds on their son's wedding day. I wish that part of it was real. And Filthy Fergus is playing the part of the priest. Hardly typecast, that bit, but he's got the costume.

'It probably does sound awful to you, Barbara, but I happen to like the steps of Brixton Town Hall.

'No, I don't find it depressing, I find it funny,' I grimace cheerfully across the telephone booth to William, who is making mad faces to cheer me over the conversation.

'That's what performance is all about.

'No, of course I don't expect you to come.

'Yes, it's alright. No. We had a lovely time on Hayling Island, we took a wind-up gramophone and played Bing Crosby and Frank Sinatra records on every picnic during the week and hardly saw a single boat. Los Angeles? Before Spain. Yes, the twenty-sixth. Anything you want me to get you, apart from Rodeo Drive shopping heaven, and a part in the next Spielberg?

'OK, I guess I'll see you sometime when we get back. Bye.'

'No, nothing to declare.'

'What is the purpose of your visit?'

'Visiting my mum.'

'Haven't you brought her any gifts?'

'Oh yes, I have. The *Evening Standard* special on the Queen Mother's Jubilee or something, do you want to see it? It's got some lovely pictures of her in her petal hats.'

'No, it's alright, you can go through. Next.'

Customs survived, we catch a cab.

'The Swanky Hotel, please,' I say rather grandly to the cabby and he replies with a jig of his lip and a jerk of his head. He's not impressed.

Mum is too busy to meet us at the airport. She will see us when we get to the hotel. She takes us for a drink and a bite to eat at the bar next door, with David of course, his charming but austere self. They lay down the law for the week's visit. They will take us out tonight, we may join in their activities of swimming twenty-five lengths at lunchtime followed by lunch at the deco diner on the corner that Anthony Perkins goes to. They are even having a cocktail party that we may attend but basically they have their routine and it is not to be tampered with even for a daughter's visit. I understand; I mean, if they had to stop every time someone came to visit they'd never get anything done.

That night I wear my wedding dress out. I can't believe everybody thinks I have just got married, buying me free drinks and yelling congratulations. To my horror I have found a hoard of black bombers in the depths of my handbag: I don't dare to contemplate the consequences if Customs had found them first. William and I are off and overriding our jet lag. One club follows another until we collapse back to our hotel room near dawn. I don't know if Mum and David returned, they were dancing in the crowds, chatting up some young girl. Who cares.

The next day we do follow the mapped-out routine but David's spikiness, grown from all that professional rejection, makes sure we realise just what an imposition we are. He is living in the city of dreams, trying to sell yet another one that nobody wants to bite. I could even start to feel sorry for this ageing ingénu with his thinning, greying flop of dark hair and his body going the way of gravity, in this young man's town where everything is pointing up, or finished.

A hardness binds Mum and him together against The Rest of the World, holds them apart from me. It is startlingly transparent, their immediate and obvious dislike of William.

William and I stick to each other, make and meet up with other friends until our return to the airport. Mum can't see us before we go, she's too busy. Seems like her life is just one big rehearsal, or show.

I didn't see my mother once on her own; it feels like David is playing, James Mason's musical svengali to Ann Todd's victim. My heart aches with disappointment and covers itself over a little bit more in protection for the next time.

Is this what growing up means? Becoming prepared for the Outside World, growing ever more self-reliant, controlled, as if nothing affects you? There are no hugs any more, no feelings, the pain is growing fainter.

Is that separate person my mother, with David? I am sitting with them in a trendy topless go-go-dancing bar, laughing. They're just another old couple trying to be young by going out to discos and taking drugs. Can nobody tell them how ridiculous they look? Who cares? Not me. I swear it doesn't touch me; it makes me untouchable.

William and I rest up in Brixton with Jester and Tony. They set an alarm clock in the morning so they can get up by nine to smoke their first bong of the day. I'm up and off to work. As the only gainfully-employed member of the flat, I'm able to whinge annoyingly at their dole-induced behaviour. I am finding it hard living with no members of my family, all of them boys and one who I share the same bed with. I nag at them. Mother hen: do the washing-up, clean the kitchen, the state of this floor! Then give up. What's the point? I sound like Barbara: 'Is that an unwashed cup I see in the sink?!'

Jester always greets my return from work with some delicious dish. Blue curry, with green rice and bright orange potatoes is a favourite – he likes experimenting, drugs, food, drink.

We hang around the estate, and it feels some days like being marooned: no buses and tubes come near here. William's bike lies in pieces around the living-room waiting for some pivotal part that no-one seems to have. 'In India,' he says over and over, 'you'd be able to buy this down the local garage, any local garage. It's like living in a third world country England is!' Taxis won't drop you off at your door. You can't blame them; after eight, the estate halls' light bulbs all seem to change to red and the women open their doors in welcome invitation once the kids are in bed.

Beneath us our neighbours are a family of skinheads who break into our flat, nick the sound system then sell it back to us for a fiver. When the cocaine disappeared one day, William discovered it had been sold down the youth club for fifty pence a packet. That's when he went mad, war was declared. I'm sure he wouldn't have been so cross if it had been sold at its real market value, it was their total ignorance of the lost revenue that annoyed him.

Each day we watched for the postman's special delivery, once we'd set upon our mission of revenge. Filling in the computer coupons.

'I wonder if Mr and Mrs Fukwit have got their ten-day free trial of the collected encyclopaedia yet?'

'I expect they're having a wonderful time, learning all sorts of things about the world they're likely to experience. If the Alsatians haven't eaten them first. A kind and thoughtful gesture, Tony. I think Jester addressed the kitchen unit to Mr and Mrs Colour Television. Do you think the postman will get confused?'

'Confused, no. Suspicious perhaps, probably not even that. Bloody tired. Carrying all those samples to number forty-eight.'

'Have you seen the cat anywhere, she seems to have gone funny since I took the teapot away. Gone in search of another friendly spout to insert up her bum, I expect.'

'What do you mean, the teapot? It's all the dope the poor cat has to inhale in this place along with you giving her a diet of baked beans and vegetarian curry leftovers. I know you're a veggie, but you really should buy her some cat food sometimes. Cats aren't natural vegetarians.'

'They are in southern India. I think it's disgusting! The mere idea of rotten meat lying around on the kitchen floor, until it gets eaten. Unhygienic.'

'Well it would feel at home then, the state of that floor. One day, Tony, you'll make somebody a terrible wife and a worse husband.'

William and I are off to Spain in ten days. I hope it'll give Spain a new slant in my eyes. Open it up from being a place of paternal guardianship and eternal boredom. Maybe we'll discover a night-life of intrigue and fascination never before allowed to me . . . Hemingway's Spain.

William just discovers dope. As though he never has before. Quality-testing. What should I expect? Of course a businessman carries his interests with him. Spain doesn't change for me. We sit beneath the orange trees in the square drinking Granitas, our lips nuzzling with the wasps at the glass's edge. I draw pictures of William and churches, William at the pool, William and the Spanish. In the evenings we go out to eat, returning to the house to sleep and make inhibited love in my father's house. I can't see it differently, I am getting bored, I am closing down.

Something has changed between William and me. Maybe just spending all this time thrown upon each other's company, each seeing the other as a lifesaving device, until, half deflated, we have drifted apart.

I am looking forward to jumping off on my own in Leeds on my degree course, now Foundation is over. I choose the course over the destination. A clear, fresh dive into unsullied waters, away from London. I can swim alone.

CHAPTER SIXTEEN

Brrrrrrring . . . Coco sat up unconsciously awake. 'What?' she thought. 'Where was the island, the sea the . . . never mind.'

She remembered the contents of the oven and made an effort to edge out of bed, stumble into her shoes, too stiff and cold for her warm toes, and bundled herself yawning down the stairs. Just in time.

The top was crisp and golden. Out of the dish's sides escaped little wisps of steam and bubbling juices, sweet and buttery.

She lifted it, hot and heavy, on to the top of the Aga and left it to cool slowly on the warm plate. There was a slam of the front door and she heard the solid, firm tread of a man's footsteps walk across the varnished wood hall and she felt herself smile without meaning to.

'I can't wait, I can't wait, slurp, slurp, slurp, let's not go up to the bedroom, pant, pant, pant, let's do it here before the children get home, oh, oh, oh yesssss . . .'

'Listening to another one of those enriching Radio Four plays, sweetheart?' He grabbed her from behind to surprise her, and imitated the actor's breathy voice into her ear.

'Let's do it here before the children get home, oh yes, yes, yes.'

'But darling, they're already home. They never left home – it's the weekend.'

'I know that, you know that, but let's for a minute pretend there aren't any. How are you, my Coco?' He kissed around each side of her face and in between, over the back of her neck, with his attentive lips.

'Heavy with child and dopey with sleep.'

'Are you talking about our beautiful, immaculate baby that you are nurturing in your divine tummy?' And with one swift movement, he swept her up into his arms as though she was a baby. He supported her laughing, shaking frame and tried to lower his face to kiss more of her body. She didn't worry that they would fall, she trusted him completely – Ben was strong and reliable.

'Even I can't hold on to this weight for ever, we're going to have to find a chair to help.'

'Behind you.'

He lowered them gently to the chair together, Coco on his lap, his arms about her. Her arms were about his neck, her head cradled to his shoulder, her body leaning into his.

'Did you have a nice day at work, dear?' she asked her husband, gently mimicking *I Love Lucy*.

'Well, wifey, it was as good as could be expected. I think I've almost finished the main painting; about another couple of days and it should be ready.'

'Gosh, that was quick, you speedy Gonzales. Won't your kindly patron be pleased?'

'And now here I am, bursting with energy to come and help you. Do your bidding. Have you really been resting?'

'Yes, doctor.'

'Good girl. Would you like a cup of tea?'

'Mmm, I should cocoa, but who will make it? My sofa and pillows can't get up.'

'I will telepathically send out for a pot of Earl Grey and it will be couriered to our door. How's that?'

'It's never quite as good as home-made, though, perhaps I'd better get up and leave my perfect mould,' she said, not moving a muscle apart from the ones about her mouth to let the words out. When she lay in Ben's arms she felt as still and as at peace as she did when alone and gazing at the sky; the feeling that comes when your child is asleep in your arms and there's nothing to do but watch the dusk descend around you.

With Ben, her heart never ached with love, only blossomed like a well-cared-for flower, safe with him.

'We could stay like this for ever and pretend we've had tea,' he whispered, and pulled her closer to him with his arms. 'But Coco must have her ten litres of liquid a day . . . sooo, I will get up and leave you while I put the kettle on.'

He gave her a kiss on the nose, while depositing her back to the armchair in the corner of the kitchen. He filled the kettle, turned it on and found her favourite yellow cups for their tea, the milk and the biscuits.

'Now what can I do?'

'Pass the green beans from the scullery and two small knives, and we can top and tail them together into the bowl on the table.'

He fetched the knives, the beans, the bowl and put them on a large stool at her side. A smaller stool he put beneath her feet and pulled up a chair for himself next to her. When the kettle was boiled he made the tea, weak with not much milk for Coco, strong and dark for him, and all the time he smiled, humming, glancing back at her as though they were sharing some delicious unspoken joke. And when he was finished, Ben sat beside Coco and together they topped and tailed the beans, talking, talking, touching, laughing, happy.

CHAPTER SEVENTEEN

'OK, OK. You can quieten down now.

'You may all think you're special just because you've managed to get into Yorkshire Poly. Special and outrageous from your
foundation courses, but you're all pretty ordinary put in one room
together . . .'

Where have I heard this before? There must be a handbook
on how to address and belittle the new occupants of colleges, read
and remembered by all beer-bellied, dirty-jeaned, rebel tutors.

This year I'm alert and half-listening to the message of
welcome, but mostly I'm alone surveying the other students.

'Your reputations do not go before you here. It doesn't make
a fuck of a difference that you were Winchester's star painter.
Remember that, and we'll get along fine.' The voice of authority
booms. My mind wanders, I'm choosing my gang.

I'm sitting next to the only obvious punk girl, Jo Crones from
Wolverhampton. We're getting on fine. Across the room is a
gorgeous-looking boy. The kind of boy you can't believe is sitting
in the same room as you. He looks like he's stepped out of a
Visconti movie. The kind of boy that must have some major defect
about him to look this good, have that hair, those clothes, more
importantly, those cheekbones. Where do boys get those cheekbones from? The ones us puppy-fat girls always want, the ones
that Marlene Dietrich had her back teeth out to perfect.

There was a boy like that; the first day at college in London –
all the girls were cooing and fainting with fascination, hanging on
with expectation as to his name and why he wanted to be there.
We were taking it in turns to speak around the room. Then he
stood up, and we waited with bated breath: he opened his mouth

and this sing-song girlie voice flew out. The deflation in that room could have plummeted the whole lot of us through the ceiling. I don't raise my expectations any higher than I can afford, to see them drop, after that one.

O perfect one Louis is standing with his exact opposite, an equal to my new friend Jo. He is like her, a punk of the original type, all safety pins and dyed, spiked hair. As a punk, I never looked that real, I was only ever playing at it, dressing up to dress down. These two look like the real things – Anthony Burgess could have thought of *A Clockwork Orange* around them. Frightening if you didn't know that they were art students. Like magnets, the four of us are drawn together in time for the first tea break, firm friends by lunch, our pacts drawn over chicken Marengo in the canteen, stuck together with its monosodium glutamate shine. Gang-bonded.

It is the afternoon of the second day: the tutors see it as a chance to slide-show us their work, a captive audience. I thought the tutors in London lived in a past of glorious olden days, but it's nothing compared to Yorkshire. The way they talk about it, you'd think they were seeking sainthood for the college's behaviour during the Sixties, a blue plaque for disgraceful behaviour. I sit back and listen, though I've heard all the stories before. About Fingers Shore, and Simon Denis and his girlfriend Cissy who offered to hold old men's dicks in the Gents of the local rough pub as part of her performance degree show.

'You seem to be having trouble, can I help you with that, sir?' she'd say, dressed in virginal white, an angelic smile primed to her lips.

The Yorkshire Ripper blights the general jollity of Leeds at the moment: going out in the evening is being clamped down on, staying out late is not advised, but we have to go to the Phonogram disco and watch live bands in the seedy prostitute part of town, though it feels risky. Everyone knows who the Ripper is, has their suspicions and gossips wildly; everyone's turned Poirot or Marple.

'Oh yeah! Everybody knows the Ripper. On the radio yesterday the police said they get sixty people a day shopping their husbands, sons and next-door neighbours.'

I can't afford to go out anyway like I used to, with no weekend job and just my savings from the glamorous past days of the Desert. London exchanged for Leeds, champagne for ginger wine, anything to keep you warm in the sub-zero damp temperatures of Yorkshire, winds howling across Hyde Park on a Sunday night. Sitting close together around the single bar of the electric heater, Louis, me, Jo and Henry, in Louis's bedsit.

William's been down for the weekend. I think he realises it's pointless.

'I'll be back for weekends. And you can come up,' might have been a slight give-away when I'm staying at the poly's hall of residence, no guests allowed. My grant, with a meagre travelling allowance. Me, relieved to get away. Sick of the sordid drug apparel, all his friends either wanting it or selling it. 'What's the Thai like, how's the black, did the Moroccan come in? Any Charlie, any acid, any grass?'

I hadn't seen William look at a book for college. Everything was about getting stoned or drunk, 'Not waving but drowning', to nick off Stevie Smith. I'm glad to get to ashore, anywhere. I'm able to justify any break, find the excuses for not committing to anything more than me. This trust is a shaky plinth.

This, here, now, seems a more balanced way of being. Dancing and singing 'New York, New York', in one of the four wedding dresses I picked up in America, now I'm across the disco floor in Leeds 1, swirling around the shopping mall on my way home.

Watching the late-night Ken Russell triple bill, *The Devils*, *The Music Lovers* and *Lisztomania* at the Hyde Park cinema. Walking home across the park, holding Louis's hand past the graffiti, CASTRATE ALL MEN, NOW.

Going home on the same bus as the Yorkshire Ripper's last victim. She would have got off at the same stop as me, crossing the road and turning right down the long unlit lane towards the university's halls of residence. I turn left and walk through the ill-lit park alone.

Sitting up through the night of the American election. Waiting for the results of Ronald Reagan's victory and the rest of our downfall. Planning and plotting our final hours of doom in our nuclear disembowelling nightmare. I shall order giant hampers from Fortnum & Mason, drink champagne in a harem of flowing silk tents, playing Charlie Parker on the sides of the River Thames while the world explodes around us, my overdraft with it. And I shall be looking at Louis's perfectly sculpted head and Cocteau profile silhouetted against a red sky. His brown eyes melting, blond hair sizzling, clear skin shrivelling, as the fallout descends . . .

Day-to-day, I'm painting the Madonna-and-Child portrait of *Jo and Her Abortion*, her latest piece of work in the studio we share together. A model of rubber, string, paint, latex, PVA and bandages, uglier than David Lynch's *Eraserhead*, comforted in this young punk mother's arms, awaiting its cradle behind them, a torn flesh crucifix, a ripped womb with a little opening for babsy to fit snugly into.

The trunk Louis buys from a local junk shop, and finds in its hidden depths human bones that he spends months drawing.

All this seems more normal to me. More real, so that I can't tell Louis, Jo or Henry about my other life. I am embarrassed at seeing things that I was brought up with to be normal looking warped, so I keep quiet to the offspring of unbroken homes. I am good at playing this part, I think. I've been taught how to act since a child. But I show something to Louis about my parents and I watch him recoil, confused. He is too sweet and lovely for my hardened cruelty; he wears beautiful wool jumpers his mother knits him, and sends with his father's letters that are full of old-fashioned worry and encouragement about food and his student accommodation.

Then my letter arrives, pushed hard beneath my door. The letter from Mum says she has left David. Left David! Left David? Left David. I reread the letter, see the tears left on the paper, mine meeting hers.

'I am not feeling very good. I am down here in Cornwall trying to finish learning this film script. Could you try to call me? Please. Reverse-charge and I will be on the other end waiting for your call . . .'

Just one letter and everything has changed. I thought I was painting a vitriolic portrait of *Mother Plus One*. I had finished just in time so it seems, to carry it up to an attic of things past. History. It can be their portrait, like Dorian Gray's, do the ageing for them, plastering the horrid ravages of life upon its smooth canvas. If we could all have one of those, plastic surgeons would be unemployed. But things are not so easy, and Mum's cracked frailty shows in her voice and touches my heart, bumping it against my ribcage. However shaky my family seemed, Mum and David, whom for much of the time I disliked, at least it was a structure, an abstract one maybe, but something I felt was safe in its solid, sick state.

Of course they thought it was me.

Mum heard it on the news and thought this last death by the Ripper was me. She said to Barbara, 'It'd be just like Coco to go and get herself killed. Attracting attention, wearing one of those wedding dresses.' This is a joke to cover her real anxiety, her fears are too sharp not to be softened with jokes these days.

Mum and a thousand other parents across the country are jamming the poly's and uni's switchboards to find out if it's their daughter that's dead and disembowelled in the bushes. Didn't make it home, let alone finish her degree, but only one parent will get the answer none of them want to hear. The child that they stayed up nights with nursing through illnesses, worked out how to tell the facts of life to, told off for smoking in the bushes and bad reports, spent all their money on, cosying and cosseting against hard realities, is dead, her skull smashed to the earth.

I'm leaving Leeds. I've applied for a transfer. I'll go to Rainbow's college, carry on my fine art degree rather than just painting or sculpture, so I'll be able to make my Bacchanalian splendour of death and rebirth and the excesses of the gods, filmed in a local graveyard. All my friends are to star with an overload of linen, a barrow-load of grapes and half an off-licence. No reason Fellini should have the copyright on excess, Bergman on death.

'Everybody is shocked by this last killing, but not everybody is leaving, Coco. Would you return once the Ripper is caught? I'm letting you go for one reason only, because I understand your mother will need you now.

'Are you sure you don't just want to take time off and return? If that's your decision, good luck. It's a shame – you would have got on well here.'

All change! I am living in Chelsea, London SW3. From the suburbs of Leeds, hall of residence, flooding the bathroom I shared with the trainee assistant librarian next door, I now have a whole apartment to myself, bathroom en suite. I have clothes from Visage, hats from David Shilling and shoes from Manolo Blahnik. I still have my wedding dresses. I have plucked my eyebrows off, completely. Sometimes I draw them in, but mostly I don't: it gives me that smooth, Elizabeth the First look, uncluttered to the hairline on my high forehead. My hair is short on one side, a sweep of hair falling over my good eye so I stumble along blindly unless I am wearing one of my twenty hats or numerous two-foot-high black, gold, silver or white fabric turbans. I dress in floor-length trailing gowns and Diaghilev opera capes, reminding me of William, picked up in auctions and second-hand shops, days of scouring for the perfect find. My make-up is matt white, rouged circles for cheeks, and eyes are crayonned panda-bear black.

I am recognisable almost anywhere I go, but then so are Barbara and Mum: we dress as the house decrees. The Rock Stars' house. Bought by John James for the beautiful Josie Green. The address that everything bad happened in, in the Sixties; now none of them can bear to remember.

'Of course you must stay in our house when you are in London,' Josie had apparently assured Mum after one of their frequent dinners, 'as long as you like.'

'But why don't they want to live here?' I ask.

'Too many bad memories,' explains Barbara, who's been there for three weeks and shows me around like an old hand.

'Too many bad trips, man! Hey, have you seen the gold discs downstairs in the Jimi Hendrix room?'

'On the first floor where his eyes follow you around the room and then reflect all over it from the disco mirror ball on the ceiling, that room? Do you think that's where the fudge bars happened?'

'Something did. Something stuck, essence of time warp.'

Mum has returned to her old life, is picking up the pieces and laying them down in some sort of order. Getting back in touch with her old friends that had become David's worst enemies when they were together. Work contacts, TV parts, the papers. Party contacts. Ricky's back in town. Invite the Johnsons. The mantelpiece groans with the postman's footsteps, the weight of the social whirl.

'God, I need some new evening dresses, everybody has seen

these – I've worn them a hundred times!'

'Haven't you been to The Sale? Frederick Fox's, the theatrical costumiers, are selling off all the old stock. Rainbow and I are going on Saturday,' Louise says on the phone.

We spend the day sifting through roomfuls of costumes from productions going back to the beginning of the century. Only five pounds for each black rubbish bag filled, we drag our booty through the backstreets of a desolate Covent Garden, vegetable detritus squidging on our shoes, barrows the only vehicles in the road.

Back home we're in time to dress up for another evening's entertainment. There's an opening, a club and a party to fit in. In all the clubs, word, annoyingly, is going round about the sale. We would've liked to have kept it to just our coterie, but now all the boys and girls are dressing as merry men to Steve Strange's Robin Hood. Medieval courtiers, Byronesque beauties, Russian gentry and peasants, Spanish matadors and Carmens, oriental exotics join in the Berlin decadence trailed across night-time London and daytime magazines, and coined the New Romantics.

This is a striking look, if somewhat off-putting for the rest of the population. It certainly seems to put boys off, but then I don't want to attract 'normals', not my kind.

What is my kind? I am confused but optimistic in my search. Somewhere out there is a boy/man who'll appreciate me for my uniqueness, not laugh, even in the cold light of day without my make-up remover . . . Where's Louis, too sweet and innocent, too beautiful for my cold-edged excitement.

I'm existing on five hours' sleep a night, commuting to Kent College, waitressing at the Desert, earning twenty-five to fifty pounds a night. I am a rich student. I catch cabs and buy bottles of champagne to drink with Ricky and Barbara. When I'm not working, I go out clubbing, to parties, openings, along the circuit. Le Kilt, Club for Heroes, the Venue, St Moritz, the Titanic. I have to commute. Who among my college peers do I have anything in common with apart from Rainbow, who I went to school and college with? I am alienated from student life, though I'm still working, painting: it's just having to fit it all in with the other life, too.

The commuting I've got down to a Fine Art. Dressed in ten minutes, out the door, on the bus to Victoria, a cappuccino from the Italian café, sleep on the train for almost an hour and into college by ten.

Some mornings, it feels like I've done a whole day's work just getting there.

I dress the same for college as I do for work, with a long painter's smock over it. Sometimes I'm a Dresden shepherdess or maybe an astrakhan-covered contessa with carmine-coated Cupid's-bow lips, painted fresh on the train. Whatever, it is not appreciated in the streets of Tonbridge, and not often, for that matter, in the metropolis of London.

I am a weirdo, an extraordinary creature that makes heads turn when I walk into an established restaurant, however fashionable. But I have this grounded belief, a cupboardful of confidence, that all stares are admiring, that all verbal abuse is ignorant jealousy.

This is the way I live.

'Of course I've ordered champagne, darling. Now come here and give Mummy a kiss.'

'How are you, Mummy? You're looking wonderful, have you had your hair done, the colour? Doesn't she, Mum?'

'Oh, do you like it? It's just a tiny bit of a tint.'

Joanna Bonnelle models her new hairdo with pride. Best profile on show, chin up, resting lightly on the tips of her beautifully manicured fingers, and smiles her enigmatic crease. It's a well-posed shot, practised before hundreds of photographers for tens of years, and the nose is her crowning point.

'Now what are we going to have for lunch?'

She turns to survey the blackboard menu with just a twist of her head. Tango d'Or, scene of so many of these lunches. Chosen for its proximity to our house and because of its liberal attitude to bad behaviour. The liberal attitude is probably because Mum has slept with two of the owners and countless of the staff. We get preferential treatment.

'Lunch, lunch! We haven't even had the sodding champagne yet. Any chance of a drink, chicken?' Mum smiles beguilingly at a nearby waiter. My eyes automatically roll back into my sockets, as for a moment I fast-forward this scene by three hours and dwell for a second upon the fate of the poor waiter. I cover over with a smile.

'Don't worry Mum, they're just bringing it. The poor buggers are rushed off their feet.'

In fact, it's probably not even her hair Joanna has had done, it's just as likely to be a nip-and-tuck job, a few lines ironed out, but we never talk of that. That or her age, Joanna, or 'Mummy' as she likes to be called by me, is a 'natural' beauty of ever-decreasing years and advancing birth date. She is coolly sophisticated to those she doesn't know, and has a cunningly successful pout for a string of private, sometimes married, businessmen. Joanna has never had children, she lives in Chelsea surrounded by a sea of yappy dogs, her 'babies'. But I am her 'daughter', surrogate, adopted from her good friend Ricky, grown-up and no responsibility. I make her laugh. Joanna makes us laugh.

'Of course when I was in Hollywood it was never like that. My film-star career was decimated because of my passionate affair with Gary Cooper – your father, darling.'

Joanna looks at me, eyes almost brimful and earnestly proclaims, 'He would have been so proud of you.' She holds my hand in hers and squeezes it meaningfully.

'Ricky, Ricky, don't you think Coco has his eyes?'

This falls on deaf ears, Mum is busy setting up 'assignations' with a man on the next table, ordering him to buy us another bottle of champagne.

'Well, I'm proud of him too, Mummy. Did you see *High Noon*, on the other afternoon? I was thinking of what a beautiful couple you must have made.'

'Thank you daughter, we were, we were. But it was not to be, the studios saw to that, but at least I was a survivor, unlike poor Marilyn. I remember her being so fluttery, so fragile . . . Now, are you keeping up with your riding? You father had such a fine seat. Oh, more champagne, thank you darling, so sweet. That was Edward's (her last husband, now divorced) problem of course, he could never live up to Gary (Cooper) or Jeffrey (her first husband, now deceased), never could bear that I'd been with anyone more successful than he was ever likely to be. I raise a toast, may they rot in hell!'

Glasses clink and heads nod in agreement.

'I suppose he's found his own level. With this wife,' I say, leading her on to her favourite topic.

'I should say!' she roars with laughter.

'What are you talking about? Not The Usherette from the Festival Hall,' Mum rejoins our conversation.

'Usherette! I thought she was just a ghastly ticket seller! Or was it ice creams?'

'Programmes?' I suggest.

'Part-time – mostly she's the lavatory attendant I expect,' says Mum.

'Good job she's had the experience for clearing up, perfect for Edward. He only sees women as good for menial tasks.'

'Lucky you escaped, before he chained you to the ironing board.'

'Poor Mary. Of course what he could never forgive me for was having it off with Michael in the afternoons.'

'Did he know?'

'Who cares? He was only one of many. Let us wish Mr and

Mrs Windbag congratulations on a stinking union. Cheers!'

'Now Ricky, you're not going off with that dreadful man, are you?'

'I might. It'll be a bit of fun.'

'Mum! Remember where "fun" got you with that awful greasy Adrian, and he's still following you around everywhere, obsessed. Like Jimi, Mum had to call the police the other night because he wouldn't get off the balcony trying to break into the house at four in the morning, after the Embassy Club. Probably thought he was directing an episode of *The Avengers*, too mean to pay a professional stuntman.'

'I didn't know The Policeman was on duty today. Thank you, Coco. I will go, if I like.'

'Well don't blame us if you end up in another frightful underground car park in Elephant and Castle, darling.'

'You were happy enough for me to pay for lunch last week, with the money that handsome devil with a tea towel had thrown me, after pushing me out of the Rolls. Didn't even give me a hanky, I had to wipe myself off on the concrete . . .'

'Mum! Do we have to have it again?'

'I did! What?'

The end of another perfect Saturday lunch . . .

This morning I have still got the flu I had last night, only now I have a hot toddy hangover too. I am not going to college, Barbara has gone to rehearsals at her theatre after mooching around unemployed for the last two months. Mum is going out to lunch. This is how she gets when she's not working. I'm surprised sometimes that the money hasn't run out, but it's always just before it does that something comes along and she squeezes herself back into shape.

Ricky has organised this lunch to matchmake Joanna off with the painter Lothario Pool and herself with Henry Wigg, another playwright, God help us. Does she never learn?

190

Mum and Henry have renewed their bodily acquaintance after a fifteen-year lapse – it is almost romantic. They make trips to the East End to buy smoked salmon and cream cheese bagels to help the champagne go down on Sunday brunchtimes in Chelsea; they talk of the old days and hold hands.

'You're staying in bed for the day, are you, poor chicken?' Mum pokes her head round the door.

'Yeah, I guess so. I just hate being ill in this house by myself. It gets so spooky and cold and depressing. The heating never works properly up here.'

'Go down to my floor, you can stay in my bed for the day and the telly's down there. Nice and cosy and warm.'

'I'd call that four-poster bed of yours many things, but cosy is not one of them. And have you changed your sheets after whoever you had last night?'

'I didn't have anyone, well, no one worth knowing. Come to lunch, doll yourself up, get a few glasses of champagne down you, then you'll feel better. I'm going with Henry, Joanna and Pool, Lothario Pool. You've met him, haven't you?'

'No. I know his work, when I was at school we went to a lecture of his at the Serpentine. He was quite good-looking in that *Virgin and the Gypsy* sort of way. Loads of the girls had crushes on him afterwards.'

'Why lunch, Mum? You're not pairing him off with Joanna, are you? Isn't he quite young?'

'Now, now. Don't be cruel about your Mummy, we thought it was time she had something a bit younger and romantic, so I thought Pool would be just the one. Now, are you coming or not?'

'Alright, alright, have you called the cab, how long have I got to get ready? Fifteen minutes, blimey, I'd better get a move on. Is the water still hot for a shower?'

We arrive at Davis's late, of course, having kept the cab waiting while I try and find my other earring and Mum is busy putting the final application of lipstick in place, but we make an entrance worth waiting for. The maître d' is over the moon at our arrival, in the knowledge that it'll keep the owner occupied, off his back, as is Frank Davies who soon settles himself on our prime table for the duration of lunch. At least with Frank at the table you know the champagne will never run out, that the service will be faster than light, that no story will remain uninterrupted, and that copulation or exposure might occur while you're eating. Certainly, he'll be bloody rude to everyone at the table, but then so will my mother if rankled. At least Frank always falls asleep and slides under the table.

'So, Frank, are you still seeing that nice girlfriend of yours that vomited all over our bathroom at our last party? We're still finding bits of it in the crevices of the tiles, you didn't do a very good job cleaning it up.'

'What do you expect, hauling me round at nine o'clock on a Sunday morning, bitch? If you'd let me have a fuck I wouldn't have brought the fucking girlfriend. How about you, are you up for a bit?' Frank inquires of a haughty Joanna.

She looks at him with a fine disgust, ignoring the crudeness of this fabled restaurant owner. Later she softens, and, relaxed by the quantities of champagne, her prudery collapses and as I come out of the loo upstairs, the first thing I hear is her aristocratic voice booming up the stairs: 'Fucking cunt . . .'

Whatever was said, or happened that lunch, sadly Pool and Joanna were not a match made in heaven. As Mum put it later, 'The problem is, he fancied you. How could you do that to your Mummy?'

'Do what? I didn't sleep with him back then.'

'Later. Later. Dirty cow.'

'Thank you very much, Mother. It was under different circumstances.'

Not so different, just another party at our house where Mum ended up with the clap and Art Souter (legendary modernist director) and I, with Pool.

There, my childhood hero disintegrated into his human form inside my bed and after two subsequent dates, hit the pavement from the elevated heights of my head. Such is the price of schoolgirl crushes. I couldn't believe this man of my romantic dreams *snored*. I didn't like the way he foamed at the mouth in sleeping anger, leaving rivulets of spit dampening my sheets and pillows; his asthmatic cough waking me in the morning, instead of a lover's tender advances. Somehow you expect painters to be different – but as I like to say, 'his art still held my heart.'

I'm hanging out with pop stars a lot these days; I'm not sure how healthy it is. All Rob Driver is interested in is his leather-skinned biker image, immaculate and imaginative as it is. There is no thought beyond the next club night, the next party, when everything he has worked for is on show. Conversation revolves around how 'out of it' we got, they got, he got, and general gossip and bitching of who's fucking who and whether it's worth ever doing it more than once with the same person. Sex, and the young boys who provide it, are a disposable commodity whose names are never remembered even at the time.

'So OK Coco, are you comin' to Lady Franny's party?'

'Yeah, Gemma and John were talking about it, it's Sunday lunch isn't it, Suzi Squirrel is coming to pick me and Stew up.'

'What are you going to wear? I've been working on my hippy look, haven't you got some old Moroccan necklaces I could borrow? I really need something to set off the dark foundation and brilliant open-necked suede shirt I got from Vivienne Westwood.'

'Sorry Dave, I'm wearing them with the ten-stone Japanese kimono I got from Fox's. Mind, I wore it the other evening to the Venue thing and I felt like I had a sumo wrestler attached to each arm it's so bloody heavy, my neck was almost coming away from my shoulders.'

'Don't. Those Manolos do the same thing to my feet!'

'The things a girl has to suffer for beauty ... See you on Sunday then, bye.'

'Cooeeee, Look at it around here, Cokes.'

'I know, Suzi, and you haven't even seen inside the house yet. Looks like Whispers is here in full form, full costume too, probably didn't have time to change between cancan shows I 'spect.'

'You never told me it was a barbie. I would have been here in my gingham pinny if I'd known ... Now, what needs doing? Frans, can I help?'

'God no. Relax. Get a drink. There should be someone around with the champagne or Buck's Fizz ... Oh, have you met ...'

Franny trails off, the party drifts on and everyone's drunk or drugged by the time lunch is ready. Well we haven't come to eat, everyone's on diets anyway – alcohol diets. I get to talk to everyone about nothing that's memorable and by eight, sober through drink, I'm thinking of Chelsea as cosy. Once again my homing instinct saves me. Suzi has said to come and find her when I'm ready to go. I could have said that ten minutes after arriving. Sometimes I stop and pull myself up to think, is this fun? Have I anything in common with this doped-out scene? I drink another glass of champagne to quell the feelings of boredom and another to try and get me there. I promise that I'll make a picture tomorrow to calm myself, place my feet back on the ground. Everybody says it's fun, it must be mustn't it, the grooviest parties with the most fashionable people, somebody must be enjoying it. Suzi doesn't drink: I'm amazed, how can she stand the drunken, drugged drivel that is this crowd's excuse for conversation?

'Meet you outside in five mins.'

After ten minutes I go in search of her and find her pressed and struggling up against the dustbins, held there in a scrawny embrace by an ageing pop legend, begging her not to go now that they are getting on so well. Poor Suzi, the feeling isn't reciprocated.

'That's the thing about Ladies' parties, you just never know who you're going to meet. Let alone who'll press their length of salami against you, do you, Suzi?' I tease her relentlessly all the way home.

'Josie Green is downstairs with Ricky and she's completely off her head. I think she's on drugs.'

'Morning Barbara!' I am stiffly catatonic from working the night before and partying for too long afterwards. 'Are we going out to lunch?'

'Yes, Ricky's booked a table at the Caprice. Groovy, eh!'

'Well that's Sunday done for. When did she turn up?'

'Four in the morning and they've been drinking brandy ever since.'

'Reliving the bliss of those LA orgies, I expect. I suppose I'd better get up, what's the time? Fucking hell – one o'clock. At least you've done your make-up.'

'Applied it.'

'What?'

'I've applied my make-up, you only have to draw yours on, it takes you two minutes.'

'Meow, "sisters, sisters, there were never such devoted sisters . . ." I thought it was Sunday lunch with Alan (Barbara's new beau) at the Chelsea Arts Club?'

'Alan had to go to Milan for the collections, so it's delayed till he comes back.'

'Oh, Ally-baby, is it? Wooeee!'

'Well how's old Cartie Jetsey-poo, then?'

'Fine. He's working hard on this play in the West End. He said he'd ring today. I might be seeing him tonight, actually. Thanks for asking,' I say, steely cold.

Barbara knows not to push it too far. I have fallen badly in love with Carter Jetts, a man who seems, age-wise, ancient. He is thirty, I am nineteen, but then I always have played with older children; or am I just taking after mother?

It was their fault, Barbara and Mum cajoled me into going to some paparazzi book launch upstairs at Davies's.

'I can't go out for another evening on the trot, I'm knackered after a long week at college. Alright, but I'm only staying out for an hour, I want an early night.'

Famous last words that disappear once I am introduced to Carter, Carter Jetts, weird name but then who am I to talk? Hmm, Coco Jetts, sounds pretty dynamic. Mum introduces me, she's worked with him, this up-and-coming, this tall, dark, gorgeous. We are inseparable. Barbara pairs up with Alan, an actor/model, and it's a foursome anxious to go somewhere quiet to seal our double-date fate. So we're in Alan's Range Rover heading towards the Desert, hardly somewhere quiet on a Friday night, but we manage to find a corner table and a banquette to snog on.

Carter and I spend the whole of that night making love and talking, drifting off to sleep to start again. In the morning I wake feeling dreadful, one of those force-nine cheap champagne hangovers. I creep out of bed, afraid he will wake before I manage to drag my bursting bladder and heaving remorse (I'm sure I will get the sack from the Desert after my behaviour last night), to the loo. I am wiping away last night's intimacy, washing off my make-up, rubbing around my eyes with toilet paper and soap till both are raw. But I still feel dirty.

Will I be able to:

a) Get my clothes in the living room and dress, doing up all the hooks and eyes on my full-length evening dress and out the door of wherever I am, before he even stirs? Where am I?

b) Get back into bed in the warmth and sleep away what I don't want to confront? Without him seeing me there, naked? The intimacy of last night.

I open the bathroom door and he is there sitting up and

looking at me. I climb back into bed and for the moment allow myself some happiness, disregarding my self-consciousness and the side that wants to tear away alone.

We go for lunch and drink Bloody Marys and eat cheese omelette, green beans and chips. It is the best meal I have ever tasted. I am in seventh heaven, so why do I lie and say I'm busy that afternoon when we are walking back towards the Embankment, holding hands? I think it will make me sound more independent, interesting, mysterious, holding myself back. When what I really want to say is, I'm here, I'm yours, let's run away together and live happily ever after. But that's what grown-ups do, isn't it, play games? I'm very grown-up.

Carter Jetts is an actor, and even though he is older than me I am impressed, smitten and lost among his words and his eyes. I think he is my boyfriend, but I'm not sure what that means any more. I am writing love poems which I cannot send him. I reread them constantly to tear at my heart to feel the pain, as though somebody has reached for my organs, squeezing them out of existence. When I'm with Carter I already feel sad, because of my inability to express any of my true feelings towards him. I have written the script and can see the end for no good reason but my own dismissal of joy. I don't deserve it. I am jeopardising my own happiness with my melancholia, my obsessive stares at the phone, damning it to ring, and what a surprise when it doesn't! Months go by as I slowly cocoon myself within a dream; I break out to sit around and watch it not happen. I can't stop myself, don't even know how or why, except that I've boarded the unstoppable train of self-destruction.

'Oh, you must be Coco, Carter's girlfriend. He's told me so much about you. Quaint name, did you have problems with it as a child, people making fun of it? What a beautiful dress you're wearing . . . is it second-hand?'

I can feel this woman's eyes examining me, taking in every

detail of my clothes, face, hair, shoes, and I have only this minute walked through the door of Carter's play's first-night party. It strikes me like lightning.

He is fucking this woman. I just know it.

This girl, the first person to approach me as I arrive. He is seeing this actress at rehearsals and giving her the benefit of his private tuition, after hours. I have no real proof but I am sickened. I can hardly concentrate on the guided tour of his director's house, where the party is being held. All I can think to contribute is, 'Carter Jett's a fucking bastard, don't you think?'

I don't actually say it, I just dumbly wander out without saying goodbye to anyone, to cry on the bus all the way home. Relieved to escape.

'You really are quite socially inadequate, aren't you, Coco?'

'What do you mean?'

'Last night, that's what I mean. What the hell's wrong with you?'

'I don't know,' I answer feebly, in our last telephone conversation. And I don't.

I am almost triumphant in my self-fulfilling prophecy. Now I have my very own bag of misery to carry with me wherever I go, and nobody will deprive me of it.

I thought he would mend me, make me whole with his half. Be my saviour. My pain is immense at his betrayal, how could he do it to me! When I loved him so much for all of those months I was willing to let him . . . give him, all of me. I am broken-hearted. I don't even have the energy to make voodoo-doll curses on the actress, leave frighteningly childish messages on her answerphone, or wake her up in the night with silent curses.

It is enough that I can get up in the morning and dress.

We are all moving out of the Chelsea house, we can't stand it any more, this era has ended. We have given up the house to the sickly ghosts and spirits of its history, adding some of our own to the mess. It was a grand house for parties and people not quite of this planet, but Barbara, Mum and me realise it's too fucked up, even for us.

I haven't spoken to Carter for three weeks. There has been no formal end to this relationship, no sorting through the baggage of recriminations. It is unfinished business that I pack with the rest of my belongings. I move to the Chelsea Arts Club for an interim two weeks, my mother stationary at its bar, a G and T in her hand, another man at her side. Makes me happy to leave. I love her too much to watch what she's doing to herself.

There's a space in Jester's council flat in Soho, sounds better.

CHAPTER EIGHTEEN

'But why can't I wear my Sleeping Beauty gown to bed as my nightdress tonight? Granny hasn't even seen it yet and she'll be sad if she doesn't see it. She will, Daddy, she will.'

'Because, sweetheart, Mummy said you were only allowed to stay up to see Granny if you were in your nightie and, though very pretty, it isn't your nightie, and what Mummy says goes. Otherwise it's to bed.'

'No, Daddy. No. You're cruel and not my friend. I shan't let you read me stories at night any more, and then what will you do?'

'I'll be very sad. Not even Cinderella, won't I even be able to read you that?'

'If you're good. I can do that by myself.'

And she twisted her rounded body away from her father to take the dress off by herself, her sulky, turned-down face now concentrated with the effort.

'I shall wear this dress for breakfast. That's a good ideal, isn't it?' Joan mispronounces, in a hurry to get the words out.

'Very, of course you must. Now is it pyjamas or nightie, pink or blue?'

'What day is it today?'

'Wednesday.'

'Well then it's pink. I only wear pink on Wednesday. Pinkie nightie. That rhymes. Pinkie nightie, pinkie nightie, pinkie nightie.'

'On it goes, here's kitty under your bed.'

'Ahh.' And she hugs the kitten to her. The poor thing with its nose half hanging off, paws split and stuffing out, loved into physical disintegration.

Joan looks down at her struggling father trying to get her slippers on her feet. 'You sweet little thing,' she capriciously strokes his cheek with her finger.

Ben stops, and, shot with the tenderness of his daughter's new tone, he does feel small. He sits up and she puts her arms around his neck, feet upon his knees, small breath upon his face and gives him a body hug, and he climbs to stand with his daughter attached to him like a monkey.

'How about going downstairs for some peeled apple and a few nuts before story-time, monkey? I think the big monster brothers and sisters are downstairs, so we'd better hurry to see if there is anything left.'

'Yes, yes, yes. You're the best daddy in the whole wide world.'

'And you're the best Joan.' And he could feel his lips sink into the pink plumpness of her cheeks with his skin.

'Have you heard my new song?

Polly put her dolly in the trolley, trolley, trolley,
She called up the doctor to see if she was well . . .'

Coco was still cooking away, making sure everything was set for Carol and Martha to do most of the rest of it all in the kitchen that evening. Then all that needed to be done was the serving of the main course and pudding. The hors d'oeuvres were already laid out along the blue and yellow painted sideboard in the dining room. The green beans, whole and glistening with the mustard vinaigrette and dots of white pine nuts; silver-skinned anchovies, their flesh turned from brown to white with pungent marinating; the red, white and black flower of tomatoes, fennel and olives layered upon the plate and the *bruschetta* crisp and brown, spread spring-green with salsa *verde*. It all looked as pretty as a picture, tasted better, but it was the smell of the soup that drifted out to the dining room from its heated container, ladle in place, that called the guests from their rooms, making their stomachs gurgle and their mouths salivate.

Bill was in his Tiger Tim pyjamas and wool tartan dressing gown and corded belt, sitting at one end of the table, assiduously intent upon finger-cleaning his plate, looking like a *Just William* illustration. A smile of bliss was upon his lips as he wiped his ice-cream finger down his tongue. His hair flopped into his eyes.

'Ahhh, that's better,' he patted his stomach and burped for final effect.

'That's my boy!' said Ben, smirking with childish pride as he came into the kitchen with Joan still vined upon his body. He was boastful at the etiquette he had managed to pass down to his son, probably because of Coco's unimpressed raised eyebrows.

'Honestly, Bill. Ben, could you be teaching Bill something more useful than burping at the end of each meal, like discussing colour theory or something?'

'Bill and Ben, the flowerpot men. That rhymes,' said Joan, her mouth full of nuts, an apple in her hand.

'It's better than Bill farting and stinking us all out of house and home,' said Mary abstractedly, more interested in peeling an apple in one piece so that she could throw the peel on to the floor and see the letter it would form, the initials of her future husband. Another of Carol's superstitions and soothsayer acts.

'More like you do!' Bill retorted.

'You do.'

'You do too.'

'We all do. There's nothing wrong with it, it's just bodily functions, shows it's all working. Better out than in.' Coco tried to smooth over what could potentially end in a fully-fledged biting, scratching, hair-pulling fight, for Bill and Mary.

'I've just done one so my body's working properly, isn't it Mummy?' chirped Joan.

'Yuck.'

'Poooheee,' sounded Joan and Bill, friends in unity.

'So what's all the fun and laughter about? I thought you'd all be up in bed by now. I'd already been up to see. Martha showed John and me to our room, he's up there changing. How are you all, my chickens?' The maternal Ricky, the grandmother, cooed at the family fledglings that gathered about her skirts.

'Silly Granny, we were down here all along.'

Coco went to her, wiping her hands down her apron before putting them around her mother, giving her a big hug and a warm kiss.

'Mum, lovely to see you. How's everything?'

'Great! Let's talk later. Do you want me to take the kids up and put them to bed?'

'Brilliant if you could, then Ben could take up his host's duties out front, where I will shortly join you, my darling?' she gave him a special loving smile, exclusively his, that could have lasted a second or a year but could only have been for Ben. The smile was replaced by another for her children's goodnight kisses and hugs while Ben turned his attention to welcoming his mother-in-law. They were friends, got on well, would have with or without Coco. Ben was that type of man who worked at any relationship to become close if it was important to the rest of his life. Far-sighted and family-bound.

'All right, puddings, bed with Granny.'

'I'm not a pudding, I'm Joan.'

'I'm not going to bed with Granny, you must be joking,' said Bill. 'Couldn't fit in my bunk with her big boobies!'

'Bill!' said Mary, stifling her laughter with the proper indignity, rolling her eyes and filing out the door and upstairs.

Ricky smiled, happy to be so easily accepted back into the fold after her months away filming. The bond was there, unbroken, unifying her with her grandchildren. All part of the family.

She sometimes pondered on how close she'd come to losing all of this. Her daughter's love, friendship, trust, all because of the drink and what she couldn't face herself, but she had faced it, been brave and gone through it all. Life only got better now that she could leave her past behind. Ricky had a loving companion in John, a gently burgeoning career as the ageing character actress who'd been there and survived it, and the warm steel strength of Coco's ever-growing family. Always there, full of unrestrained energy and excitement.

CHAPTER NINETEEN

'How much do you charge for a hand job?'

'Come 'ere, darlin', I need some quick relief round the back of the station, twenty quid do ya?'

'Are you working? How much for full sex?'

'Are you working?'

Strings of strangers shout at me as I walk down Soho's streets.

' "Are you working?" If I hear that once more I'll be done for grievous bodily harm.'

'I thought it was the flat you didn't like, that's why you were moving to Minx's.'

'The flat. The black rubbish bags full of Jester and Sidney's unwashed shirts from working, they fill the corridor, you can't get out the door. They can't be bothered to go to the launderette, so the piles just grow as each night they buy a new second-hand ironed shirt from Flip.'

And the toy-soldier manoeuvres – I tread on Dungeons and Dragons each time I go into the living room.

'That girl who's staying here called Dorothy hides her baby in a cupboard every time there's a knock on the door, in case a social worker calls, carving knife at the ready to stab through the letter box. I don't care if she's a poetic genius, she's stark raving mad. I'm beginning to know how Ted Hughes felt – fuck art, survival's the thing. Jester is the most normal thing in the flat, and that's saying something. I'll be following them too if I don't get out of Soho's pleasure pit soon.'

'Hmmm, I've never really liked the West End for living,' Louise says in her distracted manner that sounds as if it's distasteful even to mention the district.

'Minx's is just for a bit, then I'm moving to Toby's, back to Chelsea. Wandering the streets around here unnerves me. Not having a phone and having to make all my calls to my mum or dad from the prostitutes' phone booth across the road isn't nice, is it? It's almost worse than Brixton. It's nice with Berwick Street market and the delis, but quite frankly fresh salami isn't worth the hassle of stepping into some drunk's vomit all over your doorstep each morning.'

'Depressing. Better to get out. Are you going to the Sunday-afternoon tea dance at the Roof Garden – Steve's doing it.'

'I don't think so, I got so drunk there last weekend I'm ashamed to show my face. We went on post-club lunch with Mum and I ended up snogging a boy on the floor under the table, apparently. The next thing I knew I woke up with him on top of me back at the flat.'

'God! What was he like? You didn't tell me.'

'I suppose it wasn't so awful, he was quite good-looking but his name was Midge.'

'Midge's alright, different if he was called Darren or Tracey. Coco, he wasn't that moustached thing in Ultravox?'

'No it was not, thank you Louise, and not if I can help it. Midge makes me think of an irritating little insect you can't get rid of, which is not a bad description of his bedroom abilities. Not what you need on top of a force-nine hangover.'

Another club, another boy. That's about the extent of my commitment to relationships. I go off with boys and sometimes even men when I'm drunk, and then get so rattled about my behaviour I can't bear to see them again. Not in the cold light of day. How can you start a relationship with somebody when they've seen you at your worst – from there on in, there'd only be everything to look forward to. I wouldn't be able to beguile them with my sweet, innocent, true nature. Grip them tightly by the heart and superglue them to my soul, captives to the last. But somehow I do.

The phone rings and I pretend I'm not in.

What's the matter with them? Nothing.

Anything the matter with me? Everything.

That's how I've got since Carter. Mum used to call me 'Hard-hearted Hannah, the Vamp of Savannah' as a joke, a mild tease. Now I entrance them, one night of passion and they're out on their butts like used condoms, unrepeatably, soiled.

Not that I'd be seen dead using condoms. Slimy, ucky things that feel more like a plastic-wrapped cucumber than flesh. And that's if you're lucky. If you're not, a warm chipolata, an uncooked cocktail sausage, surrounded by parsley. Sex is embarrassing enough without having to look at its gossamer-pink remains over the floor; proof of the deflated, spent pleasure to dispose of. Boys' things. More slippery than banana skins, when filled with their milky residue.

Sex with another person should be an intimate hobby, but it always seems so insular to me, lonely, for those seconds after when you're catching your breath, before the talking starts again. There you can be, all damp skin pushed hard together like pressed ham, faces buried in each other's necks, shoulders, hair, willing for the same moment of release to fall apart, whatever it takes, but it's always separate. Then the sex dream is broken and you can almost forget about the way he grabbed your hand, forcing it around his cock, willing you to rub it to pleasure and the feeling of dirt and distaste that goes with it. Doing something that he wanted you to, to somebody you hardly know – intimately touching a stranger.

Carter always said he never could remember sex after he'd had it. Very convenient, slightly disconcerting if he was into S and M and bondage. I take this as a personal insult, file away under Wounds. But some people do find it so embarrassing, it's permanently placed in their subconscious: I just never expected to be having a sexual relationship with one of them.

★ ★ ★

I'm on the pill. Have been since I was fifteen, on and off. I remember taking the afternoon off double maths at school, so I could do the responsible thing down at Family Planning.

'Have you got a regular boyfriend – someone you've been going out with for six months or more, Coco?' a sixty-year-old geriatric asked me, who didn't look like she even remembered what sex was.

'No,' I'd honestly replied.

'What on earth are you coming here for, wasting my time?'

'Because I want to be on the pill.'

'Sex should be part of a responsible and loving relationship, not something you take like a biscuit when you want it.'

'Why not? I want to be prepared. It takes a month, doesn't it, until it's safe. I'm being responsible by asking for it now, fore-sight.'

'You don't seem to understand, sex and the pill are not things to be taken lightly.'

'So you don't want to give it to me?'

'No.'

'OK. Shall I see you next time I'm back, pregnant and wanting an abortion? Will I be grown-up enough to be on the pill then?'

'Alright, alright, I'll give it to you, but on the condition that you don't start taking them until you feel you've met the right boy. That you're settling into a steady relationship.'

'Fine.' Steady relationship for the night, more likely. Poor old cow, when was the last time her husband pounced on her? Probably when his secretary was away on holiday and he got desperate. Sad, really.

I'm twenty, halfway to twenty-one, with Christmas about to turn the corner. Most of the time I don't feel old enough to be this age, but when do you ever feel old enough? On Friday nights at the

Desert, usually, and some bunch of wankers, out after work with the staff secretaries instead of their wives, decide to work their way through the cocktail list. Banana daiquiris, dry Martinis, Tom and Jerries, Jamaican rum punches, Moscow Mules, tequila sunrises . . . Then they think, better just have a chilli to sober me up before driving back to the marital in Guildford, and before you know it it's Pizza Carpet sprayed across the hall, blocking the urinal, decorating the table.

'Terribly embarrassing, couldn't quite reach the loo, awfully sorry, there's an extra pound tip for you.'

Then I feel grown-up, up and over. Older than these children, whose sick I'm scrubbing out of the thick pile, wiping into a bucket, the carrots from lunch and the last strawberry daiquiri. Sticking my finger into yellow Marigolds – favourite rubber gloves to wriggle through the latrines, pulling out the fag butts marinated in urine, delicious!

'No, of course I don't mind doing it. I wouldn't do it if I did. Someone's got to, it might as well be me.'

The managers call this showing initiative: careful Coco, you know what initiative brings – responsibility. I'll be one of them soon if I'm not careful.

I'm quite cheerful about it and in the end I find it preferable when its slow to lounging around the office, aka the smoking cabin/cloakroom where beautifully scented furs are passed in to be looked after: they must smell worse than old dog-ends after we've all been in there a couple of bored, chain-smoking slow hours.

'Have a good evening, see you soon,' the receptionist politely smiles, looking discreetly sideways at her half-empty tip basket. She hands back the coat, her manicure disturbed, and a silver fox fur now delicately tipped with Revlon 'Red Hot' walks out the door.

'What are you all doing in here? Get out there, we've still got customers in the place, in case you hadn't noticed.'

'Bowie's table don't want anything more, and the people on the end tables have ordered their bill, Will.'

'Well get out there and give it to them, Coco. Ridiculous name, ever thought of changing it? You might as well say last orders to the bar.'

The Desert is now my home from home. Nothing too much like hard work. Mostly better than going to a club, at least I know everyone here, I don't get riotously drunk or sick, and I end up getting home at three in the morning with money in my pocket. This Christmas is going to be fun, I'm having it in the flat, Toby's going away so it'll be fifteen for dinner. Barbara, Jester, Tony Sledgehammer, Adrian, Louise, Ricky and some of her friends and anybody else who's not doing anything but who is affiliated to the Desert. The waifs and strays of Christmas.

Mum is down from Wales staying with me. She's living there, watching Granny die. To see her now it looks like something is fading away in her, too. She looks shrunken, like Granny, a little person sitting on the sofa. The disco diva of last year peeled back to this child from the Valleys who finds London too loud.

Mum gets drunk on Christmas Day, we all get drunk: champagne, Zybrowka and Stolichnaya vodka and Jester making his assortment of cocktails. Mum gets too drunk and starts to cry and it is my fault, I have made her cry. How could I have done it to her, gone out for a drink and left her on Christmas Eve? Alone? I help her to bed, this stumbling wreck, sodden with tears, snivelling insults, and I sit by her, holding her hand, mascara drying in its tracks over her cheeks as she falls asleep with a viper's retributions on her lips. The smallness of her translucent-skinned hand is like a child's, like Granny's.

Barbara drives me up to the valley and stands and waits outside the garage of the undertaker's where they have laid out the body. I kiss the cold, dead flesh goodbye, hold the thin-skinned blue-veined, child-size hand and cry. For what? For Granny, me, for all of us and our dying. For all of us still living. For my orphan mother. We are all still such children playing this adult game until we die and, like Granny, become as small as a child again who's played with grown-up make-up before climbing into the cradle of pure white satin, the coffin's lining, ready to be put back into a womb of earth.

How many achieve anything to change that? What power, fame, wealth, can get you off the roundabout?

'God, that was good! How was it for you?'

'OK,' I lie, and think of Glenda Jackson and George Segal in 'A Touch of Class'.

'Coco! What are you smiling about? Have you been listening? I said, Do you trust me?'

'No.' No, no, no, to everything. Trust you! You must be joking.

'Why not?'

'Well, Carter, how to put it. Do you remember when we were going out before and you were in that play, the one with Miranda Jacobs?'

'Yes, why?'

'And you were having it off with that actress, the one who played the prostitute . . .'

'Yes . . . But how did you know?'

'Because it was blatantly obvious to me. Anyway, that's why. It's as good a reason as any for not trusting you, don't you think? I'm getting dressed now, I'm going out tonight.'

'Coco that was years ago, I've changed and I thought we were spending the evening together . . . Where are you going? It's Sunday night, can't I come with you?'

'No. I'm going to see Mum do her show, it's her second time there and I said I'd support her.'

Besides, I'm thinking, if I don't get rid of you I'm going to go up the wall. The constant adulation is driving me away. Why are you so submissive when I am so mean to you? I really did want you, but what the fuck's the matter with you!

I disentangle myself from his arms and cross the room to dress at my wardrobe. I now behave as he once did to me.

'I'd really like to see Ricky's show.'

'Would you?' I reply, doing up my bra, squeezing into my tight, long black dress.

'Why don't I come with you tonight, Coco? You're so beautiful, your eyes, your smile, your hair . . .'

I grimace and close my eyes into evil slits, grab my hair away from my face and twist it into a bun.

'If only you'd suggested it earlier, dear!' I think, in reply to my sexual dissatisfaction.

'No, I don't think so. Why don't you come when she's done it a few more times? She wants to practise a bit more on people she doesn't know. I think she'd be unnerved by your presence, having worked with you. You understand.'

Bonehead, get the hint!

'OK, if that's what you think. I'll miss you tonight, Coco.'

'Will you, Carter,' I say, stony-faced, looking back at him through the mirror, not even bothering to turn around.

I'm walking down Old Compton Street towards the club and everything is shut, it being London and Sunday evening. So how come I feel so shitty, even my make-up's off balance. I should feel great after getting my own back on Carter. I'm almost twenty-two, a manager at the Desert with my own flat, a degree and still painting, even a boyfriend. I'm finally where I thought I wanted to be, with all the power in my hands and now that I've got it, do I want it? No. I don't want the power and I don't want him. Oh hell, I'm not going to think about it, I'll have a good time tonight and forget about him. I'm not working tomorrow, so I don't even have to think of the consequences. A hangover. I can nurse it alone in my bed.

'And now let's give a warm welcome for the outrageous Ricky Johnson.'

Tumultuous applause, yipeeing and shouts greet a small spotlit figure perched on a stool, centre stage, as the curtains draw back.

'Good evening all. I start the show as I mean to go on, and from here on in, it's downhill. You'll know what to expect then. Right, here we go. This is a twelfth-century aphorism, ready?

> *A ring is a hole with a rim around it.*
> *Bloody good job that all the rims fit.*
> *If the one round my bum had not been the right one,*
> *All my clothes would be covered in shit.*'

The horseshoe audience in this small, dark jazz club is with her, willing her to succeed, waiting for the punchlines, laughing at the jokes, smiling at the innuendoes. I want her to win so badly that I'm almost on stage with her, holding her constant cigarette, her pint of lager with the straws.

'So as not to spoil the lipstick,' she confides to the audience. 'I can't tell that it makes you get drunk twice as fast, but then Tallulah Bankhead said there was no way cocaine was addictive, she should know, she'd been taking it all her adult life.'

I'm sitting on a table at the front with Mum's best friends. There don't seem to be many of my friends around that I can spot from where I'm sitting. Apart from Carly the brilliant jazz singer who used to be a waitress at the Desert; tonight she's Mum's support, wearing the wildest screaming-scarlet strapless dress.

There is an unintended interval, when Lady Humphries, fashion editor of some snotty magazine, is escorted out for causing a disturbance, shouting more obscene language than my mother's.

'If you had been more coherent, dear, you could have joined

me up here on stage, but I think it's better if you go ... Ah, poor thing. Sad when they go like that.'

She is dragged screaming out of the club.

'Hiya, Coco, howya doin'? Let me introduce you to some of my friends I brought along to your mum's show. It was wild, wasn't it? Was it really all true?'

'Hello, Mike. I wasn't expecting to see you here tonight. Is Tura with you?'

Mike is an old pretty boy. A straight actor who has an American twang to his West End voice, he has big blond hair with a too-wholesome face with ready, perfect teeth. The smile and a gay aptitude land him lots of adverts for chunky chocolate bars and the occasional walk-on West End theatre part. Tura is our mutual friend and not here. So he introduces me to others: Cecily, Anne, Cameron ...

'So what's happening, are you going on anywhere? Coco always knows if anything else is going on,' he says, turning to his smiling, enquiring entourage.

'Well actually I don't know. I'll go backstage and ask Mum if she's up for anything. But I warn you, on a Sunday night it'll probably be the Mayfair place.'

'Fancy a fuck?' I say brazenly to the young boy with Mike who has been volleying with my interested glances. I have beckoned him over to my table at the restaurant. Maybe he's not that young, maybe twenty-five, but he has that dark, flopped hair, boyish charm and puppy-dog enthusiasm which I am trying to wean myself off. Too late, I am taken by his open, good-looking face and relentless smile.

'Your place or mine?' he comes back, quick as a whippet.

'Mine.'

The pact is sealed before even a kiss is exchanged, or indeed the sheets from this afternoon.

★ ★ ★

'I bought the gravlax, did you remember the glasses, Louise?'

'Yes, here they are. It was a really good idea to have a picnic on the train. I've never been to Cambridge before.'

'Well you never know when you're going to be eating next, let alone having a drink. I don't suppose they have a bar inside the Cambridge Debating Society?'

'Pass me a lager now, I've almost finished doing me eyes, I'll do the lipstick just before we arrive, it'll only be spoiling otherwise.

'So, who do you expect to be in intimate discussions with tonight, girls? The future Prime Minister or a Nobel Prize winner?' Mum asks.

'Anything, as long as it's not gay. It's not as though we're looking for long-term marriage proposals. Mind, a short-term proposal would be nice. You know, I haven't heard back from that creep who I slept with that second night of your show. Bloody cheek. Serves me right for going for somebody so normal. And don't say "He couldn't have been that normal to go with you," ' I say.

'Well, I'd hardly say "Fancy a fuck" would procure you a "normal" relationship.'

'Thank you Mother, I'll remember that next time I'm drunk and soliciting.'

'You didn't say that, did you, Coco?'

'I might have, in fact I told you, Louise, that I did. It seemed to be the right thing to say in the circumstances, but maybe with forethought . . . There goes another steady reliable.'

'It's true, you don't meet many straight men with jobs and cars and flats, these days,' Louise dismally professes.

'Somebody's getting them, because they're out there. I don't expect Sharon from the typing pool has much trouble finding a boyfriend.'

'I don't suppose she does!' Louise and I chorus back, as we

pull into Cambridge station for the performance of Mum's One-woman Show. I wonder fleetingly what David would say if he could see us now, walking into his old college.

We walk into the Debating Society hall and are seated at the front by the Chairman of the Society and the Students' Union. Mum will be on in five minutes; meanwhile we peruse the arriving audience for likely eligibles.

We stare open-mouthed at each other. Louise and I are products of Art School and are definitely not au fait with the University Image. The girls wear no make-up and their hair lies long and straight where it has been left by a brush ten hours previously. They seem careless of their dirty jeans and baggy, old jumpers, scuffed desert boots and shirt-tails hanging out; or they are prim in Laura Ashley, with neatly polished shoes, tan tights and earnest, well-scrubbed faces. And the boys are their male equivalent with spots.

Aaaargh!

We are shocked.

What were we expecting? *Brideshead Revisited*? Not that they'd all be grasping their teddies to their hearts, but maybe something a little more stylish than a tightly fitting tweed jacket with leather patches at the elbows. At least let the louche youth representatives be wearing Doc Martens with their jeans, not Clarks's grey leather range. Pul-lease.

Louise and I are currently sporting the Forties look. Joan Crawford and Ida Lupino lookalikes with our false lashes, permanently red lips, hair piled high on our heads pleated, folded, crimped and sprayed, then wrapped around old stockings and deposited in beaded net snoods at the backs of our necks. We are wearing suits with padded shoulders and nothing under the jackets, seamed stockings and high-heeled court shoes. Our nails are painted, our gloves and jewellery in place and we smell like perfume counters or whores, depending on who you ask. Of course it's worth the bother. We are just twenty-two, frightening to people our own age, frightened of anyone else.

Mum starts the show in the usual way, fifteen get up and walk out.

'If there's any more eighteen-year-old fucking Tory virgins disgusted by my foul mouth, I suggest you better sod off now. It's not going to get any better for you. If you leave now, you'll still be able to catch the last bus home.'

Thirty more get up and start fighting for the exit.

'There, that's better, now we can get on with the show.'

Mum recounts a dainty tale of menstruation and sex in a bloodied, full bathtub, with some poor innocent male victim.

When I look around at the remaining faces, some are white with horror, some aghast and fascinated, all are too terrified to leave, rabbits hypnotised by a snake. Louise and I produce the only relaxed laughter to be heard. Now this we are au fait with.

The Edinburgh Festival held wilder times ahead. Thank God.

'It's a wonder anyone can stomach it at breakfast time,' I say to Mum when she tells me that she is booked in at the Lower Assembly Room at eleven a.m. each morning for two weeks to do her show at the festival.

'They could have put me on at nine. Some shows start at nine in the morning, imagine that. I would have had to be early to bed every night, or not at all, more like.'

'Probably not at all.'

'I 'spect an afternoon rest would have seen to me. So when are you coming up, you girls?'

'Louise and I thought we'd come up for the last week, that way you would have settled in nicely, done the research for us as to where to go and what to see and then we'd just swan into it. Get the picture?'

'I do, madam, very nice. And where does madam expect to be staying, has she booked herself a suite at the Gleneagles Hotel?'

'No, not quite. We rather thought you might show us the

hospitality of your floor, Mummy dearest.'

'Oh, did you? Alright, since you ask so nicely. But I warn you it's a studio flat I'm staying in so it'll be a bit of a squash, no bringing in any waifs and strays to screw on the floor at night. I'll be needing my beauty sleep for the morning performance.'

'Mother, as if we would. Look, I'd better go, I'm at work and some mad drunk's vomiting pina coladas down his secretary's cleavage at the bar. The bliss of Friday nights! I'll call you when I've got the times of the train, OK. Lots of love, bye.'

We are stuffing it in like addicts, Louise and I, six, seven shows a day. The maximum bombardment to our senses, endless drinking and a tour of nightclub duty, at the end of a hard day's culture-vulturing. It seems pretty blissful to me with all the museums, galleries and little Italian cafés as well. But our undoing is the very open licensing hours, the pubs never seem to close. That, and the arrival of Cameron.

I hadn't heard a word from him after our assignation and I'd shrugged the whole thing off. Then Cameron turns up at my twenty-second birthday party and I think what the hell, if you can't enjoy a fuck on your birthday, when can you? The next day he sends me a belated birthday card, a montage of love.

We start seeing each other. It seems fun. Going out with somebody normal with a job, with money to pay for dinner, to go out. Not another impoverished artist, hoping for the big time, a contract with Cork Street, a show in New York, 'but you'll have to pay for my dinner till my next show'.

Cameron is a banker. He drives a fast, open-top sports car. He knows how to get his way in the world; when he decides on what he wants he gets it. He tells me all this on our fourth date, champagne at the Ritz. He wants me, but more than that, he's decided he's ready to settle down, marriage, a family. He starts showing me estate agents' bumf on castles with moats; 'I thought we should live somewhere in the country,' he says.

I'm bowled over, almost speechless. I am so used to one-night stands that even seeing somebody three times is starting to seem a little serious for me. I like him, but honestly! And as to commitment, I can't even hear the word without laughing.

I thank him in an affronted manner and assure him I am much too young to consider his proposal, except in practising the mechanics of child-making.

'I swear I didn't invite him up, honestly, Louise.'

'I thought this was going to be a girls' holiday.'

'It was, I mean it is. Look, at least he's got his open-top sports car to drive us around in.'

'Very handy for three, a two-seater.'

'Look, it's alright. We can squash in. I'm sure he won't be here for long. He works, he'll have to go back to his job. He's only up here to attend some conference. Come on, we'll have a good time.'

But the good time gets lost among the beer barrels and bottles. 'Just another pint' at lunchtime swills the jollity until evening, one more glass delays the hangover until bedtime. Maybe Cameron and I exchange intimate, excluding glances, or snog once too often over the spilling ashtrays. Cameron invites us to go and stay in his godfather's house. We have drunken, stumbling sex, and finish off the decanters of port on the sideboard.

Louise is sick and tired of it, bored to distraction probably from having to look in the other direction, with the secret whisperings of young lovers always touching. Maybe it is just the uncomfortable night on the sofa and the noise of us giggling upstairs that does it. She leaves.

Come to think of it, would any of us choose to stay in Hades any longer than we had to?

Yet still on my return to London I say, 'It's the best holiday I've ever had. It was brilliant. We had so much fun. We were so drunk . . .' and then comes another tale of drunken debauchery and the payment in hangover that my body once again sustains. Then the familiar family cry of 'The hags of Hell are perching today'.

Somehow Louise and my friendship survives the rigours of Edinburgh and back in London I am still seeing Cameron, though never the two together again. Louise says she does not trust Cameron for breaking up our holiday; maybe she doesn't trust me for still seeing him. For putting a male I've known for a few months before a girlfriend I've known for ten years. I can't blame her, I feel a cad myself, but there's something about having a man around that changes me. I say me, but it's all the women I know from my mother through to my friends. A man arrives on the horizon and everybody else becomes secondary. I can see it happening now, with Cameron, but I can't be bothered to do anything about it. It's there, he's there and it's easy if not perfect. He's a friend. I'll break it off sometime, I know I will, it's just finding the right time. He wants to make everything so serious, I don't know what he expects from me but I'm not ready. I get annoyed that he wants to be with me all the nights I'm not working, that he wants to know what I've been doing and who with. He moans about all the overtime he has to put in with his job, he complains about having to visit his parents every weekend.

'Don't do it or don't moan,' I shriek at him one day, but we drift on, in the way you do. How was it that I spent all that time moping about as a miserable teenager, with my jowls hanging down to my toes, my shoulders hunched upon the pavement, in the search of the permanent fixture, a boyfriend? The closest I could mostly find was a one-night stand, an alcohol-stained evening of exercise. And now this. It's like that song by Marilyn Monroe that I can't stop humming: 'After You Get What You Want You Don't Want It'.

That's me.

There is no way that Ricky could sustain her stage career now if a man was a permanent feature. Mind, what man would listen and laugh at the tale of the Arab and the underground car park, or the stories of defecation, or tights used as a method of contraception, or long-haul sex journeys with truck drivers, or the initiation of frightened eighteen-year-old virgins.

Not Richard, not David, for sure. Lucky David's still gaily cavorting around America.

Sometimes I catch myself between the laughter and, if I allow myself to glimpse with the morals of this society, or slyly sip at my own honesty, this surely must be the sickest of black humour. A daughter laughing at the tales of her mother's emotional, sexual and physical violation. Not just between the two of them, but in front of an audience of hundreds, and I am laughing the loudest. Of course I am, what other way is there to listen and translate these tales of horror? I even test my boyfriends to see if they'll laugh through one of my mother's shows. If they don't laugh, they don't stand a chance. Cameron laughs. I give him a sidelong glance: how can he laugh with his Jewish-Scottish upbringing and dark-eyed smile? Because it's funny, real funny, and I've always loved black humour. I've been brought up on it.

There are different degrees of black humour, there must be; some of it I don't find very funny, not at the moment anyway, call me sensitive.

Mr and Mrs Elliston are proud to announce
the wedding of their daughter
Louise
to
Cameron James Rogers
on the 23rd of August

Ha, ha, ha, who's got the last laugh,
    Ha, ha, ha, who's got the last laugh,

Ha, ha, ha, who's got the last laugh, *now*!

Dear God,

I know I haven't had much contact with you recently, life's been running away with me, but please I need your help. I know I've been unthinking, making a mess, but I promise to clear up.

I've got to get out of here. I don't care how, just something to take me away, smooth down the creases and buff up the landing mattress. Not another boy, though, not another boy. A job maybe, something. I'll keep in touch, I promise. I'll even write letters every week, well, every two to be realistic, to Barbara, Mum, Dad. I promise to be kind and good and loving to all of them, if I get out of the country. I just can't deal with those phone calls at three in the morning from some bar being asked to join in Ricky's 'good time'. Hearing from others about her three-day binges of continual bar crawls on the twenty-four-hour circuit, before they have even half ended. Going out shopping with her for the feel-good experience where she buys up half the shop to impress the shop assistant. Why couldn't she just have one jumper, she has to have it in four different colours too. Walking out of the shop justifying her extravagance, hugging it to her to warm her heart, when I know she can hear the bank manager's reprimanding voice. That's enough of a reason for having a really good lunch, and the best bit, the bottle of champagne to celebrate. What for?

The sun shining, the sky being blue, a bus being red and finding a pair of cerise gloves at Harvey Nichols that precisely match your lipstick. Any excuse.

Dear God, I'm worn with it and I've lost my sense of direction, I can't paint, I can't even see the exit signs any more.

Please God, give me a geographical, just for the time and space.

Deposit me in another country, another world. I don't even

care which one, just send me the plane ticket.
   Your ever-faithful servant,
   Coco xxxxxxxxxxxxxxxxx

'There's a woman come to see you Coco, on table five, she says she's come from Singapore to find you.'

'Really, I wonder what that's about? I better go see to it.'

'Hi, I'm Suzzi Kroner, we've never met before but I've been sent on a mission to persuade you to come and run our new club we're opening in Singapore. We've heard such a lot about you from members of our other clubs in Bangkok and Hong Kong, we'd like to offer you a contract for six months, to see if you like it. The money is good and you get to run it exactly the way you want. I can see it would have to be a good offer to draw you away from running a successful club like this in the centre of London, your family and friends. So the offer is good. Would you be interested?'

'My, isn't this sudden.'

'Pardon me?'

'It's nice to meet you, Suzzi. Yes, I would, let me think about it. I mean, as you say, leaving family and friends would be a wrench, but can we meet outside of here? I don't think it's the done thing to discuss new job prospects right on the site of the present one.'

'No of course not, how rude of me. Let me take you to lunch tomorrow to consider, talk it over. I can tell you a bit more about the project. Could you meet me at my hotel, Blakes, around twelve-thirty?'

'Sure. Nice meeting you, I look forward to talking to you tomorrow.'

Thank you God, thank you. Now that's what I call fast, express service, Heaven's DHL. I must have got on to a direct line, whatever, you're a star. Just three more weeks and I'm out of here.

I leave work singing all the way, rejuvenated by a winning wartime spirit.

'Goodbye Piccadilly, farewell Leicester Square, it's a long, long way to Singapore but my heart lies there.'

CHAPTER TWENTY

Most of the guests – there's only ten of them staying – have left the dining room to go for coffee, almond biscuits and brandy in the sitting room with the real log fire blazing away. Red leather Chesterfield sofas and armchairs, squodgy with age, are warmed by the blaze. Another sofa sits alone facing towards the windows that look across the garden, half hidden from the rest of the room by a large partitioned painted screen, a lovers' hideaway. Wendy and Luke from London were exploring its possibilities, for the short time it took to drink their coffee and refill before taking it upstairs for an 'early night'; the other couple haven't even come down for dinner. The Jameses, Todds and the two Americans have been hitting it off like old friends all through dinner and are making a party of it around the fire; armagnac and the cafetière are flowing. They've asked The Actress and her companion to join them, and have been politely rejected but thanked.

'Ricky Johnson, that's her name. She's been in loads of films, character actress . . .'

'Sure honey, you remember her in that Henry James story they made into a film, with that actor who always plays the part of those stiff old repressed Englishmen. You know . . .'

'Edward Finney?'

'No, no, the other one.'

'Which other one? Aren't they all like that?'

Back in the dining room, Coco and Ben are just sitting down for dinner with Ricky and John. It is nine-thirty and the children have been asleep for an hour, Joan for more.

'This is delicious. Come and sit down darling, you're working far too hard, and with all that baby to carry around. Are you having your afternoon sleeps, that's the important thing.'

'Just some Perrier for me, thank you.'

'It's so lovely to be back here and how the children have grown, Joan talks as though she was auditioning! We'll soon have her in RADA.'

'I know, they're all coming on in leaps and bounds. They're very pleased to see you, Mum. Don't expect a late lie-in, they'll be pounding at your door and dragging you up for breakfast.'

'I'll be dressed already. John and I always run in the morning, don't we, darling?'

'We'll probably be up before them. Your mother has so much energy. I'm dreading retirement, I won't have an office to go and recuperate in during the day.'

Ricky and John exchange loving hand-squeezes beneath the table and eye-smiles above. They are well suited at that point of their lives: good-looking, smart, older successful people with nothing more to prove than the pampered allure of wisdom from age versus youth: 'Remember firm?' was a favourite comment of Ricky's upon seeing young beauties.

John is a banker, a managing director. They met in the drying-out clinic, Hunkley Hall, where the rich go to have their lifestyles altered. Where the famous can break down in tears to become humble again and they can all learn to live without alcohol as their motivation, crutch or best friend. So much easier to say than do.

Now Ricky is like a different person, all the unreliability and coarseness scrubbed away. Coco finds her more accepting of what others wish or want to do, no longer does everybody have to be like, think like, act like Ricky Johnson, to be good enough to boost her ego, save her from her booming insecurity. She is kinder and more loving; stronger and prouder of this achievement to have given up alcohol than anything else she's done or been in her life, and Coco loves her for it.

'I hear you've got an exhibition in the summer in Zurich, Ben;

Ricky was telling me the paintings are great. I'm sure it'll do well, it's a good place to have it. The bankers I know in Switzerland seem to spend all their time and money on art,' says John.

'Thanks. I'll give you an invite when they're printed and you can bring some of them to my show.'

'Why not? Ricky could come too if she's not busy.'

'Great, let's make a party of it. Just got to finish the paintings now and we'll be all set. Come down to the studio in the morning, if you like. Then you can see that these aren't all my pictures — some are Coco's.'

John and Ben chat on in that almost familiar convivial family manner of one in-law to another, while Coco and Ricky, mother and daughter, now true friends, talk at the other side of the table.

'It looks like it's all going well here. The food is too delicious, where did you learn to cook? It's not from my side of the family, it must be from your father. How is he, have you heard from him?'

'Yes, he's fine. I spoke to him last week, he called from Spain. He's there almost all the time now, and enjoying it with Sylvie.'

'Good. How are you feeling? It's not too much for you, is it, all of this? You're going to take time off with the baby, aren't you?'

'Of course, Mum, I've been training up Ben's sister to take over for a few months, she's working in a restaurant in London at the moment. She'll be able to do it with her eyes shut. I suppose we might even be able to go off to the house in France for a week or two if you're not using it, it depends.'

'Of course, and if you want me to stay here or have the other kids, whenever, you just have to say. I'm here for you now, so make use of me,' Ricky says smiling, filled with love for her daughter. Proud of the woman she's become, proud of her own achievements as a mother, that she's managed to give her child something to sustain her through all the worst of it so that she could grow above it, like a bulb in winter pushing its way through the dark soil to emerge into the warmth of summer as a flower. A different flower: hardier, more able to survive harsher winters ahead.

'I know, Mum, unconditional love and all that, I'll ask when I need to. Thanks for offering, though, I appreciate it.' Coco puts her arm about Ricky's shoulder and gives her a squeeze, a kiss on the cheek and lots of love.

'Now let's have pudding. Who's for treacle tart and lemon syllabub ice cream, or warm bread and butter pudding?'

CHAPTER TWENTY-ONE

I could feel it the moment I walked in the door. The flare signals were set off in my stomach, igniting the rest of my body; the hairs on the back of my neck stood to attention, jaw muscles clamped rigid upon my teeth. I looked across the restaurant and saw the coterie of waiters and managers surrounding and bending to a force that made them laugh and smile and then, as quickly, be admonished to their stations. Ricky had arrived early and in full flight. Her voice zoomed beneath the ceiling and boomed under the tables, her laugh careered off the walls and landed on other diners' plates. When Ricky entered a room in certain spirits, or rather when certain spirits had entered Ricky, anywhere became her private party, it wouldn't have mattered if it was the Albert Hall.

Across the bar is my father with a face full of resignation; by his side, beautifully coutured, elegantly reposeful as though it was another quiet dinner at Claridge's, is his constant companion, Sylvie. Barbara, my cousin, the actress/starlet, sits there scowling, another boyfriend by her side who'll soon be on his way out because he's entranced with Ricky, another star's behaviour. And this is only the beginning of the evening.

I think seriously of putting everybody out of their pain by running backwards through the restaurant and out to the nearest call box, to ring and cancel on a pretext. Any, it doesn't matter. But it's my last evening, the final family dinner, I might never see these shores again if I'm lucky and I haven't seen Barbara in months because she's been away on tour. I've got to go through with it, the farewell dinner. Out with the flair as best I can with a gulp full of saliva before the glass of champagne does it properly. I grab at a smile, left over from some other time, and pin it across my chops. I'm humming 'Pack up your troubles' to spur me across the room, to bathe in the warmth of my family.

'More champagne, one bottle's not enough, what do you think we are, a bunch of bloody Muslims at Ramadan? We're here to celebrate. This is my daughter Coco and she's deserting us, leaving us for another country. We gotta send her off right, bring us the magnum. You don't have any! What kind of a restaurant is this? Where's Alan, the manager, I want him to serve us. This is a very special night, you don't seem to realise. Alan, Alan, the waiter said there was no champagne for my little girl. There's got to be champagne for my baby.'

'Ricky it's all right, I don't want any more champagne. I'll just have a glass of red wine with my food, I've still got some left. It's alright, honestly Mum, everything's fine.'

'Well if you're sure? It is your night, you just ask for anything you like.'

'It's my daughter,' she turns to the people on the next table who are entranced by the noise and commotion going on, on ours. 'My beautiful, clever daughter – don't you think she's beautiful? She's going to Singapore, incredibly important job.' She beams back over to me. 'That's her father over there but we're not married any more, are you married? No, I didn't think so. Your poor old cow stuck at home with the kids while you're on a "business meeting", I 'spect. I wouldn't marry this one if I was you, if he does it to one wife he'll do it to the next.

'Well, no need to be so fuckin' hoity-toity, he doesn't look like much of a fuck anyway. What's the packet like in his trousers? You'd be better off with this waiter, love, at least he could get it up. What's your name? Harry – that's a nice name, if you're not busy later, Harold, I think this one'll need servicing.' Ricky winks suggestively and turns her attention back to her own table.

'Now, what we got nice to eat here? Anything? Bit of old fish, do me Alan. I'm just popping to the loo. Send a search party for the chef if I'm not back in half an hour, I've always fancied him, the dusky olive complexion.'

I close my eyes for the moment of relief when she disappears. I take a sip from my glass, feel it trickle down my throat. It's not enough: I take a gulp, take a sneak at my watch and wonder how long it'll take to get to pudding and coffee. Would a Fernet Branca be better to ease the knot of my stomach, or an ice-cold kümmel? I wish Mum could return from the loo, the kitchens or wherever she's gone to, sober. If she could just hold herself together in one piece, for one hour.

Why's my father trying to tell some funny story, where's the point?

I try to follow something, keep my mind and eyes focused, but it gets too sharp, bright, loud, fast, out of control. I can't follow while slipping in and out of consciousness. Barbara's trying to send smiles of condolence from across the table but they get lost through the fog I've set up.

Just as the food arrives, Ricky has still not returned. I look at the beautifully arranged lamb and watch the glossy sauce congeal slowly over the meat. I can't move.

'Aren't you going to eat yours, it looks simply delicious, I made something rather like that last night for dinner, didn't I, darling?' Even Sylvie in her tight Germanic style was making a go of keeping the evening together.

'Yes, yes, of course I will.' I lift the meat, this foreign body, on to my lips, through and into my mouth, but I can't coordinate my teeth enough to chew it properly. I make the motions. I'm so removed I feel like I'm in a cage, pinned up on a corner wall like a security camera, the all-seeing fish-eye, able to view everything and contribute nothing.

'Ooh, lovely! This looks nice, doesn't it?' Ricky arrives back at the table still doing up her skirt, her lipstick is reapplied halfway across her face, her tights newly laddered. It doesn't do to speculate.

'You all know George, don't you? George is my new friend, aren't you George? I found him sitting by himself at the bar, so he's having dinner with us. Pull up a chair, George.' George is already slumped in a chair puffing on a large cheroot, mindless of Ricky's hand firmly clutching his crotch.

No, nobody knows George except Ricky. George who? There's something distantly familiar about him, a faded movie-star look clinging to his pampered, abused face.

The same piece of meat is still doing the rounds of my mouth, now dry and tasteless. I try to swallow it but the effort pricks my eyes and there's no getting past the boulder lodged in my throat.

'Are you all right, Coco?' Barbara asks softly across the table. But I can't lift my head from my chest, to nod a reply.

'Coco?'

All I can do is sit, feeling the dribbles falling out of my eyes and nose. I'd wanted everything of this last evening but it has disappeared before it has even begun. My disappointment and sadness at not even being able to make one evening work as a family wells up in me. I'd just wanted one snapshot to take with me; was I so naive to think that possible? Other families did it, I know, so what if it's all pretend? I'd rather have counterfeit than this. Pulling the napkin from my lap I cover my face and mop the dampness. When I look up all I can see is Ricky stuffing a mouthful of food into the loud, shrivelled, drunken, uninvited guest sitting by her side.

Resentment suddenly puffballs over everything. The glass explodes on the front of the camera.

'You couldn't fucking do it, could you? You couldn't let my last night here be nice! You couldn't bear anyone else to have any attention for a minute, could you? Ricky Johnson, centre-fucking-stage the whole bloody time. Can't you just stop for a minute? Can't you see how you've just ruined the whole bloody evening? Why couldn't you let me leave with just one nice thought about you? Now I'm never going to want to come back.

Couldn't we just play at happy families for even one night? Just one night . . .'

Ricky looks at me open-mouthed, then hurt and disarmed, suddenly sober, her eyes like a child's, full of sadness and with no tricks left to pull, no presents left to open. Nothing to say to retrieve the situation.

Barbara stands protectively with her arms around me. I cry like there is no reason left to stop; it fills the restaurant's silence, the live drama at an end for one night.

'Well done, Auntie Ricky,' Barbara says flatly. 'Can you call us a cab,' she says to a passing waiter.

CHAPTER TWENTY-TWO

'Forget the whole bloody thing! That the only thing to do. Just keep some peace and understanding. The club can rot in hell but you don't have to go with it. I'll go to LanTao. LanTao Island Monastery, escape everything that's happened in the last six months and twenty-three years.'

And Coco did feel a bit like the rat who'd jumped ship and got to shore, as she climbed off the bus at the temple and stood watching it rumble and roll its way down the dirt road, off the mountain. The mattress and the box of chickens attached with ropes to its roof almost jumping off the side at a steep-turn bump, the white and brown goat with its head out of the window, bleating, its horns knocking the slide-across windows with every jolt.

The hot dust from the bus's tyres flew back at Coco and covered her with a thin film of its rich ochre tint, and then it was gone.

She turned to look at the travelling stalls outside the temple walls lined up selling gaudy souvenirs. Business wasn't brisk, and the stallholders stood there with their turned-down faces looking like they didn't even expect a postcard sale for the day. The monastery wasn't the tourist attraction they had hoped for and the painted umbrellas that hung from their posts were fading with the sun, the cracks of their folds promising glints of richer, unseen colours. Coco wasn't sure if she did it out of sympathy or for the joy of slashing their gloomy expectations, but she went straight to the first stall and bought a blue, yellow and pink flowered wooden sunshade. It didn't change the expression of the old woman, ageless with her face a map of brown wrinkles, her hair black and shiny pulled tight against her head into its strict bun. Her body was covered by the uniform black cotton side-tied top and Mao collar, wide-legged trousers flapping at her white-socked ankles. She passed over the change and nodded unimpressed at the white westerner – now she had paid for her goods was there any need to browse? her expression seemed to shout.

Coco ignored it, and gazed across her Mao badges in porcelain and tin, the bundles of plastic-wrapped paper money adorned with pictures of cars and fur coats, houses and furniture, things to be burnt in sacrificial prayer for your deceased relatives in their afterlives. Postcards of the mountain, the temple, the prison, the island that held them all. The array of sticky sweets and cans of warm, fizzy, sweet chrysanthemum drink. The woman was right: Coco browsed with her conical striped umbrella, shading her head against a fading sun and didn't bother buying another thing. She turned and strolled through the gates, her bag upon one shoulder, the shade's stalk upon the other. The gates closed behind her; she was the last one in.

Coco found the office to pay her board and lodgings at and was pointed towards the Nissen-style hut accommodation. Inside there was a small corridor of rooms crowded with single wooden-boarded bunk beds, no mattress – just a single sheet, a straw roll mat and a mosquito net. She put her stuff down on the allotted bottom bunk and went off in search of the lie of the land. The gong for supper sounded, striking six, and Coco turned to follow it.

The monastery was the prettiest Chinese Buddhist wonderland she could imagine. The landscaped garden was full of stepping stones and bridges across water, summer houses with sloping roofs, grass of emerald green and ponds full of golden carp wafting their chiffon tails through the water lilies of blue ponds fed from the waterfalls and connecting rivers. Flowers were everywhere, shouting orange, laughing yellow and smiling pink. The temples were rich with gold and red; the Buddha guarded by their polished bronze dragons puffed out the smoke of heady perfumed incense.

Among the profusion of colour was the serene elegance of the priests with their stubbly, shaved heads and tailored grey gowns, calmly floating rather like stranger flowers. Their faces were wreathed in smiles as if they sheltered an amusing secret that kept them glowing with contentment. Little dogs shuffled and woofed by their feet, grey and white and black shih-tzus, colour-coordinated, perfect accessories for their masters whom they kept always in sight through their messy fringes.

The visitors' dining hall was sparsely furnished with large round tables and wooden chairs. By the wall were two vats with protruding ladles, one containing a pale soup with swelling, dried mushrooms, the other rice. On a table close by were bowls and chopsticks; above, a poster requested in several languages to help yourself, wash and return the bowls after use.

Coco looked around the hall at the few other visitors, all Chinese, who sat clustered in groups, the noisy clatter of chop-sticks attacking bowls, clicking from china to teeth. Their continu-ous loud chatter didn't interrupt their eating. Coco got her bowl, filled it with rice and covered it with soup, went back for her chopsticks and a glass of water and sat at a table with two others who looked up at her, smiling and interested.

Coco hadn't felt she'd been in such a foreign place for a long time, with nothing that she could understand and nobody to talk to. Alone. Why was she giving herself this forced exile, when now all she could see before her was the length of her stay? Four days seemed like an eternity; she wished she'd brought some Snickers bars with her, a bit of sugar comfort, but it would have felt like cheating. Cheating what? Herself, in the end. She knew it was important for her to be alone at this time but she didn't know how, didn't want to talk to herself. Think about what she was going to do with the rest of her life, now that this road had led to another dead end. Now that she realised that it didn't matter how far you went in the other direction, you still took whatever it was inside you that drove you away in the first place, on to the next, and the next and the next. No amount of tequila deadened the feelings; rides to expensive restaurants on private islands on luxurious junks didn't help. It just delayed it, built it up, until you were alone. Depressing but true. You can't escape your own truth in the end; you just wriggle around in it, being scratched by your own dishonesty.

She wished she'd brought a novel to read, an escape within an escape.

She smiled back at the strangers and began eating her rice, Chinese workers-style, face down into the bowl.

'Why do you come to stay at monastery?'

The man sitting opposite had spoken to Coco and for a moment she didn't quite know where to look.

'Oh I, I just wanted to see it, it looked so beautiful in pictures I'd seen, I knew I had to come here before I left Hong Kong. Have you been here before?'

'Yes, we come from the Mainland, my father and I, every year to pray, to meditate, to become whole again. It is a very beautiful place, very special. You will know this. Welcome.'

'Thank you. Yes, I think I will.'

She was nervous and unsure, speaking to these simple and honest people, unused to it from these past months in Hong Kong where the club had relocated her after Singapore, where everything was based so firmly upon the superficial. It was like speaking a foreign language, one you slip into and can't get out of.

After supper she said goodnight to her companions, embarrassed at her inadequacy to communicate, and walked back through the magical gardens. The sun's heat was fading, its body drifting down towards the sea; the sky was turning pink. She sat in one of the pagodas, listened to the tinkling music of the water and bathed under the richness of the orange and red sunset. The hum of evening prayer and bell chimes filled the warm air, but her mind still rattled with demons. Demons of the past: her behaviour, hags of indescribable horror, tadpoles of indecision that invaded her mind in teaming sets. The peace and beauty of her surroundings had opened the floodgates, without anything else to distract her, her mind had set upon itself.

In her bed on those hard boards, she rolled from one side to another, unable to find comfort or sleep. Almost weeping with frustration at her inability to change her circumstances, weighted down with tiredness, her face tight and stinging from tears, it seemed the only way to placate her mind's terrors was to admit defeat and give up the struggle.

'Fuck it! I give up! I don't know anything. Dear God, all these years and I don't know a thing. I've moved to the other side of the world and the same things are with me as though they were outside my door. The feelings of desolation and loneliness, the pointlessness of whatever I do to try and change things. I can't answer a single question – why? I don't know. Dear God, help me, please.'

Finally, with that submission, Coco drifted off into a limbo-like sleep.

The next morning Coco was woken by the deafening clang of vast bells interspersed with chimes, rings and chants. She got up, flung on her loose trousers and a vest and followed the magnificent force of noise that rose above the sky, pulling the sunrise into being. Everything seemed to be coming from the main temple. The main service of the day had begun, an army of priests attending to the rituals that had to be performed each morning, every day, for ever. The sound and the performance produced a hypnotic magic that drew Coco in. She wasn't sure whether it was simply because it was so early that she slipped into this dream state.

Coco went to lie on the grass to get back her bearings, and as she lay looking up at the sky and the sun that was trying to get through the two clouds barring its way, it seemed as if she was being drawn upwards. She could feel everything draining up through her head, as though her contents were being pulled out of her. Her spirit was within the pale steam clouds, the leftover sunrise pinks and yellows and the deepening blue sky. She was melting between sky and earth, could feel each rumble and shift of the ground beneath her, each waft of wind above her, within her. Then at some point the clouds parted, the sun peeked through and seemed to put a syphon to her head and everything flooded back into her body as though it had been through the mangle, survived, now washed and clean again, and was being returned.

Afterwards Coco wasn't quite sure how long she had been there but when she moved it was as though she was waking for the first time, not just scrubbed, but purified and invigorated, from the inside out, a colonic irrigation of the body and soul. She felt so light, so excited, that the garden now glowed in technicolor and a hunger beat at her stomach walls as though she'd been without food for days.

Coco got to the canteen just before they removed the last of the sticky, white, sweet rice porridge and black lychee tea. She sat there alone trying not to think until filled. Too much to think about on an empty stomach. When she'd finished she went back outside and wandered lazily around the garden, her mind whirring, until she realised there was nothing to think over: not one thing, not from the past, not from her childhood, not from the club she'd just got the sack from, not even about money. Everything was fine: she was being looked after, her slate had been wiped clean and now she could start again. It didn't mean she wouldn't make mistakes ever again; just that there was no need to worry about the ones of the past. Those had been taken from her and she had let them go. She could still think about the past, but it had lost its power; there was no remorse or resentment left. She had detached from it with nothing more to be said or done.

It took quite a while for Coco to absorb this understanding. The shock of it arrived upon her as though it had always been there and she'd been too damned thick to notice; now it was so clear she couldn't see it any other way. She hugged herself with joy and jumped, clicking her bare heels in the air – she would have somersaulted across the lawn if it didn't seem quite so inappropriate in the graceful serenity of the atmosphere. But you can't keep a good joy down, and she skipped and beamed like a four-year-old back to her hut to collect her drawing stuff, pastels, watercolours and paper. She would make a picture of the gardens with the main temple and when she had finished, she would leave. Return to Hong Kong, collect her stuff and get a flight back home. She had achieved whatever was meant by her journey and now she could get on with life and having fun. It seemed so clear and simple that she was beginning again.

Engrossed in her painting, which had expanded on to six pieces of paper, Coco didn't notice someone stop on the path behind her to watch her work. Shaded by the pagoda roof, she didn't feel their shadow, notice their words or footsteps as they went on, but she finally turned, feeling the constant presence of a man standing behind her unmoving for so long. Looking up at him, she smiled as if to say Can I help you? His face grew embarrassed once he realised she was looking at him, because he had had his eyes fixed upon the painting.

'I'm sorry, I don't mean to interfere or stop you working. It's good, the angle works with the colour, I think you might do more with those trees . . . but the perspective you've got just right.'

'That's an encouraging surprise, getting my perspective back.'

'Don't I know you? Coco! It is Coco, isn't it?'

'Yes. Yes, of course, Ben. You look so different. You've grown.'

'I should hope so; so do you. What are you doing here?'

'What do you mean, what am I doing here? What are you

doing here? I've been living and working first in Singapore and until recently, Hong Kong.'

'I've been travelling, visiting dying relatives, working a bit, mainly painting.'

'Snap. I didn't know you went on to college, I thought you were "university material"?'

'I was, but I changed after a year. I've been painting ever since, doing exhibitions, winning competitions, usual thing.' He laughed, bluffing boastful humility. 'But tell me about you and everything.'

'Well, where to start. I've been running this club in Singapore for the last six months but got transferred for not making my body as readily available as the powers that be thought necessary. So they decided to move me to their Hong Kong branch, but I can see things aren't panning out as expected.'

'In other words, you were too nice,' said Ben.

'Or not nice enough, depending on your view.'

Ben was tall now, brown limbs with a dusting of sun-blond hair upon the stubble of his chin and the crop of his head. His nose was large and aquiline and his face had now grown into it; clear green eyes sat like almonds on either side. His jaw was square like a boxer's, while his hands were a size to match. He sat beside Coco clumsily as though having just got those long limbs, and wasn't quite sure how to fit them into the delicacy of the gardens. His face was so wide and open, so clear and deep that Coco could not believe this was the same boy she'd gone out with at fourteen, who'd spent the holidays with her when she'd refused to communicate or have sex. It was like looking into a pool that you know you've dropped something into and you can almost see it, but the light and reflection keep it enticingly hidden. Coco thought she could almost drop into that pool, she was so close.

Ben kept chatting happily away. He was gorgeous.

They were laughing, remembering old school customs that now seemed strangely foreign, childish and ridiculous. Dipping tampons in red food colouring until they swelled, and dripping them, tied from the eaves, upon passing teachers' heads. Sunday-morning food fights, bananas and buns flying in breakfast aban-don across the refectory, no thought to who would clear up. Lying on top of each other for hours, frantic tongues firmly embedded in each other's mouths, bodies motionless. Crisp packets shrunk by the fire into miniature badges for maximum cool. Glass-sliced arms dripping in blood pacts. Cigarette currency of puffs and drags (one drag equalled three puffs) but how many drags in a fag? And could you be spotted by the history teacher, 'Just call me Jim,' in the bushes during break?

It was such a relief to be talking the same language to somebody from the same country. Not just English, but where all your common reference points were the same. Where the similari-ties went so far back there was no explaining to be done. No wonder generations stay in the same valleys and villages, marry-ing childhood sweethearts, repeating the patterns of their grand-parents and theirs before them, in the comfort of familiar surroundings.

Now we are so modern and so rich, we can jump on a plane and spend our lives searching on the other side of the world for what would have been on our doorstep in other days.

When the gong went for supper, Ben and Coco were still sitting, talking, laughing. He helped her clear her things away, set the drawing with enough fixative to make it permanent, and then she clipped it back into her pad which he picked up and carried for her. When they were both ready they walked towards the canteen, falling into an easy step with each other.

BEN RICHARDS

Don't Step On The Lines

In a flat high above London Kerry can't stop remembering Gary. Marco awaits the pleasures and temptations of summer in the city . . .

Kerry, finally taking control of her life, has returned to college to study English. Marco, friend and flatmate, deeply obsessed with sharks, roams the bars and clubs of London. Drifting in and out of various jobs, relationships and drugs, he watches Kerry's progress with a mixture of love and envy.

Then Robin appears. For Kerry, Robin – rich, good-looking, a fellow student – represents new opportunities and possibilities. For Marco, however, he is nothing but trouble.

'Scenes of London life sparkle within the narrative . . . It's all wonderfully recognisable and realistic, told with a laddish exuberance at once hilarious and touching' *Literary Review*

'Kerry is a proper nineties heroine: bright, lovely, struggling to define her life' *Mail on Sunday*

'Refreshingly unpretentious and very entertaining' *The Times*

'The London he sees is vivid and impressive' *TLS*

'A terrific book' *Time Out*

0 7472 5280 7

review

LILIAN FASCHINGER

Magdalena the Sinner

'Meet Magdalena Leitner, codename "the Sinner". She is a killer seven times over, clad in a second-skin, black leather motorcycle suit. She is Austrian – but not the yodelling type. Rather, she's bent on a singular, sinister mission: to force her confession upon the village priest she has kidnapped at gunpoint . . .

'As she tears through the European Union in search of love, liberty and in pursuit of happiness, Magdalena charges at the windmills of bourgeois mores, Church hypocrisy, nationalist instincts, and our selfish failure to listen to or care for others . . . Unfettered by moral scruples or social constraints, our leather-clad heroine acts out every woman's most subversive wish – and every man's – as she roars through conventions on her Puch . . .

'In the end, we, like the priest, are wholly in Magdalena's spell, and want this magical morality tale to go on and on and on' Cristina Odone, *Literary Review*

'Faschinger rings the changes with wit and ingenuity . . . Magdalena is a spellbinding raconteur' Margaret Walters, *The Sunday Times*

0 7472 5459 1

review

If you enjoyed this book here is a selection of other bestselling Review titles from Headline

Headline books are available at your local bookshop or newsagent. Alternatively, books can be ordered direct from the publisher. Just tick the titles you want and fill in the form below. Prices and availability subject to change without notice.

Buy four books from the selection above and get free postage and packaging and delivery within 48 hours. Just send a cheque or postal order made payable to Bookpoint Ltd to the value of the total cover price of the four books. Alternatively, if you wish to buy fewer than four books the following postage and packaging applies:

UK and BFPO £4.30 for one book; £6.30 for two books; £8.30 for three books.

Overseas and Eire: £4.80 for one book; £7.10 for 2 or 3 books (surface mail)

Please enclose a cheque or postal order made payable to *Bookpoint Limited*, and send to: Headline Publishing Ltd, 39 Milton Park, Abingdon, OXON OX14 4TD, UK.
Email Address: orders@bookpoint.co.uk

If you would prefer to pay by credit card, our call team would be delighted to take your order by telephone. Our direct line 01235 400 414 (lines open 9.00 am–6.00 pm Monday to Saturday 24 hour message answering service). Alternatively you can send a fax on 01235 400 454.

Name ....

Address ....

....

....

If you would prefer to pay by credit card, please complete:
Please debit my Visa/Access/Diner's Card/American Express (delete as applicable) card number:

Signature .... Expiry Date ....